GHOST MOVIES II

with contributions from

Algernon Blackwood
Bennett Cerf
Leon Garfield
Susan Hill
Elizabeth Jane Howard
M R James
Dean Koontz
William F Nolan
George A Romero
Elizabeth Taylor

Further Titles In This Series From Severn House

GHOST MOVIES II

Famous Supernatural Television Programmes

Collected & Introduced by
Peter Haining

SEVERN
SH
HOUSE

This first world edition published in Great Britain 1996 by
SEVERN HOUSE PUBLISHERS LTD of
9–15 High Street, Sutton, Surrey SM1 1DF.
First published in the USA 1996 by
SEVERN HOUSE PUBLISHERS INC. of
595 Madison Avenue, New York, NY 10022.

British Library Cataloguing in Publication Data

Ghost movies II : famous supernatural television programmes
    1. Short stories, English – 20th century
    I. Haining, Peter, 1940– II. Koontz, Dean R., 1945–
    823'.08733'08 [FS]

    ISBN 0-7278-4966-2

Typeset by Palimpsest Book Production Limited,
Polmont, Stirlingshire, Scotland.
Printed and bound in Great Britain by
Hartnolls Ltd, Bodmin, Cornwall.

PROGRAMME

Note: This is a list of television titles. The original works on which these television series were based may have had different titles from these listed above.

CREDITS

The Editor and publishers are grateful to the following authors, their agents and publishers for permission to include copyright stories in this collection: *Good Housekeeping* magazine and Richard Scott Simon Ltd for 'Farthing Hall' by Susan Hill; Random House Publishing Group for 'Great Ghost Stories' by Bennett Cerf; A.P. Watt Literary Agency for 'The Listener' by Algernon Blackwood; A.M. Heath & Co Ltd for 'Poor Girl' by Elizabeth Taylor; *Daily Mail* Newspapers for 'The Constable's Tale' by Leon Garfield; Robert Hale Publishers and Laurel Entertainment Corp Inc., for 'Clay' by George A.Romero; The Author for 'A Final Stone' by William F.Nolan; Peters, Fraser and Dunlop Ltd for 'Three Miles Up' by Elizabeth Jane Howard; TZ Publications and Headline Publishing Group for 'The Black Pumpkin' by Dean Koontz. While every care has been taken in seeking permission for the use of stories in this anthology, in the case of any accidental infringement interested parties are asked to write to the Editor in care of the publishers.

PROLOGUE

'A Night of Terror-Vision'

There have, over the years, been many stunts arranged on Halloween – ranging from the simple 'Trick or Treat' game played by children on their neighbours and friends, to elaborate and sometimes dangerous hoaxes for more cynical adults. But few can have had the impact or tragic aftermath of 'Ghostwatch' a BBC Screen One special drama which was broadcast on 31 October 1992. For this purported to show genuine poltergeist phenomena taking place and so convinced hundreds of viewers that it was genuine that the BBC's telephone switchboard was jammed with callers for hours afterwards. In fact, 'Ghostwatch' created a similar kind of furore to the panic that followed Orson Welles' sensational American radio version of his namesake H.G. Wells' *War of the Worlds* on the night of Halloween 1938 that so scared a considerable number of listeners that they fled from their homes in panic. Although the television drama did not cause quite such terror, it did have one tragic consequence of which more anon.

The idea for 'Ghostwatch' came from scriptwriter Stephen Volk who devised what was ostensibly an outside broadcast from 'the most haunted house in Britain' – an ordinary council house in Northolt, Middlesex in which a woman, Mrs Pamela Early, and her two daughters, Suzanne and Kim, were said to be subjected to regular and terrifying paranormal attacks which included strange noises, awful smells and even cutlery being bent. The trio of women were played by actress Brid Brennan as Mrs Early, and her children by real-life sisters, Michelle and Cherise Wesson. Investigating the poltergeist's activities during the 95 minute programme were Michael Parkinson as the presenter; Sarah Greene playing a reporter; Mike Smith and Craig Charles as interviewers and Gillian Bevan as the local GP, Dr Lin Pascoe. It was undoubtedly due in no small measure to the conviction with which all these principals played their roles under the direction of Lesley Manning, that a lot of viewers that Saturday night began to believe they were watching a real-life documentary rather than a carefully scripted and pre-recorded play. And the dramatic finale in which the TV studios were apparently struck by supernatural effects – courtesy of the BBC's special effects department – resulted in a large group of viewers being more interested in reaching for their telephones to complain to the Corporation than watching the next programme, *Match of the Day*.

Veteran journalist and chat show host, Michael Parkinson, who had hardly expected to be taken seriously as an actor was as surprised as his fellow professionals at the controversy which immediately surrounded the broadcast that had been intended to be nothing more than a Halloween night spoof. Though there could be no denying that some viewers might well have been upset by a scene in 'Ghostwatch' in which one of the Early girls had been seen disfigured and covered in blood, the BBC was quick to point out to those who complained the whole programme had been too realistic that full details of the writer and cast had been given in *Radio Times* and the programme had also been trailed several times during the previous week to make its contents clear. Notwithstanding this, there was a tragic sequel a few days later when one young teenage viewer became convinced that his own home was haunted and hanged himself.

The extraordinary impact of 'Ghostwatch' was, however, only one instance of the power the ghost story can have on television audiences. Adaptations of supernatural stories have, in fact, been a favourite with TV producers for many years, and with the ever increasing sophistication of special effects, things that go bump in the night have been depicted with increasing conviction. The white-sheeted figures who were faded in and out of the picture – or suddenly removed by dimming the lights – in the early productions of the Forties and Fifties have since given way to effects that are startlingly realistic. Television archives indicate that even before the Second World War when television in England was still in its infancy, there were productions of 'Wandering Willie's Tale' by Sir Walter Scott and Wilkie Collins 'The Dream Woman'; while in America in 1952 the ghost story genre was given a flying start with a production of Oscar Wilde's 'The Canterville Ghost' in the weekly series, *Favourite Story*. The production starred Adolphe Menjou in a role which has since been reprised on British TV by David Niven and Sir Ralph Richardson. What these pioneer shows lacked in polish and expertise they more than made up for in exploiting the love of viewers for cold chills up the spine – and once the appeal of the supernatural on TV became fully evident, the genre was set for what has proved a long and enduring history.

Today, the ghost story has become a regular feature of broadcasting schedules, especially at Christmas and Halloween. As recently as 1994, BBC 2 devoted eleven hours through the night of October 31 to stories of ghosts and horror which were screened under the banner title of *Weird Night*. This book also offers hours – perhaps even several nights – of weird tales to enjoy, all of which reflect the appeal of the ghost story on TV. Herein will be found stories by some of the most familiar names in supernatural fiction whose work has been adapted for television – often more than once. A number of their contributions are quite rare and several have not been previously anthologized. They make – if anything – even more chilling reading in print than on Terror-Vision.

It has been said that the successful suspension of disbelief is the key to good drama, and that we must never forget that there are some things in life which simply cannot be explained. I would suggest you remember both these credos before venturing further into the strange and eerie world of television's ghost movies . . .

PETER HAINING

THE WOMAN IN BLACK

(Central Television, 1989)
Starring: Adrian Rawlins, Bernard Hepton &
Pauline Moran
Directed by Charles Graham
Story 'Farthing Hall' by Susan Hill

The tradition of screening a ghost story at Christmas which has become a regular feature on television during the past half-century enjoyed another land-mark on 24 December, 1989 when Central TV pro-vided a superb adaptation of Susan Hill's best-selling novel, *The Woman in Black*, which she had written in 1983. Previewing the late-evening screening, *The Times* neatly summarized the tradition it was pre-serving. 'People like to be frightened at Christmas time,' the paper stated. 'It might be a blood memory thing – the family gathering indoors, the weather and wolves outdoors – or it might be a Puritan thing: we've just indulged ourselves rotten so now we deserve to suffer.' Whatever the case, the *Times* decided, *The Women in Black* was 'just the instrument to do it.' Susan Hill's novel about a young solicitor sent up from London to dispose of mysterious Eel Marsh House situated on a lonely stretch of coast which can only be reached by a causeway and there finds himself plunged into a maelstrom of macabre and supernatural events was faithfully adapted by one of

5

TV's most accomplished scriptwriters, Nigel Kneale of *Quatermass* fame. Adrian Rawlins was totally convincing as the inexperienced young hero who ignored the advice of the locals to avoid the lonely old house and instead came face to face with a ghostly figure in the dramatic story that most viewers found truly scary from start to finish. The success of this adaptation – which has been reshown twice in the intervening years – helped to establish *The Woman in Black* as a modern classic in the ghost story genre. This stature has been further underlined by a stage version created by Stephen Mallatratt which opened at the Fortune Theatre in London in 1988 to rave reviews – Jack Tinker in the *Daily Mail* called in 'a real theatrical spine-chiller' – and it is still playing there today: by far the theatre's longest-running production.

The events which occur at 'Farthing House' are not that dissimilar and once again demonstrate that Susan Elizabeth Hill (1942–) has few peers in the ranks of contemporary writers of supernatural fiction. Born in Scarborough on the windswept Yorkshire coast, she began writing after studying at King's College, London. In 1970 she won the prestigious Somerset Maugham Prize for her novel, *I'm The King of the Castle*, and two years later gained the Whitbread award for *The Bird of Night*. Several of her other books have also shown her knowledge and understanding of the supernatural – and apart from publishing a group of her own macabre chillers as *Ghost Stories* in 1984, she also edited the *Random House Book of Ghost Stories* in 1991. As well as her work as a playwright and screen writer, Susan reached an even larger audience recently when she wrote the sequel to Daphne du Maurier's *Rebecca*

which was called *Mrs De Winter*. 'Farthing House' is an ideal tale with which to begin this collection: not only because of its affinity to *The Woman in Black*, but also because it was only published as recently as December 1992 in *Good Housekeeping* magazine and has not yet been collected with her other works. Like the original novel, the reader will soon discover that this is a story that also deserves adapting for television. Ideally, at Christmas . . .

I have never told you any of this before – I have never told anyone, and indeed, writing it down and sealing it up in an envelope to be read at some future date may still not count as 'telling'. But I shall feel better for it, I am sure of that. Now it has all come back to me, I do not want to let it go again, I must set it down.

It is true, and for that very reason you must not hear it just now. You will be prey to enough anxieties and fancies without my adding ghosts to them; the time before the birth of a child one is so very vulnerable.

I daresay that it has made me vulnerable too, that this has brought the events to mind.

I began to be restless several weeks ago. I was burning the last of the leaves. It was a most beautiful day, clear and cold and blue and a few of them were swirling down as I raked and piled. And then a light wind blew suddenly across the grass, scuttling the leaves and making the woodsmoke drift towards me, and as I caught the smell of it, that most poignant, melancholy, nostalgic of all smells, something that had been drifting on the edges of my consciousness blurred and insubstantial, came into focus, and in a rush I remembered . . .

It was as though a door had been opened on to the past,

and I had stepped through and gazed at what I saw there again. I saw the house, the drive sweeping up to it, the countryside around it, on that late November afternoon, saw the red sun setting behind the beech copse, beyond the rising, brown fields, saw the bonfire the gardener had left to smoulder on gently by itself, and the thin pale smoke coiling up from its heart. I was there, all over again.

I went in a daze into the house, made some tea, and sat, still in my old, outdoor clothes at the kitchen table, as it went quite dark outside the window, and I let myself go back to that day, and the nights that followed, watched it all unfold again, remembered. So that it was all absolutely clear in my mind when the newspaper report appeared, a week later.

I was going to see Aunt Addy. It was November, and she had been at the place called Farthing House since the New Year, but it was only now that I had managed to get away and make the two-hundred-mile journey to visit her.

We had written, of course, and spoken on the telephone, and so far as I could tell she sounded happy. Yes, they were very nice people, she said, and yes, it was such a lovely house, and she did so like her room, everyone was most kind, oh yes dear, it was the right thing, I should have done it long ago, I really am very settled.

And Rosamund said that she was, too, said that it was fine, really, just as Addy told me, a lovely place, such kind people, and Alec had been and he agreed.

All the same, I was worried, I wasn't sure. She had been so independent always, so energetic, so very much her own person all her life, I couldn't see her in a Home, however nice and however sensible a move it was – and she was eighty-six and had had two nasty falls the previous winter – I liked to think of her as she was when we were children, and went to stay at the house in Wales, striding over the hills with the dogs, rowing on the lake, getting up those colossal picnics for us all. I always loved her, she was such fun. I wish you had known her.

And of course, I wish that one of us could have had her, but there really wasn't room to make her comfortable and, oh, other feeble-sounding reasons, which are real reasons, nonetheless.

She had never asked me to visit her, that wasn't her way. Only the more she didn't ask, the more I knew that I should, the guiltier I felt. It was just such a terrible year, what with one thing and another.

But now I was going. It had been a beautiful day for the drive too. I had stopped twice, once in a village, once in a small market town and explored churches and little shops, and eaten lunch and had a pot of tea and taken a walk along the banks of a river in the late sunshine, and the berries, I remember had been thick and heavy, clustered on the boughs. I'd seen a jay and two deer and once, like magic, a kingfisher, flashing blue as blue across a hump-backed bridge. I'd had a sort of holiday really. But now I was tired, I would be glad to get there. It was very nice that they had a guest-room, and I didn't have to stay alone in some hotel. It meant I could really spend all my time with Aunt Addy. Besides, you know how I've always hated hotels, I lie awake thinking of the hundreds of people who've slept in the bed before me.

Little Dornford 1½m.

But as I turned right and the road narrowed to a single track, between trees, I began to feel nervous, anxious, I prayed that it really would be all right, that Aunt Addy had been telling the truth.

"You'll come to the church," they had said, and a row

of three cottages, and then there is the sign to Farthing House, at the bottom of the drive.

I had seen no other car since leaving the cathedral town seven miles back on the main road. It was very quiet, very out of the way. I wondered if Addy minded. She had always been alone up there in her own house but somehow now that she was so old and infirm, I thought she might have liked to be nearer some bustle, perhaps actually in a town. And what about the others, a lot of old women isolated out here together? I shivered suddenly and peered forwards along the darkening lane. The church was just ahead, the car lights swept along a yew hedge, a lych gate, caught the shoulder of a gravestone. I slowed down.

FARTHING HOUSE. It was a neat, elegantly lettered sign, not too prominent and at least it did not proclaim itself Residential Home.

The last light was fading in the sky behind a copse of bare beech trees, the sun dropping down, a great red, frost-rimmed ball. I saw the drive, a wide lawn, the remains of a bonfire of leaves, smouldering by itself in a corner. Farthing House.

I don't know exactly what my emotions had been up to that moment. I was very tired, with that slightly dazed, confused sensation that comes after a long drive and the attendant concentration. And I was apprehensive. I so wanted to be happy about Aunt Addy, to be sure that she was in the right place to spend the rest of her life – or maybe I just wanted to have my conscience cleared so I could bowl off home again in a couple of days with a blithe heart, untroubled by guilt and be able to enjoy the coming Christmas.

But as I stood on the black and white marbled floor of the entrance porch I felt something else and it made me hesitate before ringing the bell. What was it? Not fear or anxiety, no shudders. I am being very careful now, it would be too easy to claim that I had sensed something sinister, that I was shrouded at once in the atmosphere of a haunted house.

But I did not, nothing of that sort crossed my mind. I was only overshadowed by a curious sadness – I don't know exactly how to describe it – a sense of loss, a melancholy. It descended like a damp veil about my head and shoulders. But it lifted, or almost, the cloud passed after a few moments. Well, I was tired, I was cold, it was the back end of the year, and perhaps I had caught a chill, which often manifests itself first as a sudden change of mood into a lower key.

The only other thing I noticed was the faintest smell of hospital antiseptic. That depressed me a bit more. Farthing House wasn't a hospital or even a nursing home proper and I didn't want it to seem so to Aunt Addy, not even in this slight respect.

But in fact, once I was inside, I no longer noticed it at all, there was only the pleasant smell of furniture polish, and fresh chrysanthemums and, somewhere in the background, a light, spicy smell of baking.

The smells that greeted me were all of a piece with the rest of the welcome. Farthing House seemed like an individual, private home. The antiques in the hall were good, substantial pieces and they had been well cared for over the years, there were framed photographs on a sideboard, flowers in jugs and bowls, there was an old, fraying, tapestry-covered armchair on which a fat cat slept beside a fire. It was quiet, too, there was no rattling of trolleys or buzzing of bells. And the matron did not call herself one.

"You are Mrs Flower – how nice to meet you." She put out her hand. "Janet Pearson."

She was younger than I had expected, probably in her late forties. A small King Charles spaniel hovered about her waving a frond-like tail. I relaxed.

I spent a good evening in Aunt Addy's company; she was so settled and serene, and yet still so full of life. Farthing House was well run, warm and comfortable, and there was good, home-cooked dinner, with fresh vegetables and an excellent lemon meringue pie. The rooms were spacious, the other residents pleasant but not over-obtrusive.

Something else was not as I had expected. It had been necessary to reserve the guest-room and bathroom well in advance, but when Mrs Pearson herself took my bag and led me up the handsome staircase, she told me that after a serious leak in the roof had caused damage, it was being redecorated. "So I've put you in Cedar – it happens to be free just now." She barely hesitated as she spoke. "And it's such a lovely room, I'm sure you'll like it."

How could I have failed? Cedar Room was one of the two largest in the house, on the first floor, with big bay windows overlooking the garden at the back – though now the deep red curtains had been drawn against the early evening darkness.

"Your aunt is just across the landing."

"So they've put you in Cedar," Addy said later when we were having a drink in her own room. It wasn't so large but I preferred it simply, I think, because there was so much familiar furniture, her chair, her own oak dresser, the painted screen, even the club fender we used to sit on to toast our toes as children.

"Yes. It seems a bit big for one person, but it's very handsome. I'm surprised it's vacant."

Addy winked at me. "Well, of course it *wasn't* . . ."

"Oh." For an instant, that feeling of unease and melancholy passed over me like a shadow again.

"Now buck up, don't look wan, there isn't time." And she plunged me back into family chat and cheerful recollections, interspersed with sharp observations about her fellow residents, so that I was almost entirely comfortable again.

I remained so until we parted at getting on for half-past eleven. We had spent much of the evening alone together, and then joined some of the others in one of the lounges, where an almost party-like atmosphere had developed, with laughter and banter and happy talk, which had all helped to revive my first impressions of Farthing House and Addy's place there.

It was not until I closed the door of my room and was alone that I was forced to acknowledge again what had been at the back of my mind all the time, almost like having a person at my shoulder, though just out of sight. I was in this large, high-ceilinged room because it was free, its previous occupant having recently died. I knew no more, and did not want to know, had firmly refrained from asking any questions. Why should it matter? It did not. As a matter of fact it still does not, it had no bearing at all on what happened, but I must set it down because I feel I have to tell the whole truth and part of that truth is that I was in an unsettled, slightly nervous frame of mind as I got ready for bed, because of what I knew, and because I could not help wondering whether whoever had occupied Cedar Room had died in it, perhaps even in this bed. I was, as you might say, almost expecting to have bad dreams or to see a ghost.

There is just one other thing.

When we were all in the lounge, the talk had inevitably been of former homes and families, the past in general, and Addy had wanted some photographs from upstairs. I had slipped out to fetch them for her.

It was very quiet in the hall. The doors were heavy and soundproof, though from behind one I could just hear some faint notes of recorded music, but the staff quarters down the passage were closed off and silent.

So I was quite certain that I heard it, the sound was unmistakable. It was a baby crying. Not a cat, not a dog. They are quite different, you know. What I heard from some distant room on the ground floor was the cry of a newborn baby.

I hesitated. Stopped. But it was over at once, and it did not come again. I waited, feeling uncertain. But then, from the room with the music, I heard the muffled signature tune of the ten o'clock news. I went on up the staircase. The noise had come from the television then.

Except, you see, that deep down and quite surely, I knew that it had not.

I may have had odd frissons about my room but once I was actually in bed and settling down to read a few pages of *Sense and Sensibility* before going to sleep, I felt quite composed and cheerful. The only thing wrong was that the room still seemed far too big for one person. There was ample furniture and yet it was as though someone else ought to be there. I find it difficult to explain precisely.

I was very tired. And Addy was happy, Farthing House was everything I had hoped it would be, I had had a most enjoyable evening, and the next day we were to go out and see something of the countryside and later, hear sung evensong at the cathedral.

I switched out the lamp.

At first I thought it was as quiet outside the house as in, but after a few minutes, I heard the wind sifting through the bare branches and sighing towards the windows and away. I felt like a child again, snug in my little room under the eaves.

I slept.

I dreamed almost at once and with extraordinary vividness, and it was, at least to begin with, a most happy dream. I was in St Mary's, the night after you were born, lying in my bed in that blissful, glowing, untouchable state when the whole of the rest of life seems suspended and everything irrelevant but this. You were there in your crib beside me, though I did not look at you. I don't think anything happened in the dream and it did not last very long. I was simply there in the past and utterly content.

I woke with a start, and as I came to, it was with that sound in my ears, the crying of the baby that I had heard as I crossed the hall earlier that evening. The room was quite dark. I knew at once where I was and yet I was still half within my dream – I remember that I felt a spurt of disappointment that it had *been* a dream and I was actually there, a new young mother again with you beside me in the crib.

How strange, I thought, I wonder why. And then something else happened – or no, not 'happened'. There just *was* something else, that is the only way I can describe it.

I had the absolutely clear sense that someone else had been in my room – not the hospital room of my dream, but this room in Farthing House. No one was here now, but minutes before I woke, I knew that they had been. I remember thinking, someone is in the next bed. But of course, there was no next bed, just mine.

After a while I switched on the lamp. All was as it had been when I had gone to sleep. Only that sensation, that atmosphere was still there. If nothing else had happened at Farthing House, I suppose in time I would have decided I had half-dreamed, half-imagined it, and forgotten. It was only because of what happened afterwards that I remembered so clearly and knew with such certainty that my feeling had been correct.

I got up, went over to the tall windows and opened the curtains a little. There was a clear, star-pricked sky and a thin paring of moon. The gardens and the dark countryside all around were peaceful and still.

But I felt oppressed again by the most profound melancholy of spirit, the same terrible sadness and sense of loss that had overcome me on my arrival. I stood there for a long time, unable to release myself from it, before going back to bed to read another chapter of Jane Austen, but I could not concentrate properly and in the end grew drowsy. I heard nothing, saw nothing, and I did not dream again.

The next morning my mood had lightened. There had been a slight frost during the night, and the sun rose on a countryside dusted over with rime. The sky was blue, trees set in dark pencil strokes against it.

We had a good day, Aunt Addy and I, enjoying one another's company, exploring churches and antique shops, having a pub lunch, and an old-fashioned muffin and fruitcake tea after the cathedral service.

It was as we were eating it that I asked suddenly, "What do you know about Farthing House?"

Seeing Addy's puzzled look, I went on, "I just mean, how long has Mrs Pearson been there, who had it before, all that sort of thing. Presumably it was once a family house."

"I have an idea someone told me it had been a military convalescent home during the war. Why do you ask?"

I thought of Cedar Room the previous night, and that

strange sensation. *What* had it been? Or who? But I found that I couldn't talk about it for some reason, it made me too uneasy. "Oh, nothing. Just curious." I avoided Addy's eye.

That evening, the matron invited me to her own room for sherry, and to ask if I was happy about my aunt. I reassured her, saying all the right, polite things. Then she said, "And have you been quite comfortable?"

"Oh yes." I looked straight at her. I thought she might have been giving me an opening – I wasn't sure. And I almost did tell her. But again, I couldn't speak of it. Besides, what was there to tell? I had heard a baby crying – from the television. I'd had an unusual dream, and an odd, confused sensation when I woke from it that someone had just left my room.

Nothing.

"I've been extremely comfortable," I said firmly. "I feel quite happy about everything."

Did she relax just visibly, smile a little too eagerly, was there a touch of relief in her voice when she next spoke?

I don't know whether or not I dreamed that night. It seemed that one minute I was in a deep sleep, and the next that something had woken me. As I came to, I know I heard the echo of crying in my ears, or in my inner ear, but a different sort of crying this time, not that of a baby, but a desperate, woman's sobbing. The antiseptic smell was faintly there again too, my awareness of it was mingled with that of the sounds.

I sat bolt upright. The previous night, I had had the sensation of someone having just been in my room.

Now, I saw her.

There was another bed in the opposite corner of the room, close to the window, and she was getting out of it. The room felt horribly cold. I remember being conscious of the iciness on my hands and face.

I was wide awake, I am quite sure of that, I could hear my own heart pounding, see the bedside table, and the lamp and the blue binding of *Sense and Sensibility* in the moonlight. I know I was not dreaming, so much so that I almost spoke to the woman, wondering as I saw her what on earth they were thinking of to put her and her bed in my room while I was asleep.

She was young, with a flowing, embroidered night-gown, high necked and long sleeved. Her hair was long too, and as pale as her face. Her feet were bare. But I could not speak to her, my throat felt paralysed. I tried to swallow, but even that was difficult, the inside of my mouth was so dry.

She seemed to be crying. I suppose that was what I had heard. She moved across the room towards the door and she held out her arms as if she were begging someone to give her something. And that terrible melancholy came over me again, I felt inconsolably hopeless and sad.

The door opened. I know that because a rush of air came in to the room, and it went even colder, but somehow, I did not see her put her hand to the knob and turn it. All I know is that she had gone, and that I was desperate to follow her, because I felt that she needed me in some way.

I did not switch on the lamp or put on my dressing-gown, I half ran to catch her up.

The landing outside was lit as if by a low, flickering candle flame. I saw the door of Aunt Addy's room but the wood looked darker, and there were some pictures on the walls that I had not noticed before. It was still so cold my breath made little haws of white in front of my face.

The young woman had gone. I went to the head of the staircase. Below, it was pitch dark. I heard nothing, no footstep, no creak of the floorboards. I was too frightened to go any further.

As I turned, I saw that the flickering light had faded and the landing was in darkness too. I felt my way, trembling, back to my own room and put my hand on the doorknob. As I did so I heard from far below, in the recesses of the house, the woman's sobbing and a calling – it might have been of a name, but it was too faint and far away for me to make it out.

I managed to stumble across the room and switch on the lamp. All was normal. There was just one bed, my own. Nothing had changed.

I looked at the clock. It was a little after three. I was soaked in sweat, shaking, terrified. I did not sleep again that night but sat up in the chair wrapped in the eiderdown with the lamp on, until the late grey dawn came around the curtains. That I had seen a young woman, that she had been getting out of another bed in my room, I had no doubt at all. I had not been dreaming, as I certainly had on the previous night. The difference between the two experiences was quite clear to me. She had been there.

I had never either believed or disbelieved in ghosts, scarcely ever thought about the subject at all. Now, I knew that I had seen one. And I could not throw off not only my fear but the depression her presence inflicted on me. Her distress and agitation, whatever their cause, had affected me profoundly, and from the first moment of my arrival at the door of Farthing House. It was a dark, dreadful, helpless feeling and with it there also went a sense of foreboding.

I was due to leave for home the following morning but

when I joined Aunt Addy for breakfast I felt wretched, tense and strained, quite unfit for a long drive. When I went to Mrs Pearson's office and explained simply that I had not slept well, she expressed concern at once and insisted that I stay on another night. I wanted to, but I did not want to remain in Cedar Room. When I mentioned it, very diffidently, Mrs Pearson gave me a close look and I waited for her to question me but she did not, only told me, slipping her pen nervously round and round between her fingers that there simply was not another vacant room in the house. So I said that of course it did not matter, it was only that I had always felt uneasy sleeping in very large rooms, and laughed it off, trying to reassure her. She pretended that I had.

That morning, Aunt Addy had an appointment with the visiting hairdresser. I didn't feel like sitting about reading papers and chatting in the lounge. They were nice women, the other residents, kind and friendly and welcoming but I was on edge and still enveloped in sadness and foreboding. I needed time to myself.

The weather didn't help. It had gone a degree or two warmer and the rise in temperature had brought a dripping fog and low cloud that masked the lines of the countryside. I trudged around Farthing House gardens but the grass was soaking wet and the sight of the dreary bushes and black trees lowered my spirits further. I set off down the lane, past the three cottages. A dog barked from one, but the others were silent and apparently empty. I suppose that by then I had begun to wallow slightly in my mood and I decided that I might as well go the whole hog and visit the church and its overgrown little graveyard. It was bitterly cold inside. There were some good brasses and a wonderful ornate eighteenth-century monument to a pious local squire, with florid rhymes and madly grieving angels. But the stained glass was in ugly 'uncut moquette' colours, as Stephen would have said, and besides it was actually colder inside the church than out.

I had a prowl around the graveyard, looking here and there at epitaphs. There were a couple of minor gems but otherwise, all was plain, names and dates and dullness and I was about to leave when my eye was caught by some gravestones at the far side near to the field wall. They were set a little apart and neatly arranged in two rows. I bent down and deciphered the faded inscriptions. They were all the graves of babies, newborn or a few days old, and dating from the early years of the century. I wondered why so many, and why all young babies. They had different surnames, though one or two recurred. Had there been some dreadful epidemic in the village? Had the village been much larger then, if there had been so many young families?

At the far end of the row were three adult sized stones. The inscriptions on two had been mossed over but one was clear.

Eliza Maria Dolly.
Died January 20 1902. Aged 19 years.
And also her infant daughter.

As I walked thoughtfully back I saw an elderly man dismount from a bicycle beside the gate and pause, looking towards me.

"Good morning! Gerald Manberry, vicar of the parish. Though really I am semi-retired, there isn't a great deal for a full-time man to take care of nowadays. I see you have been looking at the poor little Farthing House graves."

"Farthing House?"

"Yes, just down the lane. It was a home for young

women and their illegitimate babies from the turn of the century until the last war. Then a military convalescent home, I believe. It's a home for the elderly now of course."

How bleak that sounded. I told him that I had been staying there. "But the graves . . ." I said.

"I suppose a greater number of babies died around the time of birth then, especially in those circumstances. And mothers too, I fear. Poor girls. It's all much safer now. A better world. A better world."

I watched him wheel his ancient bicycle round to the vestry door, before beginning to walk back down the empty lane towards Farthing House. But I was not seeing my surroundings or hearing the caw-cawing of the rooks in the trees above my head. I was seeing the young woman in the night-gown, her arms outstretched, and hearing her cry and feeling again that terrible sadness and distress. I thought of the grave of Eliza Maria Dolly, 'and also her infant daughter'.

I was not afraid any more, not now that I knew who she was and why she had been there, getting out of her bed in Cedar Room, to go in search of her baby. Poor, pale, distraught young thing, she could do no one harm.

I slept well that night, I saw nothing, heard nothing, although in the morning I knew, somehow, that she had been there again, there was the same emptiness in the room and the imprint of her sad spirit upon it.

The fog had cleared and it was a pleasant winter day, intermittently sunny. I left for home after breakfast, having arranged that Aunt Addy was to come to us for Christmas.

She did so and we had a fine time, as happy as we all used to be together, with Stephen and I, Rosamund,

Alec and the others. I shall always be glad of that, for it was Addy's last Christmas. She fell down the stairs at Farthing House the following March, broke her hip and died of a stroke a few days later. They took her to hospital and I saw her there, but afterwards, when her things were to be cleared up, I couldn't face it. Stephen and Alec did everything. I never went back to Farthing House.

I often thought about it though, even dreamed of it. An experience like that affects you profoundly and for ever. But I could not have spoken about it, not to anyone at all. If ever a conversation touched upon the subject of ghosts I kept silent. I had seen one. I knew. That was all.

Some years afterwards, I learned that Farthing House had closed to residents, been sold and then demolished, to make room for a new development – the nearby town was spreading out now. Little Dornford had become a suburb.

I was sad. It had been, in most respects, such a good and happy place.

Then, only a week ago, I saw the name again, quite by chance, it leaped at me from the newspaper. You may remember the case, though you would not have known of any personal connection.

A young woman stole a baby, from its pram outside a shop. The child had only been left for a moment or two but apparently she had been following and keeping watch, waiting to take it. It was found eventually, safe and well. She had looked after it, so I suppose things could have been worse, but the distress caused to the parents was obviously appalling. You can imagine that now, can't you?

They didn't send her to prison, she was taken into medical care. Her defence was that she had stolen the child when she was out of her right mind after the death of her own baby not long before. The child was two days old. Her address was given as Farthing House Close, Little Dornford.

I think of it constantly, see the young, pale, distraught woman, her arms outstretched, searching, hear her sobbing, and the crying of her baby.

But I imagine that she has gone, now that she has what she was looking for.

GREAT GHOST STORIES

(NBC, 1961)
Starring: Lois Nettleton and Vincent Gardenia
Directed by Art Millerman
Story 'Room For One More' by Bennett Cerf

The very earliest television series to specialize in tales of the supernatural was *Great Ghost Stories* which the NBC network in New York launched in July 1961. The episodes were all half an hour long, were broadcast between 9.30 and 10 p.m. and screened 'live'. Like so many productions of this kind during television's infancy, *Great Ghost Stories* was subject to unexpected technical and artistic problems. In one scene set in a haunted house, for example, the studio lighting suddenly failed which added considerably to the atmosphere of the drama, but forced the actors to continue speaking their lines in total darkness until a generator was cut in several moments later! Rumour also has it that on another occasion an actor playing a ghost accidentally tripped over a chair during a haunting scene and, falling painfully, let out a most unspiritual epithet. Notwithstanding such hitches, the series featured dramatizations of a number of classic ghost stories including Edward Bulwer-Lytton's 'The Haunted and the Haunters', 'William Wilson' by Edgar Allan Poe and Saki's little masterpiece of terror, 'Sredi Vashtar' starring Judith Evans and

25

a young Richard Thomas. Among the other actors who starred in the series – quite a few of whom were drawn from the New York stage – were Arthur Hill, Kevin McCarthy, Joanna Linville and Robert Duvall. The quality of the material brought to the screen owed much to the expertise of the show's consultants, Bennett Cerf (1898–1971), already a well-known TV personality, and his wife, Phyllis Fraser, who in 1944 had edited a landmark anthology of ghost stories, *Great Tales of Terror and the Supernatural*, published by Random House and subsequently kept in print in America and Britain until well into the Seventies.

A year after his wife's anthology, Cerf, a former columnist for King Features, New York publisher and writer, and star member of the panel of TV's 'What's My Line', also produced a similar volume, *Famous Ghost Stories*, for Random House, in which he included his own favourites, ranging from Ambrose Bierce's 'The Damned Thing' to contemporary writer August Derleth's 'The Return of Andrew Bentley'. In his introduction to the book, Cerf revealed, 'I never have enjoyed a literary task more genuinely than the compilation of this volume – what unalloyed pleasure it was to escape from the omniscient strategists bent upon planning new world orders and self-appointed critics of the government and military, and lose myself in a world of fantasy and macabre goings-on! Do I believe in ghost stories? Of course, I do!' In the book, Cerf also included what he called 'a few of the current ghost stories that are guaranteed to rivet the attention of any dinner party'. It was from this that *Great Ghost Stories* drew the inspiration for the episode entitled 'Room For One More' which was dramatized live on July 10, 1961 with Lois Nettleton

and Vincent Gardenia. Later the same year, Cerf's story was purchased again for Rod Serling's new series of the unexplained, *The Twilight Zone*, where it formed the basis for an episode entitled, 'Twenty-Two'. Rod Serling himself adapted the story, remaining generally faithfull to the original, although he changed the setting from a Carolina plantation to a hospital and the 'ghostly vision' from a coach to a morgue. Barbara Nichols, Fredd Wayne and Jonathan Harris starred in this second version of Cerf's eerie little tale which is generally considered to have been one of the poorer *Zone* stories and certainly inferior to the *Great Ghost Stories* presentation which effectively launched the ghost story on TV . . .

Do you suffer from dinner parties that sag after the soup course? Do spells of lethargy seize you at literary salons? Are you allergic to moonlight picnics? Try introducing a couple of neatly contrived ghost stories the next time the going is slow, and watch the electrifying results! Guests perk up, goose pimples do likewise, and soon everybody is remembering a story *he* heard about a haunted house, or an ill-mannered ghost, or a thing that behaved in no fashion that was human!

In the following pages I have set down a few of the memorable ghost anecdotes that have been told me in the past few years. Several of them I heard more than once. The minor details varied, but the essentials were always the same. I have tried to keep the stories brief. It seems to me that they are more effective that way.

An intelligent, comely New York girl of twenty-odd summers was invited for the first time to the Carolina estate of some distant relatives. She looked forward to the visit, and bought quite an extensive wardrobe with which to impress her Southern cousins.

The plantation fulfilled her fondest expectations. The grounds, the manor house, the relatives themselves were perfect. She was assigned to a room in the western wing, and prepared to retire for the night in a glow of satisfaction. Her room was drenched with the light of a full moon. Outside was a gravel roadway which curved up to the main entrance of the building.

Just as she was climbing into her bed, she was startled by the sound of horses' hooves on the gravel roadway. She walked to the window, and saw, to her astonishment, a magnificent old coach, drawn by four coal-black horses, pull up sharply directly in front of her window. The coachman jumped from his perch, looked up, and pointed a long, bony finger at her. He was hideous. His face was chalk-white. A deep scar ran the length of his left cheek. His nose was beaked. As he pointed at her, he droned in sepulchral tones: "There is room for one more!" Then, as she recoiled in terror, the coach, the horses and the ominous coachman disappeared completely. The roadway stretched empty before her in the moonlight.

The girl slept little that night, but in the reassuring sunlight of the following morning, she was able to convince herself that the sight she had seen had been nothing more than a nightmare, or an obsession caused by a disordered stomach. She said nothing about it to her hosts.

The next night, however, provided an exact repetition of the first night's procedure. The same coach drove up the roadway. The same coachman pointed to her and croaked: "There is room for one more!" Then the entire equipage disappeared again.

The girl, in complete panic, could scarcely wait for morning. She trumped up some excuse to her hosts, and rushed back to New York. Her doctor had an office on the eighteenth floor of a modern medical center. She taxied there from the station, and told him her story in tremulous tones.

The doctor's matter-of-fact acceptance of her tale did much to quiet her nerves. He persuaded her that she had been the victim of a peculiar hallucination, laughed at her terror, kissed her paternally on the brow, and dismissed her in a state of infinite relief. She rang the bell for the elevator, and a door swung open before her.

The elevator was very crowded. She was about to squeeze her way inside when a familiar voice rang in her ear. "There is room for one more!" it said. The operator was the coachman who had pointed at her! She saw his chalk-white face, the livid scar, the beaked nose! She drew back and screamed, and the elevator door banged shut in her face.

A moment later the building shook with a terrific crash. The elevator that had gone on without her broke loose from its cables and plunged eighteen stories to the ground. Everybody in it, of course, was crushed to a pulp.

Ellison was a person who generally minded his own business, but it was impossible to concentrate on his evening paper after the young man had entered the car and slumped into the seat beside him. In all his years of commuting between New York and Stamford, Ellison had never seen anybody so obviously demoralized and on the verge of collapse. His hands trembled violently, his body twitched, he gave the air of seeing nothing around him and neither knowing nor caring exactly where he was. He mumbled to himself occasionally too, but when

Ellison pointedly sighed and folded up his newspaper, he pulled himself together sufficiently to apologize for fidgeting and making a nuisance of himself. Ellison did not encourage him in any way, and was rather surprised to find himself suddenly plunged into the middle of the young man's story. He had to tell it to *somebody*, he explained.

Nine years ago, he said, I was elected head of the most exclusive fraternity at —College. We had a strict rule that only three members of every new Freshman class be admitted to membership. That kept our active list to an even dozen. Nobody ever refused our bids. Everybody recognized that we were the kingpins of the campus. In what was probably a subconscious effort to prove to ourselves what superior beings we were, our initiations became more and more elaborate and fantastic as the years went by.

I guess it was my idea to take the three neophytes that we selected at the start of my senior year, and bundle them out to a deserted house about fifteen miles from the campus. It had been unoccupied for as long as anybody could remember; it was windowless, sagging, and ugly as it possibly could be. The village legend had it that the house was haunted by the spirit of the man who had lived in it last – a blackguard who murdered his wife and two children, and was probably hanged for his crime. We picked a black, starless night for the initiation, and all the way out to the place poured tales of horror and the supernatural into the ears of our three apprehensive Freshmen.

I picked the frailest of the kids to go into the house first. He was the son of a famous novelist who had won the Pulitzer Prize the year before, and was by way of being a boy prodigy himself. His eyes betrayed his fear when we shipped him off, but he compressed his lips and set out bravely enough. The rest of us built a bonfire and relaxed around it. Ted Williams had brought his guitar. Everybody joined in the songs except the other two Freshmen, who sat off to one side silently, their hands clasped about their knees.

I watched the kid enter the deserted house myself. It was about two hundred yards from where we were gathered. His instructions were to stay inside for a half hour, and then come back to us. When forty-five minutes went by without signs of hide or hair of him, I experienced my first uneasiness.

"We'll pay him back for these smart-aleck shenanigans," I said, and despatched the second Freshman to go fetch him. The boy set out across the field without a word, and entered the house. Ten minutes more went by. Nothing happened. There wasn't a sound anywhere. The fire was burning low. Williams had put aside his guitar. We just sat there watching.

"Damn these kids," I said at last. "They're a little too smart for their own good. Davis, get in there and bring them back fast, or by cracky, we'll skin you alive!" Davis was our prize conquest – a handsome, two-hundred-pound boy whose scholastic records foreshadowed an almost certain place on the next year's All-American squad. He had already been elected President of the Freshman class.

"I'll get 'em," grinned Davis, and loped toward the house. "Come out of there, you lugs," we heard him call before he disappeared from view.

And then we just sat there. I guess it was only ten minutes, but it seemed like hours. "It looks like my move, fellows," I said finally. "We'll have to teach these brats that they can't play tricks on their elders this way." Nobody said anything at all, and I got up and walked slowly over to the deserted house.

The first thing that struck me when I entered was a musty smell – like the smell of an attic full of old books and newspapers. I yelled for the boys, and poked my flashlight into every corner, but there wasn't a sign of them. Only a faint, steady tap that seemed to come from the roof. Filled with a dread I can't describe to you, I climbed the creaking stairway to the second floor, and the ladder leading to the roof. I stuck my head through the open skylight. There was Davis, stretched out on his stomach! His hair had turned snow white. His eyes rolled in his head. He was mad as a hatter. In his hand he had a hammer covered with blood. He was rapping weakly with it on the tin parapet, in a senseless rhythm. I screamed to him, but he paid no attention to me at all. He just went on tapping with that bloody hammer. I got back to the fellows waiting for me somehow or other, and we managed to carry Davis down from the roof. He died in the college hospital the next morning without uttering a single syllable. We never found the slightest trace of the other two boys . . .

Ellison fidgeted in his seat, not quite certain whether or not he was being gulled. The young man certainly was in a desperate condition. A drunkard, perhaps, or dope fiend? All this had happened nine years ago according to the young man's own story, he pointed out carefully; surely he had not been in such a state all that time! The young man turned burning eyes upon him.

On the anniversary of that night every year, he explained, one of the nine men who had been on that hazing party had gone stark, raving mad. They were found gibbering nonsense, and tapping the floor with a blood-soaked hammer. They all died within twenty-four hours' time.

Tomorrow, said the young man in low and precise tones, is the ninth anniversary of that night. And I'm the only one left . . .

A young lady dreamed one night that she was walking along a strange country lane. It led her up a wooded hill whose summit was crowned with the loveliest little white frame house and garden she ever had seen. Unable to conceal her delight, she knocked loudly on the door of the house, and finally it was opened by an old, old man with a long white beard. Just as she started to talk to him, she woke up. Every detail of this dream was so vivid in her memory that she carried it about in her head for days. Then, on three successive nights, she had precisely the same dream again. Always she awakened at the point where her conversation with the old man was about to begin.

A few weeks later, the young lady was motoring to Litchfield for a week-end party, when she suddenly tugged at the driver's sleeve, and begged him to stop. There, at the right of the concrete highway, was the country lane of her dreams! "Wait for me a few moments," she pleaded, and, her heart beating wildly, set out on the lane. She was no longer surprised when it wound to the top of the wooded hill and the house whose every feature was now so familiar to her. The old man responded to her impatient summons. "Tell me," she began, "is this little house for sale?" "That it is," said the man, "but I would scarcely advise you to buy it. You see, young lady, this house is haunted!" "Haunted," echoed the girl. "For heaven's sake, by whom?" "By you," said the old man, and softly closed the door . . .

*   *   *

John Sullivan was the only son of a doting mother, widowed during the First World War. He was handsome, richly endowed with Irish charm, and a particular favorite of the ladies. They could not resist his fetching smile. In fact, they never tried.

John couldn't explain how he suddenly came to be walking up Euclid Avenue. He had no memory of how he got there, nor of what he had been doing previously that morning. "I must be walking in my sleep," he said to himself in some perplexity. Two lovely young girls were approaching him. John stopped them with the confidence born of years of easy conquest. "Could you be telling me the time?" he asked with his easy smile. To his surprise, one of the girls screamed, and both of them careened past him. Several other people, he noticed, seemed terrified by the sight of him. One man flattened himself against a show window of the Halle Store to get out of his way.

Greatly puzzled, John Sullivan started to climb into a taxi. Just as he was giving the address of his home, however, the driver looked at him for the first time, smothered an exclamation, pushed him out of the cab, and drove off with a grinding of gears.

John's head was spinning. He entered a drugstore, and phoned to his mother. A strange voice answered.

"Mrs Sullivan?" it echoed. "Now who would be expecting to find her in now? Don't you know that her poor son John was caught in a machine at the bindery yesterday and mangled to death? She's out at the cemetery where they're burying him now!"

Two ladies from the faculty of a famous New England college for women decided to spend one of their vacations in an automobile tour to California and back. They traveled westward by way of the Petrified Forest and the Grand Canyon, and headed for home on the Salt Lake City route. They were two normal, unimaginative women, enjoying to the full a tour of their native country.

Late one evening, they were driving through the flat and monotonous fields of Kansas, intent upon reaching a hostel some thirty miles distant, when their car broke down. They were the kind of drivers who knew nothing whatever about motors. They had no choice but to wait for some good Samaritan to come driving along and help them – and it soon became obvious that no other car was likely to come that way until the next morning.

It was then that one of the ladies noticed a two-story, unpainted farmhouse, set back some distance from the road. They approached it gingerly, wary of watchdogs, and knocked timidly on the front door. Nobody answered. The impression grew on them that the house was uninhabited. When they discovered that the door was unlocked, they entered, calling loudly, and flashing their pocket searchlight in every corner. They found the living room and kitchen in good order, but an undisturbed layer of dust indicated that no human had been in them for days.

The ladies blessed their luck, and decided to spend the night in the living room. The couch was fairly comfortable, and they bundled themselves up in robes which they fetched from the stalled automobile. There were dry logs in the fireplace; the ladies soon had a roaring fire going, and, in the light of the flickering embers, went peacefully to sleep.

Some hours later, one of the ladies awoke with the distinct feeling that somebody had entered the house. Her friend jumped up at precisely the same moment. A chill seemed to run through the room, followed by the unmistakable scent of the salt sea, although the nearest ocean front was over a thousand miles away. Then a young man walked into the room! Rather he *floated* in, because they heard no footsteps. He was dressed in boots and oilskins; seaspray glistened on his rough stubble of reddish beard. He moved to the dying fire, shivering violently, and knelt down before it.

One of the women screamed. The figure turned slowly, gave a sort of mournful sigh, and slowly dissolved into nothingness. The terrified women clutched each other desperately, and lay there until the morning sun poured through the dusty window panes. "I saw it; I know I did!" said one of them. "Of course you did; I saw it too," the other reassured her, and then pointed dramatically to the fireplace. Before it was a small puddle of brackish water, and a piece of slimy green weed!

The ladies made for the open air, but the bolder of the two snatched up the piece of weed before they bolted, and held it gingerly at arm's length. When it dried, she placed it carefully in her bag.

Eventually a car rattled along the highway, and the driver cheerfully consented to tow the ladies to the nearest garage. While the mechanic tinkered with the engine, the ladies asked him about the deserted house some miles back on the road. "That must have been the Newton place," he said with no special show of interest. "Been empty nigh on to two years now. When Old Man Newton died, he left it lock, stock and barrel to his son Tom, who said he didn't like farming, and lit out one day for the East. Spoke of taking to the sea, like his great-grandfather did. Ain't none of us seen hide nor hair of him since that day!"

When the ladies returned to their college, they took the green weed, which still seemed clammy and damp, to the head of the botany department. He readily confirmed their suspicions. "It's seaweed, all right," he told them. "Furthermore, it's a kind that's only found on dead bodies!" The ship news reporter of the *Evening Sun* reported that a Thomas Newton had sailed as first-class seaman on a freighter called the *Robert B. Anthony* on April 14, 1937. It had gone down with all hands aboard in a storm off the Greenland coast six weeks thereafter.

A favorite story of New York literary circles a few years ago concerned the beautiful young girl in the white satin dress. It was one of those anecdotes that everybody swore had actually happened to his first cousin or next-door neighbor, and several narrators got very testy when they were informed that several other people's cousins had evidently undergone the same experience a few weeks before.

At any rate, the legend maintained that a very lovely but poverty-stricken damsel was invited to a formal dance. It was her chance to enter a brand-new world. Who knew but what some rich young man would fall in love with her and lift her out of her life in a box factory? The catch in the matter was that she had no suitable dress to wear for such a great occasion.

"Why don't you rent a costume for the evening?" suggested a friend. She did. She went to a pawnshop near her little flat and for a surprisingly reasonable sum rented a beautiful white satin evening gown with all the accessories to match. Miraculously, it fit her like a glove, and she looked so radiant when she arrived at the party that she created a minor sensation. She was cut in on again and again, and as she whirled happily around the floor she felt that her luck indeed had changed for good.

Then she began to feel faint and nauseated. She fought against a growing discomfort as long as she could, but finally she stole out of the house and had just sufficient strength to stagger into a cab and creep up the stairs to her room. She threw herself onto her bed, broken-hearted, and it was then, possibly in her delirium, that she heard a woman's voice whispering into her ear. It was harsh and bitter. "Give me back my dress," it said. "Give me back my dress! It belongs to the dead . . ."

The next morning the lifeless body of the young girl was found stretched out on her bed. The unusual circumstances led the coroner to order an autopsy. The girl had been poisoned by embalming fluid, which had entered her pores when she grew overheated from dancing. The pawnbroker was reluctant to admit that he knew where the dress came from, but spoke out when he heard that the District Attorney's office was involved. It had been sold him by an undertaker's assistant, who had taken it from the body of a dead girl just before the casket was nailed down for the last time.

A dozen miles outside of Baltimore, the main road from New York (Route Number One) is crossed by another important highway. It is a dangerous intersection, and there is talk of building an underpass for the east-west road. To date, however, the plans exist only on paper.

Dr Eckersall was driving home from a country-club dance late one Saturday night. He slowed up for the intersection, and was surprised to see a lovely young girl, dressed in the sheerest of evening gowns, beckoning to him for a lift. He jammed on his brakes, and motioned her to climb into the back seat of his roadster. "All cluttered up with golf clubs and bags up here in front," he explained. "But what on earth is a youngster like you doing out here all alone at this time of night?"

"It's too long a story to tell you now," said the girl. Her

voice was sweet and somewhat shrill – like the tinkling of sleigh bells. "Please, please take me home. I'll explain everything there. The address is —North Charles Street. I do hope it's not too far out of your way!"

The doctor grunted, and set the car in motion. He drove rapidly to the address she had given him, and as he pulled up before the shuttered house, he said, "Here we are." Then he turned around. The back seat was empty!

"What the devil?" the doctor muttered to himself. The girl couldn't possibly have fallen from the car. Nor could she simply have vanished. He rang insistently on the house bell, confused as he had never been in his life before. At long last the door opened. A gray-haired, very tired-looking man peered out at him.

"I can't tell you what an amazing thing has happened," began the doctor. "A young girl gave me this address a while back. I drove her here and —"

"Yes, yes, I know," said the man wearily. "This has happened several other Saturday evenings in the past month. That young girl, sir, was my daughter. She was killed in an automobile accident at that intersection where you saw her almost two years ago . . ."

MYSTERY AND IMAGINATION

> (ABC TV, 1966–1970)
> Starring: Edward Woodward, Clifford Rose &
> Elizabeth Begley
> Directed by Bill Bain
> Story 'The Listener' by Algernon Blackwood

Mystery and Imagination **was the first British ghost story series, and during the four years of its transmission brought to the small screen a number of excellect short stories from literary sources as well as several of the classic supernatural novels including** *Frankenstein* **(with Ian Holm as the scientist and Ron Pember his creature),** *Dracula* **(Denholm Elliott unforgettable as the Count, and ably supported by Susan George and Bernard Archard) and** *Sweeney Todd* **(with Freddie Jones giving one of his most charismatic performances as the Demon Barber of Fleet Street alongside Heather Canning as his pie-making accomplice, Mrs Lovett). Amongst the short stories used by the programme were several by Robert Louis Stevenson, Edgar Allan Poe, Joseph Sheridan Le Fanu, M.R. James (of whom more in the next selection) and Algernon Blackwood (1869–1951). Blackwood was, in fact, a name already familiar to many members of the audience as 'The Ghost Man' – because for years he had been a regular broadcaster on radio telling supernatural stories, after which he had graduated naturally to television during** its early years to recount similar yarns of ghostly happenings and hauntings. It was in 1949 that the tall, distinguished-looking Blackwood with his weather-beaten face, piercing eyes and sombre voice was invited by BBC producer Stephen McCormack to be one of the guests on *Saturday Night Story* and entertain the ever-growing audience of viewers. According to a contemporary report, Blackwood did not rehearse for these appearances and often extemporized his stories as he went along. He was never known to over-run, however, and was said to have held the studio crew every bit as spellbound as the watchers at home. Algernon Blackwood's contributions to the medium – which had actually begun on the BBC's very first public broadcast in 1936 – were later marked with the award of the Television Society's Medal for Outstanding Artistic Achievement.

Blackwood, who was described by H.P.Lovecraft as, 'the one absolute and unquestioned master of weird atmosphere', became interested in the occult while he was still a young man, and after a considerable amount of travel in North America, he finally found work as a journalist on the *New York Evening Sun* and then the *New York Times*. It was around the turn of the century that he returned to Britain and began writing the short stories and novels – including *A Haunted Island* (1899), *The Empty House* (1906) and *The Lost Valley* (1910) – which made him popular with the reading public and, in turn, lead to his appearances on radio and television. Many of Blackwood's stories were based on his own strange experiences or were drawn from the accounts of eyewitnesses to inexplicable phenomena: facts which gave such a frisson to his appearances on *Saturday Night Story*.

His work was equally well treated on *Mystery and Imagination* by producer Jonathan Alwyn, a man with a real feel for the macabre which he demonstrated with startling effect in his version of *Dracula* when Denholm Elliott was seen visibly disintigrating during the closing moments in a display of special effects the like of which had not been witnessed before on television. The well-known writer William Trevor adapted Blackwood's story about a shy lepidopterist and what happens to him in a strange old house – and according to *TV Times*, director Bill Bain got an 'award winning performance' from Edward Woodward as Reeve. Here is the story from which that groundbreaking production was made and screened on March 30, 1968.

Sept. 4. – I have hunted all over London for rooms suited to my income – £120 a year – and have at last found them. Two rooms, without modern conveniences, it is true, and in an old, ramshackle building, but within a stone's throw of P—Place and in an eminently respectable street. The rent is only £25 a year. I had begun to despair when at last I found them by chance. The chance was a mere chance, and unworthy of record. I had to sign a lease for a year, and I did so willingly. The furniture from our old place in H—shire, which has been stored so long, will just suit them.

Oct. 1. – Here I am in my two rooms, in the centre of London, and not far from the offices of the periodicals where occasionally I dispose of an article or two. The building is at the end of a *cul-de-sac*. The alley is well paved and clean, and lined chiefly with the backs of sedate and institutional-looking buildings. There is a stable in it. My own house is dignified with the title of 'Chambers.' I feel as if one day the honour must prove too much for it, and it will swell with pride – and fall asunder. It is very old. The floor of my sitting-room has valleys and low hills on it, and the top of the door slants away from the ceiling with a glorious disregard of what is usual. They must have quarrelled – fifty years ago – and have been going apart ever since.

Oct. 2. – My landlady is old and thin, with a faded, dusty face. She is uncommunicative. The few words she utters seem to cost her pain. Probably her lungs are half choked with dust. She keeps my rooms as free from this commodity as possible, and has the assistance of a strong girl who brings up the breakfast and lights the fire. As I have said already, she is not communicative. In reply to pleasant efforts on my part she informed me briefly that I was the only occupant of the house at present. My rooms had not been occupied for some years. There had been other gentlemen upstairs, but they had left.

She never looks straight at me when she speaks, but fixes her dim eyes on my middle waistcoat button, till I get nervous and begin to think it isn't on straight, or is the wrong sort of button altogether.

Oct. 8. – My week's book is nicely kept, and so far is reasonable. Milk and sugar 7d., bread 6d., butter 8d., marmalade 6d., eggs 1s. 8d., laundress 2s. 9d., oil 6d., attendance 5s.; total 12s. 2d.

The landlady has a son who, she told me, is "somethink on a homnibus." He comes occasionally to see her. I think he drinks, for he talks very loud, regardless of the hour

43

of the day or night, and tumbles about over the furniture downstairs.

All the morning I sit indoors writing—articles; verses for the comic papers; a novel I've been 'at' for three years, and concerning which I have dreams; a children's book, in which the imagination has free rein; and another book which is to last as long as myself, since it is an honest record of my soul's advance or retreat in the struggle of life. Besides these, I keep a book of poems which I use as a safety valve, and concerning which I have no dreams whatsoever. Between the lot I am always occupied. In the afternoons I generally try to take a walk for my health's sake, through Regent's Park, into Kensington Gardens, or farther afield to Hampstead Heath.

Oct. 10. – Everything went wrong to-day. I have two eggs for breakfast. This morning one of them was bad. I rang the bell for Emily. When she came in I was reading the paper, and, without looking up, I said, "Egg's bad." "Oh, is it, sir?" she said; "I'll get another one," and went out, taking the egg with her. I waited my breakfast for her return, which was in five minutes. She put the new egg on the table and went away. But, when I looked down, I saw that she had taken away the good egg and left the bad one – all green and yellow – in the slop basin. I rang again.

"You've taken the wrong egg," I said.

"Oh!" she exclaimed; "I thought the one I took down didn't smell so *very* bad." In due time she returned with the good egg, and I resumed my breakfast with two eggs, but less appetite. It was all very trivial, to be sure, but so stupid that I felt annoyed. The character of that egg influenced everything I did. I wrote a bad article, and tore it up. I got a bad headache. I used bad words – to myself.

Everything was bad, so I 'chucked' work and went for a long walk.

I dined at a cheap chop-house on my way back, and reached home about nine o'clock.

Rain was just beginning to fall as I came in, and the wind was rising. It promised an ugly night. The alley looked dismal and dreary, and the hall of the house, as I passed through it, felt chilly as a tomb. It was the first stormy night I had experienced in my new quarters. The draughts were awful. They came criss-cross, met in the middle of the room, and formed eddies and whirlpools and cold silent currents that almost lifted the hair of my head. I stuffed up the sashes of the windows with neckties and odd socks, and sat over the smoky fire to keep warm. First I tried to write, but found it too cold. My hand turned to ice on the paper.

What tricks the wind did play with the old place! It came rushing up the forsaken alley with a sound like the feet of a hurrying crowd of people who stopped suddenly at the door. I felt as if a lot of curious folk had arranged themselves just outside and were staring up at my windows. Then they took to their heels again and fled whispering and laughing down the lane, only, however, to return with the next gust of wind and repeat their impertinence. On the other side of my room a single square window opens into a sort of shaft, or well, that measures about six feet across to the back wall of another house. Down this funnel the wind dropped, and puffed and shouted. Such noises I never heard before. Between these two entertainments I sat over the fire in a great-coat, listening to the deep booming in the chimney. It was like being in a ship at sea, and I almost looked for the floor to rise in indulations and rock to and fro.

*   *   *

45

Oct. 12. – I wish I were not quite so lonely – and so poor. And yet I love both my loneliness and my poverty. The former makes me appreciate the companionship of the wind and rain, while the latter preserves my liver and prevents me wasting time in dancing attendance upon women. Poor, ill-dressed men are not acceptable 'attendants.'

My parents are dead, and my only sister is – no, not dead exactly, but married to a very rich man. They travel most of the time, he to find his health, she to lose herself. Through sheer neglect on her part she has long passed out of my life. The door closed when, after an absolute silence of five years, she sent me a cheque for £50 at Christmas. It was signed by her husband! I returned it to her in a thousand pieces and in an unstamped envelope. So at least I had the satisfaction of knowing that it cost her something! She wrote back with a broad quill pen that covered a whole page with three lines, 'You are evidently as cracked as ever, and rude and ungrateful into the bargain.' It had always been my special terror lest the insanity in my father's family should leap across the generations and appear in me. This thought haunted me, and she knew it. So after this little exchange of civilities the door slammed, never to open again. I heard the crash it made, and, with it, the falling from the walls of my heart of many little bits of china with their own peculiar value – rare china, some of it, that only needed dusting. The same walls, too, carried mirrors in which I used sometimes to see reflected the misty lawns of childhood, the daisy chains, the wind-torn blossoms scattered through the orchard by warm rains, the robbers' cave in the long walk, and the hidden store of apples in the hay-loft. She was my inseparable companion then – but, when the door slammed, the mirrors cracked across their entire length, and the visions they held vanished for ever. Now I am quite alone. At forty one cannot begin all over again to build up careful friendships, and all others are comparatively worthless.

Oct. 14. – My bedroom is 10 by 10. It is below the level of the front room, and a step leads down into it. Both rooms are very quiet on calm nights, for there is no traffic down this forsaken alley-way. In spite of the occasional larks of the wind, it is a most sheltered strip. At its upper end, below my windows, all the cats of the neighbourhood congregate as soon as darkness gathers. They lie undisturbed on the long ledge of a blind window of the opposite building, for after the postman has come and gone at 9.30, no footsteps ever dare to interrupt their sinister conclave, no step but my own, or sometimes the unsteady footfall of the son who "is somethink on a homnibus."

Oct. 15. – I dined at an 'A.B.C.' shop on poached eggs and coffee, and then went for a stroll round the outer edge of Regent's Park. It was ten o'clock when I got home. I counted no less than thirteen cats, all of a dark colour, crouching under the lee side of the alley walls. It was a cold night, and the stars shone like points of ice in a blue-black sky. The cats turned their heads and stared at me in silence as I passed. An odd sensation of shyness took possession of me under the glare of so many pairs of unblinking eyes. As I fumbled with the latch-key they jumped noiselessly down and pressed against my legs, as if anxious to be let in. But I slammed the door in their faces and ran quickly upstairs. The front room, as I entered to grope for the matches, felt as cold as a stone vault, and the air held an unusual dampness.

*   *   *

Oct. 17. – For several days I have been working on a ponderous article that allows no play for the fancy. My imagination requires a judicious rein; I am afraid to let it loose, for it carries me sometimes into appalling places beyond the stars and beneath the world. No one realises the danger more than I do. But what a foolish thing to write here – for there is no one to know, no one to realise! My mind of late has held unusual thoughts, thoughts I have never had before, about medicines and drugs and the treatment of strange illnesses. I cannot imagine their source. At no time in my life have I dwelt upon such ideas as now constantly throng my brain. I have had no exercise lately, for the weather has been shocking; and all my afternoons have been spent in the reading-room of the British Museum, where I have a reader's ticket.

I have made an unpleasant discovery: there are rats in the house. At night from my bed I have heard them scampering across the hills and valleys of the front room, and my sleep has been a good deal disturbed in consequence.

Oct. 19. – The landlady, I find, has a little boy with her, probably her son's child. In fine weather he plays in the alley, and draws a wooden cart over the cobbles. One of the wheels is off, and it makes a most distracting noise. After putting up with it as long as possible, I found it was getting on my nerves, and I could not write. So I rang the bell. Emily answered it.

"Emily, will you ask the little fellow to make less noise? It's impossible to work."

The girl went downstairs, and soon afterwards the child was called in by the kitchen door. I felt rather a brute for spoiling his play. In a few minutes, however, the noise began again, and I felt that he was the brute. He dragged the broken toy with a string over the stones till the rattling noise jarred every nerve in my body. It became unbearable, and I rang the bell a second time.

"That noise *must* be put a stop to!" I said to the girl, with decision.

"Yes, sir," she grinned, "I know; but one of the wheels is hoff. The men in the stable offered to mend it for 'im, but he wouldn't let them. He says he likes it that way."

"I can't help what he likes. The noise must stop. I can't write."

"Yes, sir; I'll tell Mrs Monson."

The noise stopped for the day then.

Oct. 23. – Every day for the past week that cart has rattled over the stones, till I have come to think of it as a huge carrier's van with four wheels and two horses; and every morning I have been obliged to ring the bell and have it stopped. The last time Mrs Monson herself came up, and said she was sorry I had been annoyed; the sounds should not occur again. With rare discursiveness she went on to ask if I was comfortable, and how I liked the rooms. I replied cautiously. I mentioned the rats. She said they were mice. I spoke of the draughts. She said, "Yes, it were a draughty 'ouse." I referred to the cats, and she said they had been as long as she could remember. By way of conclusion, she informed me that the house was over two hundred years old, and that the last gentleman who had occupied my rooms was a painter who "'ad real Jimmy Bueys and Raffles 'anging all hover the walls." It took me some moments to discern that Cimabue and Raphael were in the woman's mind.

Oct. 24. – Last night the son who is "somethink on a

homnibus" came in. He had evidently been drinking, for I heard loud and angry voices below in the kitchen long after I had gone to bed. Once, too, I caught the singular words rising up to me through the floor, "Burning from top to bottom is the only thing that'll ever make this 'ouse right." I knocked on the floor, and the voices ceased suddenly, though later I again heard their clamour in my dreams.

These rooms are very quiet, almost too quiet sometimes. On windless nights they are silent as the grave, and the house might be miles in the country. The roar of London's traffic reaches me only in heavy, distant vibrations. It holds an ominous note sometimes, like that of an approaching army, or an immense tidal-wave very far away thundering in the night.

Oct. 27. – Mrs Monson, though admirably silent, is a foolish, fussy woman. She does such stupid things. In dusting the room she puts all my things in the wrong places. The ash-trays, which should be on the writing-table, she sets in a silly row on the mantelpiece. The pen-tray, which should be beside the inkstand, she hides away cleverly among the books on my reading-desk. My gloves she arranges daily in idiotic array upon a half-filled book-shelf, and I always have to rearrange them on the low table by the door. She places my armchair at impossible angles between the fire and the light, and the tablecloth – the one with Trinity Hall stains – she puts on the table in such a fashion that when I look at it I feel as if my tie and all my clothes were on crooked and awry. She exasperates me. Her very silence and meekness are irritating. Sometimes I feel inclined to throw the inkstand at her, just to bring an expression into her watery eyes and a squeak from those colourless lips. Dear me! What violent expressions I am making use of!

How very foolish of me! And yet it almost seems as if the words were not my own, but had been spoken into my ear – I mean, I never make use of such terms naturally.

Oct. 30. – I have been here a month. The place does not agree with me, I think. My headaches are more frequent and violent, and my nerves are a perpetual source of discomfort and annoyance.

I have conceived a great dislike for Mrs Monson, a feeling I am certain she reciprocates. Somehow, the impression comes frequently to me that there are goings on in this house of which I know nothing, and which she is careful to hide from me.

Last night her son slept in the house, and this morning as I was standing at the window I saw him go out. He glanced up and caught my eye. It was a loutish figure and a singularly repulsive face that I saw, and he gave me the benefit of a very unpleasant leer. At least, so I imagined.

Evidently I am getting absurdly sensitive to trifles, and I suppose it is my disordered nerves making themselves felt. In the British Museum this afternoon I noticed several people at the readers' table staring at me and watching every movement I made. Whenever I looked up from my books I found their eyes upon me. It seemed to me unnecessary and unpleasant, and I left earlier than was my custom. When I reached the door I threw back a last look into the room, and saw every head at the table turned in my direction. It annoyed me very much, and yet I know it is foolish to take not of such things. When I am well they pass me by. I must get more regular exercise. Of late I have had next to none.

Nov. 2. – The utter stillness of this house is beginning

to oppress me. I wish there were other fellows living upstairs. No footsteps ever sound overhead, and no tread ever passes my door to go up the next flight of stairs. I am beginning to feel some curiosity to go up myself and see what the upper rooms are like. I feel lonely here and isolated, swept into a deserted corner of the world and forgotten . . . Once I actually caught myself gazing into the long, cracked mirrors, trying to see the sunlight dancing beneath the trees in the orchard. But only deep shadows seemed to congregate there now, and I soon desisted.

It has been very dark all day, and no wind stirring. The fogs have begun. I had to use a reading-lamp all this morning. There was no cart to be heard to-day. I actually missed it. This morning, in the gloom and silence, I think I could almost have welcomed it. After all, the sound is a very human one, and this empty house at the end of the alley holds other noises that are not quite so satisfactory.

I have never once seen a policeman in the lane, and the postmen always hurry out with no evidence of a desire to loiter.

10 P.M. – As I write this I hear no sound but the deep murmur of the distant traffic and the low sighing of the wind. The two sounds melt into one another. Now and again a cat raises its shrill, uncanny cry upon the darkness. The cats are always there under my windows when the darkness falls. The wind is dropping into the funnel with a noise like the sudden sweeping of immense distant wings. It is a dreary night. I feet lost and forgotten.

Nov. 3. – From my windows I can see arrivals. When any one comes to the door I can just see the hat and shoulders and the hand on the bell. Only two fellows have been to see me since I came here two months ago. Both of them I saw from the window before they came up, and heard their voices asking if I was in. Neither of them ever came back.

I have finished the ponderous article. On reading it through, however, I was dissatisfied with it, and drew my pencil through almost every page. There were strange expressions and ideas in it that I could not explain, and viewed with amazement, not to say alarm. They did not sound like my *very own*, and I could not remember having written them. Can it be that my memory is beginning to be affected?

My pens are never to be found. That stupid old woman puts them in a different place each day. I must give her due credit for finding so many new hiding places; such ingenuity is wonderful. I have told her repeatedly, but she always says, "I'll speak to Emily, sir." Emily always says, "I'll tell Mrs Monson, sir." Their foolishness makes me irritable and scatters all my thoughts. I should like to stick the lost pens into them and turn them out, blind-eyed, to be scratched and mauled by those thousand hungry cats. Whew! What a ghastly thought! Where in the world did it come from? Such an idea is no more my own than it is the policeman's. Yet I felt I *had* to write it. It was like a voice singing in my head, and my pen wouldn't stop till the last word was finished. What ridiculous nonsense! I must and will restrain myself. I must take more regular exercise; my nerves and liver plague me horribly.

Nov. 4. – I attended a curious lecture in the French quarter on 'Death,' but the room was so hot and I was so weary that I fell asleep. The only part I heard, however, touched my imagination vividly. Speaking of suicides, the lecturer

53

said that self-murder was no escape from the miseries of the present, but only a preparation of greater sorrow for the future. Suicides, he declared, cannot shirk their responsibilities so easily. They must return to take up life exactly where they laid it so violently down, but with the added pain and punishment of their weakness. Many of them wander the earth in unspeakable misery till they can *reclothe* themselves in the body of some one else – generally a lunatic, or weak-minded person, who cannot resist the hideous obsession. This is their only means of escape. Surely a weird and horrible idea! I wish I had slept all the time and not heard it at all. My mind is morbid enough without such ghastly fancies. Such mischievous propaganda should be stopped by the police. I'll write to the *Times* and suggest it. Good idea.

I walked home through Greek Street, Soho, and imagined that a hundred years had slipped back into place and De Quincey was still there, haunting the night with invocations to his 'just, subtle, and mighty' drug. His vast dreams seemed to hover not very far away. Once started in my brain, the pictures refused to go away; and I saw him sleeping in that cold, tenantless mansion with the strange little waif who was afraid of its ghosts, both together in the shadows under a single horseman's cloak; or wandering in the companionship of the spectral Anne; or, later still, on his way to the eternal rendezvous at the foot of Great Titchfield Street, the rendezvous she never was able to keep. What an unutterable gloom, what an untold horror of sorrow and suffering comes over me as I try to realise something of what that man – boy he then was – must have taken into his lonely heart.

As I came up the alley I saw a light in the top window, and a head and shoulders thrown in an exaggerated shadow upon the blind. I wondered what the son could be doing up there at such an hour.

Nov. 5. – This morning, while writing, some one came up the creaking stairs and knocked cautiously at my door. Thinking it was the landlady, I said, "Come in!" The knock was repeated, and I cried louder, "Come in, come in!" But no one turned the handle, and I continued my writing with a vexed "Well, stay out, then!" under my breath. Went on writing? I tried to, but my thoughts had suddenly dried up at their source. I could not set down a single word. It was a dark, yellow-fog morning, and there was little enough inspiration in the air as it was, but that stupid woman standing just outside my door waiting to be told again to come in roused a spirit of vexation that filled my head to the exclusion of all else. At last I jumped up and opened the door myself.

"What do you want, and why in the world don't you come in?" I cried out. But the words dropped into empty air. There was no one there. The fog poured up the dingy staircase in deep yellow coils, but there was no sign of a human being anywhere.

I slammed the door, with imprecations upon the house and its noises, and went back to my work. A few minutes later Emily came in with a letter.

"Were you or Mrs Monson outside a few minutes ago knocking at my door?"

"No, sir."

"Are you sure?"

"Mrs Monson's gone to market, and there's no one but me and the child in the 'ole 'ouse, and I've been washing the dishes for the last hour, sir."

I fancied the girl's face turned a shade paler. She fidgeted towards the door with a glance over her shoulder.

"Wait, Emily," I said, and then told her what I had heard. She stared stupidly at me, though her eyes shifted now and then over the articles in the room.

"Who was it?" I asked when I had come to the end.

"Mrs Monson says it's honly mice," she said, as if repeating a learned lesson.

"Mice!" I exclaimed; "it's nothing of the sort. Some one was feeling about outside my door. Who was it? Is the son in the house?"

Her whole manner changed suddenly, and she became earnest instead of evasive. She seemed anxious to tell the truth.

"Oh no, sir; there's no one in the house at all but you and me and the child, and there couldn't 'ave been nobody at your door. As for them knocks—" She stopped abruptly, as though she had said too much.

"Well, what about the knocks?" I said more gently.

"Of course," she stammered, "the knocks isn't mice, nor the footsteps neither, but then—" Again she came to a full halt.

"Anything wrong with the house?"

"Lor', no, sir; the drains is splendid!"

"I don't mean drains, girl. I mean, did anything – anything bad ever happen here?"

She flushed up to the roots of her hair, and then turned suddenly pale again. She was obviously in considerable distress, and there was something she was anxious, yet afraid to tell – some forbidden thing she was not allowed to mention.

"I don't mind what it was, only I should like to know," I said encouragingly.

Raising her frightened eyes to my face, she began to blurt out something about "that which 'appened once to a gentleman that lived hupstairs," when a shrill voice calling her name sounded below.

"Emily, Emily!" It was the returning landlady, and the girl tumbled downstairs as if pulled backward by a rope, leaving me full of conjectures as to what in the world could have happened to a gentleman *upstairs* that could in so curious a manner affect my ears *downstairs*.

Nov. 10. – I have done capital work; have finished the ponderous article and had it accepted for the—*Review*, and another one ordered. I feel well and cheerful, and have had regular exercise and good sleep; no headaches, no nerves, no liver! Those pills the chemist recommended are wonderful. I can watch the child playing with his cart and feel no annoyance; sometimes I almost feel inclined to join him. Even the grey-faced landlady rouses pity in me; I am sorry for her: so worn, so weary, so oddly put together, just like the building. She looks as if she had once suffered some shock of terror, and was momentarily dreading another. When I spoke to her to-day very gently about not putting the pens in the ash-tray and the gloves on the book-shelf she raised her faint eyes to mine for the first time, and said with the ghost of a smile, "I'll try and remember, sir," I felt inclined to pat her on the back and say, "Come, cheer up and be jolly. Life's not so bad after all." Oh! I am much better. There's nothing like open air and success and good sleep. They build up as if by magic the portions of the heart eaten down by despair and unsatisfied yearnings. Even to the cats I feel friendly. When I came in at eleven o'clock to-night they followed me to the door in a stream, and I stooped down to stroke the one nearest to me. Bah! The brute hissed and spat, and struck at me with her paws. The claw caught my hand and drew blood in a thin line. The others danced sideways into the darkness, screeching, as though I had done them an injury. I believe these cats really hate me. Perhaps they are only waiting to be reinforced. Then they will attack me. Ha, ha! In spite of the momentary annoyance, this fancy sent me laughing upstairs to my room.

The fire was out, and the room seemed unusually cold. As I groped my way over to the mantelpiece to find the matches I realised all at once that there was another person standing beside me in the darkness. I could, of course, see nothing, but my fingers, feeling along the ledge, came into forcible contact with something that was at once withdrawn. It was cold and moist. I could have sworn it was somebody's hand. My flesh began to creep instantly.

"Who's that?" I exclaimed in a loud voice.

My voice dropped into the silence like a pebble into a deep well. There was no answer, but at the same moment I heard some one moving away from me across the room in the direction of the door. It was a confused sort of footstep, and the sound of garments brushing the furniture on the way. The same second my hand stumbled upon the matchbox, and I struck a light. I expected to see Mrs Monson, or Emily, or perhaps the son who is something on an omnibus. But the flare of the gas jet illumined an empty room; there was not a sign of a person anywhere. I felt the hair stir upon my head, and instinctively I backed up against the wall, lest something should approach me from behind. I was distinctly alarmed. But the next minute I recovered myself. The door was open on to the landing, and I crossed the room, not without some inward trepidation, and went out. The light from the room fell upon the stairs, but there was no one to be seen anywhere, nor was there any sound on the creaking wooden staircase to indicate a departing creature.

I was in the act of turning to go in again when a sound overhead caught my ear. It was a very faint sound, not unlike the sigh of wind; yet it could not have been the wind, for the night was still as the grave. Though it was not repeated, I resolved to go upstairs and see for myself what it all meant. Two senses had been affected – touch and hearing – and I could not believe that I had been deceived. So, with a lighted candle, I went stealthily forth or my unpleasant journey into the upper regions of this queer little old house.

On the first landing there was only one door, and it was locked. On the second there was also only one door, but when I turned the handle it opened. There came forth to meet me the chill musty air that is characteristic of a long unoccupied room. With it there came an indescribable odour. I use the adjective advisedly. Though very faint, diluted as it were, it was nevertheless an odour that made my gorge rise. I had never smelt anything like it before, and I cannot describe it.

The room was small and square, close under the roof, with a sloping ceiling and two tiny windows. It was cold as the grave, without a shred of carpet or a stick of furniture. The icy atmosphere and the nameless odour combined to make the room abominable to me, and, after lingering a moment to see that it contained no cupboards or corners into which a person might have crept for concealment, I made haste to shut the door, and went downstairs again to bed. Evidently I had been deceived after all as to the noise.

In the night I had a foolish but very vivid dream. I dreamed that the landlady and another person, dark and not properly visible, entered my room on all fours, followed by a horde of immense cats. They attacked me as I lay in bed, and murdered me, and then dragged my body upstairs and deposited it on the floor of that cold little square room under the roof.

*   *   *

Nov. 11. – Since my talk with Emily – the unfinished talk – I have hardly once set eyes on her. Mrs Monson now attends wholly to my wants. As usual, she does everything exactly as I don't like it done. It is all too utterly trivial to mention, but it is exceedingly irritating. Like small doses of morphine often repeated, she has finally a cumulative effect.

Nov. 12. – This morning I woke early, and came into the front room to get a book, meaning to read in bed till it was time to get up. Emily was laying the fire.

"Good morning!" I said cheerfully. "Mind you make a good fire. It's very cold."

The girl turned and showed me a startled face. It was not Emily at all!

"Where's Emily?" I exclaimed.

"You mean the girl as was 'ere before me?"

"Has Emily left?"

"I came on the 6th," she replied sullenly, "and she'd gone then." I got my book and went back to bed. Emily must have been sent away almost immediately after our conversation. This reflection kept coming between me and the printed page. I was glad when it was time to get up. Such prompt energy, such merciless decision, seemed to argue something of importance – to somebody.

Nov. 13. – The wound inflicted by the cat's claw has swollen, and causes me annoyance and some pain. It throbs and itches. I'm afraid my blood must be in poor condition, or it would have healed by now. I opened it with a penknife soaked in an antiseptic solution, and cleansed it thoroughly. I have heard unpleasant stories of the results of wounds inflicted by cats.

*   *   *

Nov. 14. – In spite of the curious effect this house certainly exercises upon my nerves, I like it. It is lonely and deserted in the very heart of London, but it is also for that reason quiet to work in. I wonder why it is so cheap. Some people might be suspicious, but I did not even ask the reason. No answer is better than a lie. If only I could remove the cats from the outside and the rats from the inside. I feel that I shall grow accustomed more and more to its peculiarities, and shall die here. Ah, that expression reads queerly and gives a wrong impression: I meant *live and die* here. I shall renew the lease from year to year till one of us crumbles to pieces. From present indications the building will be the first to go.

Nov. 16. – It is abominable the way my nerves go up and down with me – and rather discouraging. This morning I woke to find my clothes scattered about the room, and a cane chair overturned beside the bed. My coat and waistcoat looked just as if they had been *tried on* by some one in the night. I had horribly vivid dreams, too, in which some one covering his face with his hands kept coming close up to me, crying out as if in pain, "Where can I find covering? Oh, who will clothe me?" How silly, and yet it frightened me a little. It was so dreadfully real. It is now over a year since I last walked in my sleep and woke up with such a shock on the cold pavement of Earl's Court Road, where I then lived. I thought I was cured, but evidently not. This discovery has rather a disquieting effect upon me. To-night I shall resort to the old trick of tying my toe to the bed-post.

Nov. 17. – Last night I was again troubled by most oppressive dreams. Some one seemed to be moving in the night up and down my room, sometimes passing into the front room, and then returning to stand beside the bed and stare intently down upon me. I was being watched by this person all night long. I never actually awoke, though I was often very near it. I suppose it was a nightmare from indigestion, for this morning I have one of my old vile headaches. Yet all my clothes lay about the floor when I awoke, where they had evidently been flung (had I so tossed them?) during the dark hours, and my trousers trailed over the step into the front room.

Worse than this, though – I fancied I noticed about the room in the morning that strange, fetid odour. Though very faint, its mere suggestion is foul and nauseating. What in the world can it be, I wonder? . . . In future I shall lock my door.

Nov. 26. – I have accomplished a lot of good work during this past week, and have also managed to get regular exercise. I have felt well and in an equable state of mind. Only two things have occurred to disturb my equanimity. The first is trivial in itself, and no doubt to be easily explained. The upper window where I saw the light on the night of November 4, with the shadow of a large head and shoulders upon the blind, is one of the windows in the square room under the roof. In reality it has *no blind at all!*

Here is the other thing. I was coming home last night in a fresh fall of snow about eleven o'clock, my umbrella low down over my head. Half-way up the alley, where the snow was wholly untrodden, I saw a man's legs in front of me. The umbrella hid the rest of his figure, but on raising it I saw that he was tall and broad and was walking, as I was, towards the door of my house. He could not have been four feet ahead of me. I had thought the alley was empty when I entered it, but might of course have been mistaken very easily.

A sudden gust of wind compelled me to lower the umbrella, and when I raised it again, not half a minute later, there was no longer any man to be seen. With a few more steps I reached the door. It was closed as usual. I then noticed with a sudden sensation of dismay that the surface of the freshly fallen snow was *unbroken*. My own footmarks were the only ones to be seen anywhere, and though I retraced my way to the point where I had first seen the man, I could find no slightest impression of any other boots. Feeling creepy and uncomfortable, I went upstairs, and was glad to get into bed.

Nov. 28. – With the fastening of my bedroom door the disturbances ceased. I am convinced that I walked in my sleep. Probably I untied my toe and then tied it up again. The fancied security of the locked door would alone have been enough to restore sleep to my troubled spirit and enable me to rest quietly.

Last night, however, the annoyance was suddenly renewed in another and more aggressive form. I woke in the darkness with the impression that some one was standing outside my bedroom door *listening*. As I became more awake the impression grew into positive knowledge. Though there was no appreciable sound of moving or breathing, I was so convinced of the propinquity of a listener that I crept out of bed and approached the door. As I did so there came faintly from the next room the unmistakable sound of some one retreating stealthily across the floor. Yet, as I heard it, it was neither the tread of a man nor a regular footstep, but rather, it seemed to me, a confused sort of crawling, almost as of some one on his hands and knees.

I unlocked the door in less than a second, and passed quickly into the front room, and I could feel, as by the subtlest imaginable vibrations upon my nerves, that the spot I was standing in had just that instant been vacated! The Listener had moved; he was now behind the other door, standing in the passage. Yet this door was also closed. I moved swiftly, and as silently as possible, across the floor, and turned the handle. A cold rush of air met me from the passage and sent shiver after shiver down my back. There was no one in the doorway; there was no one on the little landing; there was no one moving down the staircase. Yet I had been so quick that this midnight Listener could not be very far away, and I felt that if I persevered I should eventually come face to face with him. And the courage that came so opportunely to overcome my nervousness and horror seemed born of the unwelcome conviction that it was somehow necessary for my safety as well as my sanity that I should find this intruder and force his secret from him. For was it not the intent action of his mind upon my own, in concentrated listening, that had awakened me with such a vivid realisation of his presence?

Advancing across the narrow landing, I peered down into the well of the little house. There was nothing to be seen; no one was moving in the darkness. How cold the oilcloth was to my bare feet.

I cannot say what it was that suddenly drew my eyes upwards. I only know that, without apparent reason, I looked up and saw a person about half-way up the next turn of the stairs, leaning forward over the balustrade and staring straight into my face. It was a man. He appeared to be clinging to the rail rather than standing on the stairs. The gloom made it impossible to see much beyond the general outline, but the head and shoulders were seemingly enormous, and stood sharply silhouetted against the skylight in the roof immediately above. The idea flashed into my brain in a moment that I was looking into the visage of something monstrous. The huge skull, the mane-like hair, the wide-humped shoulders, suggested, in a way I did not pause to analyse, that which was scarcely human; and for some seconds, fascinated by horror, I turned the gaze and stared into the dark, inscrutable countenance above me, without knowing exactly where I was or what I was doing.

Then I realised in quite a new way that I was face to face with the secret midnight Listener, and I steeled myself as best I could for what was about to come.

The source of the rash courage that came to me at this awful moment will ever be to me an inexplicable mystery. Though shivering with fear, and my forehead wet with an unholy dew, I resolved to advance. Twenty questions leaped to my lips: What are you? What do you want? Why do you listen and watch? Why do you come into my room? But none of them found articulate utterance.

I began forthwith to climb the stairs, and with the first signs of my advance *he* drew himself back into the shadows and began to move too. He retreated as swiftly as I advanced. I heard the sound of his crawling motion a few steps ahead of me, ever maintaining the same distance. When I reached the landing he was half-way up the next flight, and when I was half-way up the next flight he had already arrived at the top landing. I then heard him open the door of the little square room under the roof and go in. Immediately, though the door did not close after him, the sound of his moving entirely ceased.

At this moment I longed for a light, or a stick, or any weapon whatsoever; but I had none of these things, and it was impossible to go back. So I marched steadily up the rest of the stairs, and in less than a minute found myself standing in the gloom face to face with the door through which this creature had just entered.

For a moment I hesitated. The door was about half-way open, and the Listener was standing evidently in his favourite attitude just behind it – listening. To search through that dark room for him seemed hopeless; to enter the same small space where he was seemed horrible. The very idea filled me with loathing, and I almost decided to turn back.

It is strange at such times how trivial things impinge on the consciousness with a shock as of something important and immense. Something – it may have been a beetle or a mouse – scuttled over the bare boards behind me. The door moved a quarter of an inch, closing. My decision came back with a sudden rush, as it were, and thrusting out a foot, I kicked the door so that it swung sharply back to its full extent, and permitted me to walk forward slowly into the aperture of profound blackness beyond. What a queer soft sound my bare feet made on the boards! How the blood sang and buzzed in my head!

I was inside. The darkness closed over me, hiding even the windows. I began to grope my way round the walls in a thorough search; but in order to prevent all possibility of the other's escape, I first of all *closed the door*.

There we were, we two, shut in together between four walls, within a few feet of one another. But with what, with whom, was I thus momentarily imprisoned? A new light flashed suddenly over the affair with a swift, illuminating brilliance – and I knew I was a fool, an utter fool! I was wide awake at last, and the horror was evaporating. My cursed nerves again; a dream, a nightmare, and the old result – walking in my sleep. The figure was a dream-figure. Many a time before had the actors in my dreams stood before me for some moments after I was awake . . . There was a chance match in my pyjamas' pocket, and I struck it on the wall. The room was utterly empty. It held not even a shadow. I went quickly down to bed, cursing my wretched nerves and my foolish, vivid dreams. But as soon as ever I was asleep again, the same uncouth figure of a man crept back to my bedside, and bending over me with his immense head close to my ear, whispered repeatedly in my dreams, "I want your body; I want its covering. I'm waiting for it, and listening always." Words scarcely less foolish than the dream.

But I wonder what that queer odour was up in the square room. I noticed it again, and stronger than ever before, and it seemed to be also in my bedroom when I woke this morning.

Nov. 29. – Slowly, as moonbeams rise over a misty sea in June, the thought is entering my mind that my nerves and somnambulistic dreams do not adequately account for the influence this house exercises upon me. It holds me as with a fine, invisible net. I cannot escape if I would. It draws me, and it means to keep me.

Nov. 30. – The post this morning brought me a letter from Aden, forwarded from my old rooms in Earl's Court. It was from Chapter, my former Trinity chum, who is on his way home from the East, and asks for my address. I sent it to him at the hotel he mentioned, 'to await arrival.'

As I have already said, my windows command a view of the alley, and I can see an arrival without difficulty. This morning, while I was busy writing, the sound of footsteps coming up the alley filled me with a sense of vague alarm that I could in no way account for. I went over to the window, and saw a man standing below waiting for the door to be opened. His shoulders were broad, his top-hat glossy, and his overcoat fitted beautifully round the collar. All this I could see, but no more. Presently the door was opened, and the shock to my nerves was unmistakable when I heard a man's voice ask, "Is Mr— still here?" mentioning my name. I could not catch the answer, but it could only have been in the affirmative, for the man entered the hall and the door shut to behind him. But I waited in vain for the sound of his steps on the stairs. There was no sound of any kind. It seemed to me so strange that I opened my door and looked out. No one was anywhere to be seen. I walked across the narrow landing, and looked through the window that commands the whole length of the alley. There was no sign of a human being, coming or going. The lane was deserted. Then I deliberately walked downstairs into the kitchen, and asked the grey-faced landlady if a gentleman had just that minute called for me.

The answer, given with an odd, weary sort of smile, was "*No!*"

Dec. 1. – I feel genuinely alarmed and uneasy over the state of my nerves. Dreams are dreams, but never before have I had dreams in broad daylight.

I am looking forward very much to Chapter's arrival. He is a capital fellow, vigorous, healthy, with no nerves, and even less imagination; and he has £2000 a year into the bargain. Periodically he makes me offers – the last was to travel round the world with him as secretary, which was a delicate way of paying my expenses and giving me some pocket-money – offers, however, which I invariably decline. I prefer to keep his friendship. Women could not come between us; money might – therefore I give it no opportunity. Chapter always laughed at what he called my "fancies," being himself possessed only of that thin-blooded quality of imagination which is ever associated with the prosaic-minded man. Yet, if taunted with this obvious lack, his wrath is deeply stirred. His psychology is that of the cross materialist – always a rather funny article. It will afford me genuine relief, none the less, to hear the cold judgment his mind will have to pass upon the story of this house as I shall have it to tell.

Dec. 2. – The strangest part of it all I have not referred to in this brief diary. Truth to tell, I have been afraid to set it down in black and white. I have kept it in the background of my thoughts, preventing it as far as possible from taking shape. In spite of my efforts, however, it has continued to grow stronger.

Now that I come to face the issue squarely, it is harder to express than I imagined. Like a half-remembered melody that trips in the head but vanishes the moment you try to sing it, these thoughts form a group in the background of my mind, *behind* my mind, as it were, and refuse to come forward. They are crouching ready to spring, but the actual leap never takes place.

In these rooms, except when my mind is strongly concentrated on my own work, I find myself suddenly dealing in thoughts and ideas that are not my own! New, strange conceptions, wholly foreign to my temperament, are for ever cropping up in my head. What precisely they are is of no particular importance. The point is that they are entirely apart from the channel in which my thoughts have hitherto been accustomed to flow. Especially they come when my mind is at rest, unoccupied; when I'm dreaming over the fire, or sitting with a book which fails to hold my attention. Then these thoughts which are not mine spring into life and make me feel exceedingly uncomfortable. Sometimes they are so strong that I almost feel as if some one were in the room beside me, thinking aloud.

Evidently my nerves and liver are shockingly out of order. I must work harder and take more vigorous exercise. The horrid thoughts never come when my mind is much occupied. But they are always there – waiting and as it were *alive*.

What I have attempted to describe above came first upon me gradually after I had been some days in the house, and then grew steadily in strength. The other strange thing has come to me only twice in all these weeks. *It appals me*. It is the consciousness of the propinquity of some deadly and loathsome disease. It comes over me like a wave of fever heat, and then passes off, leaving me cold and trembling. The air seems for a few seconds to become tainted. So penetrating and convincing is the thought of this sickness, that on both occasions my brain has turned momentarily dizzy, and through my mind, like flames of white heat, have flashed the ominous names of all the dangerous illnesses I know. I can no more explain these visitations than I can fly, yet I know there is no dreaming about the clammy skin and palpitating heart which they always leave as witnesses of their brief visit.

Most strongly of all was I aware of this nearness of a mortal sickness when, on the night of the 28th, I went upstairs in pursuit of the listening figure. When we were shut in together in that little square room under the roof, I felt that I was face to face with the actual essence of this invisible and malignant disease. Such a feeling never entered my heart before, and I pray to God it never may again.

There! Now I have confessed. I have given some expression at least to the feelings that so far I have been afraid to see in my own writing. For – since I can no longer deceive myself – the experiences of that night (28th) were no more a dream than my daily breakfast is a dream; and the trivial entry in this diary by which I sought to explain away an occurrence that caused me unutterable horror was due solely to my desire not to acknowledge in words what I really felt and believed to be true. The increase that would have accrued to my horror by so doing might have been more than I could stand.

Dec. 3. – I wish Chapter would come. My facts are all ready marshalled, and I can see his cool, grey eyes fixed incredulously on my face as I relate them: the knocking at my door, the well-dressed caller, the light in the upper window and the shadow upon the blind, the man who preceded me in the snow, the scattering of my clothes at night, Emily's arrested confession, the landlady's suspicious reticence, the midnight Listener on the stairs, and those awful subsequent words in my sleep; and above all, and hardest to tell, the presence of the abominable sickness, and the stream of thoughts and ideas that are not my own.

I can see Chapter's face, and I can almost hear his deliberate words, "You've been at the tea again, and underfeeding, I expect, as usual. Better see my nerve doctor, and then come with me to the south of France." For this fellow, who knows nothing of disordered liver or high-strung nerves, goes regularly to a great nerve specialist with the periodical belief that his nervous system is beginning to decay.

Dec. 5. – Ever since the incident of the Listener, I

71

have kept a night-light burning in my bedroom, and my sleep has been undisturbed. Last night, however, I was subjected to a far worse annoyance. I woke suddenly, and saw a man in front of the dressing-table regarding himself in the mirror. The door was locked, as usual. I knew at once it was the Listener, and the blood turned to ice in my veins. Such a wave of horror and dread swept over me that it seemed to turn me rigid in the bed, and I could neither move nor speak. I noted, however, that the odour I so abhorred was strong in the room.

The man seemed to be tall and broad. He was stooping forward over the mirror. His back was turned to me, but in the glass I saw the reflection of a huge head and face illumined fitfully by the flicker of the night-light. The spectral grey of very early morning stealing in round the edges of the curtains lent an additional horror to the picture, for it fell upon hair that was tawny and mane-like, hanging loosely about a face whose swollen, rugose features bore the once seen never forgotten leonine expression of— I dare not write down that awful word. But, by way of corroborative proof, I saw in the faint mingling of the two lights that there were several bronze-coloured blotches on the cheeks which the man was evidently examining with great care in the glass. The lips were pale and very thick and large. One hand I could not see, but the other rested on the ivory back of my hair-brush. Its muscles were strangely contracted, the fingers thin to emaciation, the back of the hand closely puckered up. It was like a big grey spider crouching to spring, or the claw of a great bird.

The full realisation that I was alone in the room with this nameless creature, almost within arm's reach of him, overcame me to such a degree that, when he suddenly turned and regarded me with small beady eyes, wholly out of proportion to the grandeur of their massive setting, I sat bolt upright in bed, uttered a loud cry, and then fell back in a dead swoon of terror upon the bed.

Dec. 6. – . . . When I came to this morning, the first thing I noticed was that my clothes were strewn all over the floor . . . I find it difficult to put my thoughts together, and have sudden accesses of violent trembling. I determined that I would go at once to Chapter's hotel and find out when he is expected. I cannot refer to what happened in the night; it is too awful, and I have to keep my thoughts rigorously away from it. I feel light-headed and queer, couldn't eat any breakfast, and have twice vomited with blood. While dressing to go out, a hansom rattled up noisily over the cobbles, and a minute later the door opened, and to my great joy in walked the very subject of my thoughts.

The sight of his strong face and quiet eyes had an immediate effect upon me, and I grew calmer again. His very handshake was a sort of tonic. But, as I listened eagerly to the deep tones of his reassuring voice, and the visions of the night time paled a little, I began to realise how very hard it was going to be to tell him my wild, intangible tale. Some men radiate an animal vigour that destroys the delicate woof of a vision and effectually prevents its reconstruction. Chapter was one of these men.

We talked of incidents that had filled the interval since we last met, and he told me something of his travels. He talked and I listened. But, so full was I of the horrid thing I had to tell, that I made a poor listener. I was for ever watching my opportunity to leap in and explode it all under his nose.

Before very long, however, it was borne in upon me that he too was merely talking for time. He too held something of importance in the background of his mind, something too weighty to let fall till the right moment presented itself. So that during the whole of the first half-hour we were both waiting for the psychological moment in which properly to release our respective bombs; and the intensity of our minds' action set up opposing forces that merely sufficed to hold one another in check – and nothing more. As soon as I realised this, therefore, I resolved to yield. I renounced for the time my purpose of telling my story, and had the satisfaction of seeing that his mind, released from the restraint of my own, at once began to make preparations for the discharge of its momentous burden. The talk grew less and less magnetic; the interest waned; the descriptions of his travels became less alive. There were pauses between his sentences. Presently he repeated himself. His words clothed no living thoughts. The pauses grew longer. Then the interest dwindled altogether and went out like a candle in the wind. His voice ceased, and he looked up squarely into my face with serious and anxious eyes.

The psychological moment had come at last!

"I say—" he began, and then stopped short.

I made an unconscious gesture of encouragement, but said no word. I dreaded the impending disclosure exceedingly. A dark shadow seemed to precede it.

"I say," he blurted out at last, "what in the world made you ever come to this place – to these rooms, I mean?"

"They're cheap, for one thing," I began, "and central and —"

"They're too cheap," he interrupted. "Didn't you ask what made 'em so cheap?"

"It never occurred to me at the time."

There was a pause in which he avoided my eyes.

"For God's sake, go on, man, and tell it!" I cried, for

the suspense was getting more than I could stand in my nervous condition.

"This was where Blount lived so long," he said quietly, "and where he – died. You know, in the old days I often used to come here and see him, and do what I could to alleviate his—" He stuck fast again.

"Well!" I said with a great effort. "*Please* go on – faster."

"But," Chapter went on, turning his face to the window with a perceptible shiver, "he finally got so terrible I simply couldn't stand it, though I always thought I could stand anything. It got on my nerves and made me dream, and haunted me day and night."

I stared at him, and said nothing. I had never heard of Blount in my life, and didn't know what he was talking about. But, all the same, I was trembling, and my mouth had become strangely dry.

"This is the first time I've been back here since," he said almost in a whisper, "and, 'pon my word, it gives me the creeps. I swear it isn't fit for a man to live in. I never saw you look so bad, old man."

"I've got it for a year," I jerked out, with a forced laugh; "signed the lease and all. I thought it was rather a bargain."

Chapter shuddered, and buttoned his overcoat up to his neck. Then he spoke in a low voice, looking occasionally behind him as though he thought some one was listening. I too could have sworn some one else was in the room with us.

"He did it himself, you know, and no one blamed him a bit; his sufferings were awful. For the last two years he used to wear a veil when he went out, and even then it was always in a closed carriage. Even the attendant who had nursed him for so long was at length obliged to leave. The extremities of both the lower limbs were gone, dropped off, and he moved about the ground on all fours with a sort of crawling motion. The odour, too, was —"

I was obliged to interrupt him here. I could hear no more details of that sort. My skin was moist, I felt hot and cold by turns, for at last I was beginning to understand.

"Poor devil," Chapter went on; "I used to keep my eyes closed as much as possible. He always begged to be allowed to take his veil off, and asked if I minded very much. I used to stand by the open window. He never touched me, though. He rented the whole house. Nothing would induce him to leave it."

"Did he occupy – these very rooms?"

"No. He had the little room on the top floor, the square one just under the roof. He preferred it because it was dark. These rooms were too near the ground, and he was afraid people might see him through the windows. A crowd had been known to follow him up to the very door, and then stand below the windows in the hope of catching a glimpse of his face."

"But there were hospitals."

"He wouldn't go near one, and they didn't like to force him. You know, they say it's *not* contagious, so there was nothing to prevent his staying here if he wanted to. He spent all his time reading medical books, about drugs and so on. His head and face were something appalling, just like a lion's."

I held up my hand to arrest further description.

"He was a burden to the world, and he knew it. One night I suppose he realised it too keenly to wish to live. He had the free use of drugs – and in the morning he was found dead on the floor. Two years ago, that was, and they said then he had still several years to live."

"Then, in Heaven's name!" I cried, unable to bear the

suspense any longer, "tell me what it was he had, and be quick about it."

"I thought you knew!" he exclaimed, with genuine surprise. "I thought you knew!"

He leaned forward and our eyes met. In a scarcely audible whisper I caught the words his lips seemed almost afraid to utter:

"He was a leper!"

GHOST STORY FOR CHRISTMAS

(BBC 1971–)
Starring: Robert Hardy, Clive Swift &
Thelma Barlow
Directed by Lawrence Gordon Clark
Story 'The Stalls of Barchester Cathedral' by
M.R.James

Although the ABC series *Mystery and Imagination* can claim to have first brought some of the classic ghost stories of M.R. James to the television screen – the series adapted four in all: 'The Tractate Middoth', 'Lost Hearts' and 'Room 13' (all shown in 1966) plus 'Casting The Runes' and a re-run of 'The Tractate Middoth' in 1968 – it was the BBC who really established the donnish author's popularity with viewers in 1971 when they began what has subsequently become an almost annual event featuring a Jamesian tale, *Ghost Stories For Christmas*. Thanks to these faithfully adapted and stylishly made productions of his ghost stories, no Christmas viewing seems quite the same without one! The series was undoubtedly given an outstanding send-off with the hour-long version of 'The Stalls of Barchester Cathedral' which was first shown on Christmas Eve 1971 (and has since been reshown several times) and provided a benchmark against which all the following productions have been judged. Produced and directed by Lawrence Gordon

Clark – a long-time devotee of James who remained at the helm of the series for several years therefter – the story of an investigation into an old box in Barchester Cathedral which leads to the uncovering of the facts about the strange death of a former archdeacon, was well served by its stars: in particular Robert Hardy who believes in ghosts. Hardy, who played Archdeacon Hayes, confessed in the special Christmas issue of *Radio Times*, 'Of course I believe in ghosts. I saw one when I was nine years old and another a few years ago when I was in France with my wife. If you admit to the existence of Good and Evil and to life after death, the way is open for a belief in ghosts, is it not?' The story was atmospherically filmed almost entirely on location at ancient Norwich Cathedral in Norfolk, and the programme earned one of the highest audience ratings of the Christmas season as well as initiating a tradition.

The author, Montague Rhodes James (1862–1936) is one of the most famous ghost story writers of this century, yet lived for much of his life in quiet scholarship as a Fellow of King's College, Cambridge and latterly Provost of Eton. He only began writing his chilling and understated little stories of the unknown as entertainments to tell his friends at Christmas, but once he was persuaded to collect them in books such as *Ghost Stories of an Antiquary* (1904), *More Ghost Stories of an Antiquary* (1910) and *A Thin Ghost* (1919), he was quickly recognized as a seminal influence on the genre and his work has remained largely in print ever since. Although many of his stories have now been televised, only one 'Casting the Runes', has been adapted for the cinema as *Night of the Demon* (1957). James' life and contribution to

the supernatural genre was recently celebrated in an hour-long drama-documentary *A Pleasant Terror* produced by Clive Dunn for Anglia TV in December 1995.

This matter began, as far as I am concerned, with the reading of a notice in the obituary section of the *Gentleman's Magazine* for an early year in the nineteenth century: —

'On February 26th, at his residence in the Cathedral Close of Barchester, the Venerable John Benwell Haynes, D.D., aged 57, Archdeacon of Sowerbridge and Rector of Pickhill and Candley. He was of—College, Cambridge, and where, by talent and assiduity, he commanded the esteem of his seniors; when, at the usual time, he took his first degree, his name stood high in the list of *wranglers*. These academical honours procured for him within a short time a Fellowship of his College.

In the year 1783 he received Holy Orders, and was shortly afterwards presented to the perpetual Curacy of Ranxton-sub-Ashe by his friend and patron the late truly venerable Bishop of Lichfield ... His speedy preferments, first to a Prebend, and subsequently to the dignity of Precentor in the Cathedral of Barchester, form an eloquent testimony to the respect in which he was held and to his eminent qualifications. He succeeded to the Archdeaconry upon the sudden decease of Archdeacon Pulteney in 1810. His sermons, ever conformable to the principles of the religion and Church which he adorned, displayed in no ordinary degree, without the least trace of enthusiasm, the refinement of the scholar united with the graces of the Christian. Free from sectarian violence, and informed by the spirit of the truest charity, they will long dwell in the memories of his hearers. (Here a further omission.) The productions of his pen include an able defence of Episcopacy, which, though often perused by the author of this tribute to his memory, afford but one additional instance of the want of liberality and enterprise which is a too common characteristic of the publishers of our generation. His published works are, indeed, confined to a spirited and elegant version of the *Argonautica* of Valerius Flaccus, a volume of *Discourses upon the Several Events in the Life of Joshua*, delivered in his Cathedral, and a number of the charges which he pronounced at various visitations to the clergy of his Archdeaconry. These are distinguished by etc., etc. The urbanity and hospitality of the subject of these lines will not readily be forgotten by those who enjoyed his acquaintance. His interest in the venerable and awful pile under whose hoary vault he was so punctual an attendant, and particularly in the musical portion of its rites, might be termed filial, and formed a strong and delightful contrast to the polite indifference displayed by too many of our Cathedral dignitaries at the present time.'

The final paragraph, after informing us that Dr Haynes died a bachelor, says: —

'It might have been augured that an existence so placid and benevolent would have been terminated in a ripe old age by a dissolution equally gradual and calm. But how unsearchable are the workings of Providence! The peaceful and retired seclusion amid which the honoured evening of Dr Haynes' life was mellowing to its close was destined to be disturbed, nay, shattered, by a tragedy as appalling as it was unexpected. The morning of the 26th of February —'

But perhaps I shall do better to keep back the remainder

of the narrative until I have told the circumstances which led up to it. These, as far as they are now accessible, I have derived from another source.

I had read the obituary notice which I have been quoting, quite by chance, along with a great many others of the same period. It had excited some little speculation in my mind, but, beyond thinking that, if I ever had an opportunity of examining the local records of the period indicated, I would try to remember Dr Haynes, I made no effort to pursue his case.

Quite lately I was cataloguing the manuscripts in the library of the college to which he belonged. I had reached the end of the numbered volumes on the shelves, and I proceeded to ask the librarian whether there were any more books which he thought I ought to include in my description. "I don't think there are," he said, "but we had better come and look at the manuscript class and make sure. Have you time to do that now?" I had time. We went to the library, checked off the manuscripts, and, at the end of our survey, arrived at a shelf of which I had seen nothing. Its contents consisted for the most part of sermons, bundles of fragmentary papers, college exercises, *Cyrus*, an epic poem in several cantos, the product of a country clergyman's leisure, mathematical tracts by a deceased professor, and other similar material of a kind with which I am only too familiar. I took brief notes of these. Lastly, there was a tin box, which was pulled out and dusted. Its label, much faded, was thus inscribed: 'Papers of the Ven. Archdeacon Haynes. Bequeathed in 1834 by his sister, Miss Letita Haynes.'

I knew at once that the name was one which I had somewhere encountered, and could very soon locate it. "That must be the Archdeacon Haynes who came to a very odd end at Barchester. I've read his obituary in the

Gentleman's Magazine. May I take the box home? Do you know if there is anything interesting in it?"

The librarian was very willing that I should take the box and examine it at leisure. "I never looked inside it myself," he said, "but I've always been meaning to. I am pretty sure that is the box which our old Master once said ought never to have been accepted by the college. He said that to Martin years ago; and he said also that as long as he had control over the library it should never be opened. Martin told me about it, and said that he wanted terribly to know what was in it; but the Master was librarian, and always kept the box in the lodge, so there was no getting at it in his time, and when he died it was taken away by mistake by his heirs, and only returned a few years ago. I can't think why I haven't opened it; but, as I have to go away from Cambridge this afternoon, you had better have first go at it. I think I can trust you not to publish anything undesirable in our catalogue."

I took the box home and examined its contents, and thereafter consulted the librarian as to what should be done about publication, and, since I have his leave to make a story out of it, provided I disguise the identity of the people concerned, I will try what can be done.

The materials are, of course, mainly journals and letters. How much I shall quote and how much epitomise must be determined by considerations of space. The proper understanding of the situation has necessitated a little – not very arduous – research, which has been greatly facilitated by the excellent illustrations and text of the Barchester volume in Bell's *Cathedral Series*.

When you enter the choir of Barchester Cathedral now, you pass through a screen of metal and coloured marbles, designed by Sir Gilbert Scott, and find yourself in what I must call a very bare and odiously furnished place. The stalls are modern, without canopies. The places of the dignitaries and the names of the prebends have fortunately been allowed to survive, and are inscribed on small brass plates affixed to the stalls. The organ is in the triforium, and what is seen of the case is Gothic. The reredos and its surroundings are like every other.

Careful engravings of a hundred years ago show a very different state of things. The organ is on a massive classical screen. The stalls are also classical and very massive. There is a baldacchino of wood over the altar, with urns upon its corners. Further east is a solid altar screen, classical in design, of wood, with a pediment, in which is a triangle surrounded by rays, enclosing certain Hebrew letters in gold. Cherubs contemplate these. There is a pulpit with a great sounding-board at the eastern end of the stalls on the north side, and there is a black and white marble pavement. Two ladies and a gentleman are admiring the general effect. From other sources I gather that the archdeacon's stall then, as now, was next to the bishop's throne at the south-eastern end of the stalls. His house almost faces the western part of the church, and is a fine red-brick building of William the Third's time.

Here Dr Haynes, already a mature man, took up his abode with his sister in the year 1810. The dignity had long been the object of his wishes, but his predecessor refused to depart until he had attained the age of ninety-two. About a week after he had held a modest festival in celebration of that ninety-second birthday, there came a morning, late in the year, when Dr Haynes, hurrying cheerfully into his breakfast-room, rubbing his hands and humming a tune, was greeted, and checked in his genial flow of spirits, by the sight of his sister, seated, indeed, in her usual place behind the tea-urn, but bowed forward and sobbing unrestrainedly into her handkerchief. "What

– what is the matter? What bad news?" he began. "Oh, Johnny, you've not heard? The poor dear archdeacon!" "The archdeacon, yes? What is it – ill, is he?" "No, no; they found him on the staircase this morning; it is so shocking." "Is it possible! Dear, dear, poor Pulteney! Had there been any seizure?" "They don't think so, and that is almost the worst thing about it. It seems to have been all the fault of that stupid maid of theirs, Jane." Dr Haynes paused. "I don't quite understand, Letitia. How was the maid at fault?" "Why, as far as I can make out, there was a stair-rod missing, and she never mentioned it, and the poor archdeacon set his foot quite on the edge of the step – you know how slippery that oak is – and it seems he must have fallen almost the whole flight and broken his neck. It *is* so sad for poor Miss Pulteney. Of course, they will get rid of the girl at once. I never liked her." Miss Haynes's grief resumed its sway, but eventually relaxed so far as to permit of her taking some breakfast. Not so her brother, who, after standing in silence before the window for some minutes, left the room, and did not appear again that morning.

I need only add that the careless maid-servant was dismissed forthwith, but that the missing stair-rod was very shortly afterwards found *under* the stair-carpet – an additional proof, if any were needed, of extreme stupidity and carelessness on her part.

For a good many years Dr Haynes had been marked out by his ability, which seems to have been really considerable, as the likely successor of Archdeacon Pulteney, and no disappointment was in store for him. He was duly installed, and entered with zeal upon the discharge of those functions which are appropriate to one in his position. A considerable space in his journals is occupied with exclamations upon the confusion in which Archdeacon Pulteney had left the business of his office and the documents appertaining to it. Dues upon Wringham and Barnswood have been uncollected for something like twelve years, and are largely irrecoverable; no visitation has been held for seven years; four chancels are almost past mending. The persons deputised by the archdeacon have been nearly as incapable as himself. It was almost a matter for thankfulness that this state of things had not been permitted to continue, and a letter from a friend confirms this view. '*ó karéXwv*,' it says (in rather cruel allusion to the Second Epistle to the Thessalonians), 'is removed at last. My poor friend! Upon what a scene of confusion will you be entering! I give you my word that, on the last occasion of my crossing his threshold, there was no single paper that he could lay hands upon, no syllable of mine that he could hear, and no fact in connection with my business that he could remember. But now, thanks to a negligent maid and a loose stair-carpet, there is some prospect that necessary business will be transacted without a complete loss alike of voice and temper.' This letter was tucked into a pocket in the cover of one of the diaries.

There can be no doubt of the new archdeacon's zeal and enthusiasm. 'Give me but time to reduce to some semblance of order the innumerable errors and complications with which I am confronted, and I shall gladly and sincerely join with the aged Israelite in the canticle which too many, I fear, pronounce but with their lips.' This reflection I find, not in a diary, but a letter; the doctor's friends seem to have returned his correspondence to his surviving sister. He does not confine himself, however, to reflections. His investigation of the rights and duties of his office are very searching and businesslike, and there is a calculation in one place that a period of three years will just suffice to set the business of the Archdeaconry upon a proper footing. The estimate appears to have been an exact one. For just three years he is occupied in reforms; but I look in vain at the end of that time for the promised *Nunc dimittis*. He has now found a new sphere of activity. Hitherto his duties have precluded him from more than an occasional attendance at the Cathedral services. Now he begins to take an interest in the fabric and the music. Upon his struggles with the organist, an old gentleman who had been in office since 1786, I have no time to dwell; they were not attended with any marked success. More to the purpose is his sudden growth of enthusiasm for the Cathedral itself and its furniture. There is a draft of a letter to Sylvanus Urban (which I do not think was ever sent) describing the stalls in the choir. As I have said, these were of fairly late date – of about the year 1700, in fact.

'The archdeacon's stall, situated at the south-east end, west of the episcopal throne (now so worthily occupied by the truly excellent prelate who adorns the See of Barchester), is distinguished by some curious ornamentation. In addition to the arms of Dean West, by whose efforts the whole of the internal furniture of the choir was completed, the prayer-desk is terminated at the eastern extremity by three small but remarkable statuettes in the grotesque manner. One is an exquisitely modelled figure of a cat, whose crouching posture suggests with admirable spirit the suppleness, vigilance, and craft of the redoubted adversary of the genus *Mus*. Opposite to this is a figure seated upon a throne and invested with the attributes of royalty; but it is no earthly monarch whom the carver has sought to portray. His feet are studiously concealed by the long robe in which he is draped: but neither the crown nor the cap which he wears suffice to

87

hide the prick-ears and curving horns which betray his
Tartarean origin; and the hand which rests upon his knee
is armed with talons of horrifying length and sharpness.
Between these two figures stands a shape muffled in a
long mantle. This might at first sight be mistaken for a
monk or "friar of orders gray," for the head is cowled
and a knotted cord depends from somewhere about the
waist. A slight inspection, however, will lead to a very
different conclusion. The knotted cord is quickly seen to
be a halter, held by a hand all but concealed within the
draperies; while the sunken features and, horrid to relate,
the rent flesh upon the cheek-bones, proclaim the King
of Terrors. These figures are evidently the production
of no unskilled chisel; and should it chance that any of
your correspondents are able to throw light upon their
origin and significance, my obligations to your valuable
miscellany will be largely increased.'

There is more description in the paper, and, seeing that
the woodwork in question has now disappeared, it has
a considerable interest. A paragraph at the end is worth
quoting: —

'Some late researches among the Chapter accounts have
shown me that the carving of the stalls was not, as was
very usually reported, the work of Dutch artists, but
was executed by a native of this city or district named
Austin. The timber was procured from an oak copse
in the vicinity, the property of the Dean and Chapter,
known as Holywood. Upon a recent visit to the parish
within whose boundaries it is situated, I learned from
the aged and truly respectable incumbent that traditions
still lingered amongst the inhabitants of the great size and
age of the oaks employed to furnish the materials of the
stately structure which has been, however imperfectly,

described in the above lines. Of one in particular, which stood near the centre of the grove, it is remembered that it was known as the Hanging Oak. The propriety of that title is confirmed by the fact that a quantity of human bones was found in the soil about its roots, and that at certain times of the year it was the custom for those who wished to secure a successful issue to their affairs, whether of love or the ordinary business of life, to suspend from its boughs small images or puppets rudely fashioned of straw, twigs, or the like rustic materials.'

So much for the archdeacon's archaeological investigations. To return to his career as it is to be gathered from his diaries. Those of his first three years of hard and careful work show him throughout in high spirits, and, doubtless, during this time, that reputation for hospitality and urbanity which is mentioned in his obituary notice was well deserved. After that, as time goes on, I see a shadow coming over him – destined to develop into utter blackness – which I cannot but think must have been reflected in his outward demeanour. He commits a good deal of his fears and troubles to his diary; there was no other outlet for them. He was unmarried, and his sister was not always with him. But I am much mistaken if he has told all that he might have told. A series of extracts shall be given: —

'*Aug.* 30, 1816. – The days begin to draw in more perceptibly than ever. Now that the Archdeaconry papers are reduced to order, I must find some further employment for the evening hours of autumn and winter. It is a great blow that Letitia's health will not allow her to stay through these months. Why not go on with my *Defence of Episcopacy?* It may be useful.

*   *   *

'*Sept*. 15. – Letitia has left me for Brighton.

'*Oct*. 11. – Candles lit in the choir for the first time at evening prayers. It came as a shock: I find that I absolutely shrink from the dark season.

'*Nov*. 17. – Much struck by the character of the carving on my desk: I do not know that I had ever carefully noticed it before. My attention was called to it by an accident. During the *Magnificat* I was, I regret to say, almost overcome with sleep. My hand was resting on the back of the carved figure of a cat which is the nearest to me of the three figures on the end of my stall. I was not aware of this, for I was not looking in that direction, until I was startled by what seemed a softness, a feeling as of rather rough and coarse fur, and a sudden movement, as if the creature were twisting round its head to bite me. I regained complete consciousness in an instant, and I have some idea that I must have uttered a suppressed exclamation, for I noticed that Mr Treasurer turned his head quickly in my direction. The impression of the unpleasant feeling was so strong that I found myself rubbing my hand upon my surplice. This accident led me to examine the figures after prayers more carefully than I had done before, and I realised for the first time with what skill they are executed.

'*Dec*. 6. – I do indeed miss Letitia's company. The evenings, after I have worked as long as I can at my *Defence*, are very trying. The house is too large for a lonely man, and visitors of any kind are too rare. I get an uncomfortable impression when going to my room that there *is* company of some kind. The fact is (I may as well formulate it to myself) that I hear voices. This, I am well aware, is a common symptom of incipient decay of the brain – and I believe that I should be less disquieted than I am if I had any suspicion that this was the cause. I have none – none whatever, nor is there anything in my family history to give colour to such an idea. Work, diligent work, and a punctual attention to the duties which fall to me is my best remedy, and I have little doubt that it will prove efficacious.

'*Jan.* 1. – My trouble is, I must confess it, increasing upon me. Last night, upon my return after midnight from the Deanery, I lit my candle to go upstairs. I was nearly at the top when something whispered to me, "Let me wish you a happy New Year." I could not be mistaken: it spoke distinctly and with a peculiar emphasis. Had I dropped my candle, as I all but did, I tremble to think what the consequences must have been. As it was, I managed to get up the last flight, and was quickly in my room with the door locked, and experienced no other disturbance.

'*Jan.* 15. – I had occasion to come downstairs last night to my workroom for my watch, which I had inadvertently left on my table when I went up to bed. I think I was at the top of the last flight when I had a sudden impression of a sharp whisper in my ear "*Take care.*" I clutched the balusters and naturally looked round at once. Of course, there was nothing. After a moment I went on – it was no good turning back – but I had as nearly as possible fallen: a cat – a large one by the feel of it – slipped between my feet, but again, of course, I saw nothing. It *may* have been the kitchen cat, but I do not think it was.

'*Feb.* 27. – A curious thing last night, which I should like to forget. Perhaps if I put it down here I may see it in its true proportion. I worked in the library from about 9 to 10. The hall and staircase seemed to be unusually full of what I can only call movement without sound: by this I mean that there seemed to be continuous going and coming, and that whenever I ceased writing to listen, or looked out into the hall, the stillness was absolutely unbroken. Nor, in going to my room at an earlier hour than usual – about half-past ten – was I conscious of anything that I could call a noise. It so happened that I had told John to come to my room for the letter to the bishop which I wished to have delivered early in the morning at the Palace. He was to sit up, therefore, and come for it when he heard me retire. This I had for the moment forgotten, though I had remembered to carry the letter with me to my room. But when, as I was winding up my watch, I heard a light tap at the door, and a low voice saying, "May I come in?" (which I most undoubtedly did hear), I recollected the fact, and took up the letter from my dressing-table, saying, "Certainly : come in." No one, however, answered my summons, and it was now that, as I strongly suspect, I committed an error: for I opened the door and held the letter out. There was certainly no one at that moment in the passage, but, in the instant of my standing there, the door at the end opened and John appeared carrying a candle. I asked him whether he had come to the door earlier; but am satisfied that he had not. I do not like the situation; but although my senses were very much on the alert, and though it was some time before I could sleep, I must allow that I perceived nothing further of an untoward character.'

With the return of spring, when his sister came to live with him for some months, Dr Haynes' entries become more cheerful, and, indeed, no symptom of depression is discernible until the early part of September, when he was again left alone. And now, indeed, there is evidence that he was incommoded again, and that more pressingly. To this matter I will return in a moment, but I digress to put in a document which, rightly or wrongly, I believe to have a bearing on the thread of the story.

The account-books of Dr Haynes, preserved along with his other papers, show, from a date but little later than that of his institution as archdeacon, a quarterly payment of £25 to J.L. Nothing could have been made of this, had it stood by itself. But I connect with it a very dirty and ill-written letter, which, like another that I have quoted, was in a pocket in the cover of a diary. Of date or postmark there is no vestige, and the decipherment was not easy. It appears to run: —

'Dr Sr.

'I have bin expctin to her off you theis last wicks, and not Haveing done so must supose you have not got mine witch was saying how me and my man had met in with bad times this season all seems to go cross with us on the farm and which way to look for the rent we have no knowledge of it this been the sad case with us if you would have the great [liberality *probably, but the exact spelling defies reproduction*] to send fourty pounds otherwise steps will have to be took which I should not wish. Has you was the Means of me losing my place with Dr Pulteney I think it is only just what I am asking and you know best what I could say if I was Put to it but I do not wish anything of that unpleasant Nature being one that always wish to have everything Pleasant about me.

'Your obedt Servt,
'JANE LEE.'

93

About the time at which I suppose this letter to have been written there is, in fact, a payment of £40 to J.L.

We return to the diary: —

'*Oct.* 22. – At evening prayers, during the Psalms, I had that same experience which I recollect from last year. I was resting my hand on one of the carved figures, as before (I usually avoid that of the cat now), and – I was going to have said – a change came over it, but that seems attributing too much importance to what must, after all, be due to some physical affection in myself: at any rate, the wood seemed to become chilly and soft as if made of wet linen. I can assign the moment at which I became sensible of this. The choir were singing the words (*Set thou an ungodly man to be ruler over him and) let Satan stand at his right hand.*

'The whispering in my house was more persistent to-night. I seemed not to be rid of it in my room. I have not noticed this before. A nervous man, which I am not, and hope I am not becoming, would have been much annoyed, if not alarmed, by it. The cat was on the stairs to-night. I think it sits there always. There *is* no kitchen cat.

'*Nov.* 15. – Here again I must note a matter I do not understand. I am much troubled in sleep. No definite image presented itself, but I was pursued by the very vivid impression that wet lips were whispering into my ear with great rapidity and emphasis for some time together. After this, I suppose, I fell asleep, but was awakened with a start by a feeling as if a hand were laid on my shoulder. To my intense alarm I found myself standing at the top of the lowest flight of the first staircase. The moon was shining brightly enough through the large window to let me see that there was a large cat on the second or third step. I can make no comment. I crept up to bed again, I do not know how. Yes, mine is a heavy burden. [Then follows a line or two which has been scratched out. I fancy I read something like "acted for the best."]'

Not long after this it is evident to me that the archdeacon's firmness began to give way under the pressure of these phenomena. I omit as unnecessarily painful and distressing the ejaculations and prayers which, in the months of December and January, appear for the first time and become increasingly frequent. Throughout this time, however, he is obstinate in clinging to his post. Why he did not plead ill-health and take refuge at Bath or Brighton I cannot tell; my impression is that it would have done him no good; that he was a man who, if he had confessed himself beaten by the annoyances, would have succumbed at once, and that he was conscious of this. He did seek to palliate them by inviting visitors to his house. The result he has noted in this fashion: —

'*Jan.* 7. – I have prevailed on my cousin Allen to give me a few days, and he is to occupy the chamber next to mine.

'*Jan.* 8. – A still night. Allen slept well, but complained of the wind. My own experiences were as before: still whispering and whispering: what is it that he wants to say?

'*Jan.* 9. – Allen thinks this a very noisy house. He thinks, too, that my cat is an unusually large and fine specimen, but very wild.

*   *   *

'*Jan.* 10. – Allen and I in the library until 11. He left me twice to see what the maids were doing in the hall: returning the second time he told me he had seen one of them passing through the door at the end of the passage, and said if his wife were here she would soon get them into better order. I asked him what coloured dress the maid wore; he said grey or white. I supposed it would be so.

'*Jan.* 11. – Allen left me to-day. I must be firm.'

These words, *I must be firm*, occur again and again on subsequent days; sometimes they are the only entry. In these cases they are in an unusually large hand, and dug into the paper in a way which must have broken the pen that wrote them.

Apparently the archdeacon's friends did not remark any change in his behaviour, and this gives me a high idea of his courage and determination. The diary tells us nothing more than I have indicated of the last days of his life. The end of it all must be told in the polished language of the obituary notice: —

'The morning of the 26th of February was cold and tempestuous. At an early hour the servants had occasion to go into the front hall of the residence occupied by the lamented subject of these lines. What was their horror upon observing the form of their beloved and respected master lying upon the landing of the principal staircase in an attitude which inspired the gravest fears. Assistance was procured, and an universal consternation was experienced upon the discovery that he had been the object of a brutal and a murderous attack. The vertebral column was fractured in more than one place. This might have been the result of a fall: it appeared that the stair-carpet was loosened at one point. But, in addition to this, there were injuries inflicted upon the eyes, nose and mouth, as if by the agency of some savage animal, which, dreadful to relate, rendered those features unrecognisable. The vital spark was, it is needless to add, completely extinct, and had been so, upon the testimony of respectable medical authorities, for several hours. The author or authors of this mysterious outrage are alike buried in mystery, and the most active conjecture has hitherto failed to suggest a solution of the melancholy problem afforded by this appalling occurrence.'

The writer goes on to reflect upon the probability that the writings of Mr Shelley, Lord Byron, and M. Voltaire may have been instrumental in bringing about the disaster, and concludes by hoping, somewhat vaguely, that this event may 'operate as an example to the rising generation'; but this portion of his remarks need not be quoted in full.

I had already formed the conclusion that Dr Haynes was responsible for the death of Dr Pulteney. But the incident connected with the carved figure of death upon the archdeacon's stall was a very perplexing feature. The conjecture that it had been cut out of the wood of the Hanging Oak was not difficult, but seemed impossible to substantiate. However, I paid a visit to Barchester, partly with the view of finding out whether there were any relics of the woodwork to be heard of. I was introduced by one of the canons to the curator of the local museum, who was, my friend said, more likely to be able to give me information on the point than any one else. I told this gentleman of the description of certain carved figures and arms formerly on the stalls, and asked whether any had survived. He was able to show me the arms of Dean West and some other fragments. These, he said, had been got from an old resident, who had also once owned a figure – perhaps one of those which I was inquiring for. There was a very odd thing about that figure, he said. "The old man who had it told me that he picked it up in a wood-yard, whence he had obtained the still extant pieces, and had taken it home for his children. On the way home he was fiddling about with it and it came in two in his hands, and a bit of paper dropped out. This he picked up and, just noticing that there was writing on it, put it into his pocket, and subsequently into a vase on his mantelpiece. I was at his house not very long ago, and happened to pick up the vase and turn it over to see whether there were any marks on it, and the paper fell into my hand. The old man, on my handing it to him, told me the story I have told you, and said I might keep the paper. It was crumpled and rather torn, so I have mounted it on a card, which I have here. If you can tell me what it means I shall be very glad, and also, I may say, a good deal surprised."

He gave me the card. The paper was quite legibly inscribed in an old hand, and this is what was on it: —

'When I grew in the Wood
I was water'd wth Blood
Now in the Church I stand
Who that touches me with his Hand
If a Bloody hand he bear
I councell him to be ware
Lest he be fetcht away
Whether by night or day,
But chiefly when the wind blows high
In a night of February.'

'This I drempt, 26 Febr. A° 1699. JOHN AUSTIN.'

"I suppose it is a charm or a spell: wouldn't you call it something of that kind?" said the curator.

"Yes," I said, "I suppose one might. What became of the figure in which it was concealed?"

"Oh, I forgot," said he. "The old man told me it was so ugly and frightened his children so much that he burnt it."

HAUNTED

(GRANADA TELEVISION, 1976)
Starring: Lynne Miller, Stuart Wilson &
Matthew Pollock
Directed by Michael Apted
Story 'Poor Girl' by Elizabeth Taylor

Granada Television who have created so many land-
mark TV series from *Coronation Street* to the *Adven-
tures of Sherlock Holmes* and, most recently, *Cracker*,
also produced a notable supernatural series, *Haunted*,
in 1976. The programme, which was launched in
the Christmas season, was the brainchild of Derek
Granger, the former theatre critic turned producer
who is today best remembered for his magnificent adaptation of Evelyn Waugh's classic novel,
Brideshead Revisited (1981). I was one of the consultants on the series which drew its material from classic
and contemporary sources. One curiously prophetic
tale was 'The Ferryman' based on a short story
by Kingsley Amis about a writer who investigates a
haunting in an old inn: it starred Jeremy Brett who,
of course, would later return to star for the network
as the great detective, Sherlock Holmes. 'Poor Girl',
which was first shown on New Year's Eve, combined
sexuality and the supernatural in a story about an
Edwardian governess who takes up her first post and
soon finds herself in danger of possession by strange

forces. Lynne Miller gave a compelling performance as the unfortunate Florence Chasty torn between a love-sick boy and the advances of his womanising father. Derek Granger's sumptuous production was enjoyed by a large prime-time audience and well reviewed – especially by *The Guardian* which said the story, 'took viewers to the very edge of a haunted world.'

Elizabeth Taylor (1912–1975), the author of 'Poor Girl' – and not to be confused with the famous film star – was for half a century one of the leading British short story writers whose work appeared regularly in the *New Yorker* and was much admired by fellow authors including Paul Bailey, Anne Tyler and Elizabeth Jane Howard (who also contributes a story to this collection.) In her stories, Elizabeth Taylor often concentrated on the undertones of English family life, in particular the superstitions and fears that could unexpectedly disturb even the most well-balanced men and women. This was seen to vivid effect in her books such as *The Sleeping Beauty* (1953), *The Soul of Kindness* (1964) and *The Excursion to the Source* (1970). Recently, renewed tribute to the durability and poignancy of her work has been made through the publication of a selection of 21 of her best stories in a collection entitled *Dangerous Calm* (1995). Granada scriptwriter Robin Chapman was also faithful to her work in his adaptation of 'Poor Girl' which was for many viewers the highlight of the *Haunted* series. It remains a mystery to this day why the programme did not return for a second season . . .

Miss Chasty's first pupil was a flirtatious little boy. At seven years, he was alarmingly precocious and sometimes she thought that he despised his childhood, regarding it as a waiting time which he used only as a rehearsal for adult life. He was already more sophisticated than his young governess and disturbed her with his air of dalliance, the mockery with which he set about his lessons, the preposterous conversations he led her into, guiding her skilfully away from work, confusing her with bizarre conjectures and irreverent ideas, so that she would clasp her hands tightly under the plush table-cloth and pray that his father would not choose such a moment to observe her teaching, coming in abruptly as he sometimes did and signalling her to continue her lesson.

At those times, his son's eyes were especially lively, fixed cruelly upon his governess as he listened, smiling faintly, to her faltering voice, measuring her timidity. He would answer her questions correctly, but significantly, as if he knew that by his aptitude he rescued her from dismissal. There were many governesses waiting employment, he implied – and this was so at the beginning of the century. He underlined her good fortune at having a pupil who could so easily learn, could display the results of her teaching to such advantage for the benefit of the rather sombre, pompous figure seated at the window. When his father, apparently satisfied, had left them without a word, the boy's manner changed. He seemed fatigued and too absent-minded to reply to any more questions.

"Hilary!" she would say sharply. "Are you attending to me?" Her sharpness and her foolishness amused him, coming as he knew they did from the tension of the last ten minutes.

"Why, my dear girl, of course."

"You must address me by my name."

"Certainly, dear Florence."

"Miss Chasty."

His lips might shape the words, which he was too weary to say.

Sometimes, when she was correcting his sums, he would come round the table to stand beside her, leaning against her heavily, looking closely at her face, not at his book, breathing steadily down his nose so that tendrils of hair wavered on her neck and against her cheeks. His stillness, his concentration on her and his too heavy leaning worried her. She felt something experimental in his attitude, as if he were not leaning against her at all, but against someone in the future. "He is only a baby," she reminded herself, but she would try to shift from him, feeling a vague distaste. She would blush, as if he were a grown man, and her heart could be heard beating quickly. He was aware of this and would take up the corrected book and move back to his place. Once he proposed to her and she had the feeling that it was a proposal-rehearsal and that he was making use of her, as an actor might ask her to hear his lines.

"You must go on with your work," she said.

"I can shade in a map and talk as well."

"Then talk sensibly."

"You think I am too young, I daresay; but you could wait for me to grow up. I can do that quickly enough."

"You are far from grown-up at the moment."

"You only say these things because you think the governesses ought to. I suppose you don't know *how* governesses go on, because you have never been one until now, and you were too poor to have one of your own when you were young."

"That is impertinent, Hilary."

"You once told me yourself that your father couldn't afford one."

"Which is a different way of putting it."

"I shouldn't have thought they cost much." He had a way of *just* making a remark, of breathing it so gently that it was scarcely said, and might conveniently be ignored.

He was a dandified little boy. His smooth hair was like a silk cap, combed straight from the crown to a level line above his topaz eyes. His sailor-suits were spotless. The usual boldness changed to an agonized fussiness if his serge sleeve brushed against chalk or if he should slip on the grassy terrace and stain his clothes with green. On their afternoon walks he took no risks and Florence, who had younger brothers, urged him in vain to climb a tree or jump across puddles. At first, she thought him intimidated by his mother or nurse; but soon she realized that his mother entirely indulged him and the nurse had her thoughts all bent upon the new baby: his fussiness was just another part of his grown-upness come too soon.

The house was comfortable, although to Florence rather too sealed-up and overheated after her own damp and draughty home. Her work was not hard and her loneliness only what she had expected. Cut off from the kitchen by her education, she lacked the feuds and camaraderie, gossip and cups of tea, which made life more interesting for the domestic staff. None of the maids – coming to light the lamp at dusk or laying the schoolroom-table for tea – ever presumed beyond a remark or two about the weather.

One late afternoon, she and Hilary returned from their walk and found the lamps already lit. Florence went to her room to tidy herself before tea. When she came down to the schoolroom, Hilary was already there, sitting on the window-seat and staring out over the park as his father did. The room was bright and warm and a maid had put a white cloth over the plush one and was beginning to lay the table.

The air was full of a heavy scent, dry and musky. To Florence, it smelt quite unlike the Eau de Cologne she sometimes sprinkled on her handkerchief when she had a headache and she disapproved so much that she returned the maid's greeting coldly and bade Hilary open the window.

"Open the window, dear girl?" he said. "We shall catch our very deaths."

"You will do as I ask and remember in future how to address me."

She was angry with the maid who now seemed to her an immoral creature and angry to be humiliated before her.

"But why?" asked Hilary.

"I don't approve of my schoolroom being turned into a scented bower." She kept her back to the room and was trembling, for she had never rebuked a servant before.

"I approve of it," Hilary said, sniffing loudly.

"I think it's lovely," the maid said. "I noticed it as soon as I opened the door."

"Is this some joke, Hilary?" Florence asked when the maid had gone.

"No. What?"

"This smell in the room?"

"No. You smell of it most, anyhow." He put his nose to her sleeve and breathed deeply.

It seemed to Florence that this was so, that her clothes had caught the perfume among their folds. She lifted her palms to her face, then went to the window and leant out into the air as far as she could.

"Shall I pour out the tea, dear girl?"

"Yes, please."

She took her place at the table abstractedly, and as she drank her tea she stared about the room, frowning. When

Hilary's mother looked in, as she often did at this time, Florence stood up in a startled way.

"Good-evening, Mrs Wilson. Hilary, put a chair for your Mamma."

"Don't let me disturb you."

Mrs Wilson sank into the rocking-chair by the fire and gently tipped to and fro.

"Have you finished your tea, darling boy?" she asked. "Are you going to read me a story from your book? Oh, there is Lady scratching at the door. Let her in for Mama."

Hilary opened the door and a balding old pug-dog with bloodshot eyes waddled in.

"Come Lady! Beautiful one. Come to Mistress! What is wrong with her, poor pet lamb?"

The bitch had stopped just inside the room and lifted her head and howled. "What has frightened her, then? Come, beauty! Coax her with a sponge-cake, Hilary."

She reached forward to the table to take the dish and doing so noticed Florence's empty tea-cup. On the rim was a crimson smear, like the imprint of a lip. She gave a sponge-finger to Hilary, who tried to quieten the pug, then she leaned back in her chair and studied Florence again as she had studied her when she had engaged her a few weeks earlier. The girl's looks were appropriate enough, appropriate to a clergyman's daughter and a governess. Her square chin looked resolute, her green eyes innocent, her dress was modest and unbecoming. Yet Mrs Wilson could detect an excitability, even feverishness, which she had not noticed before and she wondered if she had mistaken guardedness for innocence and deceit for modesty.

She was reaching this conclusion – rocking back and forth when she saw Florence's hand stretch out and turn the cup round in its saucer so that the red stain was out of sight.

"What is wrong with Lady?" Hilary asked, for the dog would not be pacified with sponge-fingers, but kept making barking advances farther into the room, then growling in retreat.

"Perhaps she is crying at the new moon," said Florence and she went to the window and drew back the curtain. As she moved, her skirts rustled. If she has silk underwear as well! Mrs Wilson thought. She had clearly heard the sound of taffetas and she imagined the drab, shiny alpaca dress concealing frivolity and wantonness.

"Open the door, Hilary!" she said. "I will take Lady away. Vernon shall give her a run in the park. I think a quiet read for Hilary and then an early bed-time, Miss Chasty. He looks pale this evening."

"Yes, Mrs Wilson." Florence stood respectfully by the table, hiding the cup.

The hypocrisy, Mrs Wilson thought and she trembled as she crossed the landing and went downstairs.

She hesitated to tell her husband of her uneasiness, knowing his susceptibilities to women whom his conscience taught him to deplore. Hidden below the apparent urbanity of their married life were old unhappinesses – little acts of treachery and disloyalty which pained her to remember, bruises upon her peace of mind and her pride: letters found, a pretty maid dismissed, an actress who had blackmailed him. As he read the Lesson in Church, looking so perfectly upright and honourable a man, she sometimes thought of his escapades; but not with bitterness or cynicism, only with pain at her memories and a whisper of fear about the future. For some time she had been spared those whispers and had hoped that their marriage had at last achieved its calm. To speak of

Florence as she must might both arouse his curiosity and revive the past. Nevertheless, she had her duty to her son to fulfil and her own anger to appease and she opened the library door very determinedly.

"Oliver, I am sorry to interrupt your work, but I must speak to you."

He put down the *Strand Magazine* quite happily, aware that she was not a sarcastic woman.

Oliver and his son were extraordinarily alike. "As soon as Hilary has grown a moustache we shall not know them apart," Mrs Wilson often said, and her husband liked this little joke which made him feel more youthful. He did not know that she added a silent prayer – O God, please do not let him *be* like him, though.

"You seem troubled, Louise." His voice was rich and authoritative. He enjoyed setting to rights her little domestic flurries and waited indulgently to hear of some trades-man's misdemeanour or servant's laziness.

"Yes. I am troubled about Miss Chasty."

"Little Miss Mouse? I was rather troubled myself. I noticed two spelling-faults in Hilary's botany essay, which she claimed to have corrected. I said nothing before the boy; but I shall acquaint her with it when the opportunity arises."

"Do you often go to the schoolroom, then?"

"From time to time. I like to be sure that our choice was wise."

"It was not. It was misguided *and* unwise."

"All young people seem slip-shod nowadays."

"She is more than slip-shod. I believe she should go. I think she is quite brazen. Oh, yes, I should have laughed at that myself if it had been said to me an hour ago, but I have just come from the schoolroom and it occurs to me that now she has settled down and feels more secure –

since you pass over her mistakes – she is beginning to take advantage of your leniency and to show herself in her true colours. I felt a sinister atmosphere up there and I am quite upset and exhausted by it. I went up to hear Hilary's reading. They were finishing tea and the room was full of the most overpowering scent – *her* scent. It was disgusting."

"Unpleasant?"

"No, not at all. But upsetting."

"Disturbing?"

She would not look at him or reply, hearing no more indulgence or condescension in his voice, but the quality of warming interest.

"And then I saw her tea-cup and there was a mark on it – a read smear where her lips had touched it. She did not know I saw it and as soon as she noticed it herself she turned it round, away from me. She is an immoral woman and she has come into our house to teach our son."

"I have never noticed a trace of artificiality in her looks. It seemed to me that she was rather colourless."

"She has been sly. This evening she looked quite different, quite flushed and excitable. I know that she had rouged her lips or painted them, or whatever those women do." Her eyes filled with tears.

"I shall observe her for a day or two," Oliver said, trying to keep anticipation from his voice.

"I should like her to go at once."

"Never act rashly. She is entitled to a quarter's notice unless there is definite blame. We could make ourselves very foolish if you have been mistaken. Oh, I know that you are sure; but it has been known for you to misjudge others. I shall take stock of her and decide if she is suitable. She is still Miss Mouse to me and I cannot think otherwise until I see the evidence with my own eyes."

"There was something else as well," Mrs Wilson said wretchedly.

"And what was that?"

"I should rather not say." She had changed her mind about further accusations. Silk underwear would prove, she guessed, too inflammatory.

"I shall go up ostensibly to mention Hilary's faults." He could not go fast enough and stood up at once.

"But Hilary will be in bed."

"I could not mention the spelling-faults if he were not."

"Shall I come with you?"

"My dear Louise, why should you? It would look very strange – a deputation about two spelling-faults."

"Then don't be long will you? I hope you won't be long."

He went to the schoolroom, but there was no one there. Hilary's story-book lay closed upon the table and Miss Chasty's sewing was folded neatly. As he was standing there looking about him and sniffing hard, a maid came in with a tray of crockery.

"Has Master Hilary gone to bed?" he asked, feeling rather foolish and confused.

The only scent in the air was a distant smell – even a haze – of cigarette smoke.

"Yes, sir."

"And Miss Chasty – where is she?"

"She went to bed, too, sir."

"Is she unwell?"

"She spoke of a chronic head, sir."

The maid stacked the cups and saucers in the cupboard and went out. Nothing was wrong with the room apart from the smell of smoke and Mr Wilson went downstairs. His wife was waiting in the hall. She looked up expectantly, in some relief at seeing him so soon.

"Nothing," he said dramatically. "She had gone to bed with a headache. No wonder she looked feverish."

"You noticed the scent."

"There was none," he said. "No trace. Nothing. Just imagination, dear Louise. I thought that it must be so."

He went to the Library and took up his magazine again, but he was too disturbed to read and thought with impatience of the following day.

Florence could not sleep. She had gone to her room, not with a headache but to escape conversations until she had faced her predicament alone. This she was doing, lying on the honeycomb quilt which, since maids do not wait on governesses, had not been turned down.

The schoolroom this evening seemed to have been wreathed about with a strange miasma; the innocent nature of the place polluted in a way which she could not understand or have explained. Something new it seemed, had entered the room which had not belonged to her or became a part of her – the scent had clung about her clothes: the stained cup was her cup and her handkerchief with which she had rubbed it clean was still reddened; and, finally, as she had stared in the mirror, trying to re-establish her personality, the affected little laugh which startled her had come from herself. It had driven her from the room.

I cannot explain the inexplicable, she thought wearily and began to prepare herself for bed. Homesickness hit her like a blow on the head. Whatever they do to me, I have always my home, she promised herself. But she could not think who *they* might be; for no one in this house had threatened her. Mrs Wilson had done no more than irritate her with her commonplace fussing over Hilary and her dog, and Florence was prepared to overcome much more than irritations. Mr Wilson's pomposity, his constant watch on her work, intimidated her, but she knew that all who must earn their living must have fears lest their work should not seem worth the payment. Hilary was easy to manage; she had quickly seen that she could always deflect him from rebelliousness by opening a new subject for conversation; any idea would be a counter-attraction to naughtiness; he wanted her to sharpen his wits upon. And is that all that teaching is, or should be? she had wondered. The servants had been good to her, realizing that she would demand nothing of them. She had suffered great loneliness, but had foreseen it as part of her position. Now she felt fear nudging it away. I am not lonely any more, she thought. I am not alone any more. And I have lost something. She said her prayers; then sitting up in bed, kept the candle alight while she brushed her hair and read the Bible.

Perhaps I have lost my reason, she suddenly thought, resting her finger on her place in the Psalms. She lifted her head and saw her shadow stretch up the powdery, rose-sprinkled wall. Now can I keep *that* secret? she wondered. When there is no one to help me to do it? Only those who are watching to see it happen.

She was not afraid in her bedroom as she had been in the schoolroom, but her perplexed mind found no replies to its questions. She blew out the candle and tried to fall asleep but lay and cried for a long time, and yearned to be at home again and comforted in her mother's arms.

In the morning she met kind enquiries. Nurse was so full of solicitude that Florence felt guilty. "I came up with a warm drink and put my head round the door but you were in the land of Nod so I drank it myself. I should take a grey powder if I were you. Or I could mix you a gargle. There are a lot of throats about."

"I am quite better this morning," said Florence and she felt calmer as she sat down at the schoolroom-table with

Hilary. Yet it was all true, her reason whispered. The morning hasn't altered that.

"You have been crying," said Hilary. "Your eyes are red."

"Sometimes people's eyes are red from other causes – headaches and colds." She smiled brightly.

"And sometimes from crying, as I said, I should think *usually* from crying."

"Page fifty-one," she said, locking her hands together in her lap.

"Very well." He opened the book, pressed down the pages and lowered his nose to them, breathing the smell of print. He is utterly sensuous, she thought. He extracts every pleasure, every sensation, down to the most trivial.

They seemed imprisoned in the schoolroom, by the silence of the rest of the house and by the rain outside. Her calm began to break up into frustration and she put her hands behind her chair and pressed them against the hot mesh of the fireguard to steady herself. As she did so, she felt a curious derangement of both mind and body; of desire unsettling her once sluggish, peaceful nature, desire horribly defined, though without direction.

"I have soon finished those," said Hilary, bringing his sums and placing them before her. She glanced at her palms which were criss-crossed deep with crimson where she had pressed them against the fireguard, then she took up her pen and dipped it into the red ink.

"Don't lean against me, Hilary," she said.

"I love the scent so much."

It had returned, musky, enveloping, varying as she moved. She ticked the sums quickly, thinking that she would set Hilary more work and escape for a moment to calm herself – change her clothes or cleanse herself in the rain. Hearing Mr Wilson's footsteps along the passage, she knew that her escape was cut off and raised wild-looking eyes as he came in. He mistook panic for passion, thought that by opening the door suddenly he had caught her out and laid bare her secret, her pathetic adoration.

"Good-morning," he said musically and made his way to the window-seat. "Don't let me disturb you." He said this without irony, although he thought: So it is that way the wind blows! Poor creature! He had never found it difficult to imagine that women were in love with him.

"I will hear you verbs," Florence told Hilary, and opened the French Grammar as if she did not know them herself. Her eyes – from so much crying – were a pale and brilliant green and, as the scent drifted in his direction and he turned to her, she looked fully at him.

Ah, the still waters! he thought and stood up suddenly. "Ils vont," he corrected Hilary and touched his shoulder as he passed. "Are you attending to Miss Chasty?"

"Is she attending to me?" Hilary murmured. The risk was worth taking, for neither heard. His father appeared to be sleep-walking and Florence deliberately closed her eyes, as if looking down were not enough to blur the outlines of her desire.

"I find it difficult," Oliver said to his wife, "to reconcile your remarks about Miss Chasty with the young woman herself. I have just come from the schoolroom and she was engaged in nothing more immoral than teaching French verbs – that not very well, incidentally."

"But can you *explain* what I have told you?"

"I can't do that," he said gaily. For who can explain a jealous woman's fancies? he implied.

He began to spend more time in the schoolroom; from surveillance, he said. Miss Chasty, though not outwardly of an amorous nature, was still not what he had at first supposed. A suppressed wantonness hovered beneath her primness. She was the ideal governess in his eyes – irreproachable, yet not unapproachable. As she was so conveniently installed, he could take his time in divining the extent of her willingness; especially as he was growing older and the game was beginning to be worth more than the triumph of winning it. To his wife, he upheld Florence, saw nothing wrong save in her scholarship, which needed to be looked into – the explanation for his more frequent visits to the schoolroom. He laughed teasingly at Louise's fancies.

The schoolroom indeed became a focal point of the house – the stronghold of Mr Wilson's desire and his wife's jealousy.

"We are never alone," said Hilary. "Either Papa or Mamma is here. Perhaps they wonder if you are good enough for me."

"Hilary!" His father had heard the last sentence as he opened the door and the first as he hovered outside listening. "I doubt if my ears deceived me. You will go to your room while you think of a suitable apology and I think of an ample punishment."

"Shall I take my history book with me or shall I just waste time?"

"I have indicated how to spend your time."

"That won't take long enough," said Hilary beneath his breath as he closed the door.

"Meanwhile, I apologize for him," said his father. He did not go to his customary place by the window, but came to the hearthrug where Florence stood behind her chair. "We have indulged him too much and he has been too much with adults. Have there been other occasions?"

"No, indeed, sir."

"You find him tractable?"

"Oh, yes."

"And you are happy in your position?"

"Yes."

As the dreaded, the now familiar scent began to wreathe about the room, she stepped back from him and began to speak rapidly, as urgently as if she were dying and must make some explanation while she could. "Perhaps, after all, Hilary is right and you do wonder about my competence – and if I can give him all he should have. Perhaps a man would teach him more . . ."

She began to feel a curious infraction of the room and of her personality, seemed to lose the true Florence, and the room lightened as if the season had been changed.

"You are mistaken," he was saying. "Have I ever given you any hint that we were not satisfied?"

Her timidity had quite dissolved and he was shocked by the sudden boldness of her glance.

"No, no hint," she said, smiling. As she moved, he heard the silken swish of her clothes.

"I should rather give you a hint of how well pleased I am."

"Then why don't you?" she asked.

She leaned back against the chimney-piece and looped about her fingers a long necklace of glittering green beads. Where did these come from? she wondered. She could not remember ever having seen them before, but she could not pursue her bewilderment, for the necklace felt familiar to her hands, much more familiar than the rest of the room.

"*When* shall I?" he was insisting. "This evening, per-haps? when Hilary is in bed?"

Then who is *he*, if Hilary is to be in bed? she won-dered. She glanced at him and smiled again. "You are extraordinarily alike," she said. "You and Hilary." But

Hilary is a little boy, she reminded herself. It is silly to confuse the two.

"We must discuss Hilary's progress," he said, his voice so burdened with meaning that she began to laugh at him.

"Indeed we must," she agreed.

"Your necklace is the colour of your eyes." He took it from her fingers and leaned forward, as if to kiss her. Hearing footsteps in the passage she moved sharply aside, the necklace broke and the beads were scattered over the floor.

"Why is Hilary in the garden at this hour?" Mrs Wilson asked. Her husband and the governess were on their knees, gathering up the beads.

"Miss Chasty's necklace broke," her husband said. She had heard that submissive tone before: his voice lacked authority only when he was caught out in some infidelity.

"I was asking about Hilary. I have just seen him running in the shrubbery without a coat."

"He was sent to his room for being impertinent to Miss Chasty."

"Please fetch him at once," Mrs Wilson told Florence. Her voice always gained in authority what her husband's lacked.

Florence hurried from the room, still holding a handful of beads. She felt badly shaken – as if she had been brought to the edge of some experience which had then retreated beyond her grasp.

"He was told to stay in his room," Mr Wilson said feebly.

"Why did her beads break?"

"She was fidgeting with them. I think she was nervous. I was making it rather apparent to her that I regarded

Hilary's insubordination as proof of too much leniency on her part."

"I didn't know that she had such a necklace. It is the showiest trash that I have ever seen."

"We cannot blame her for the cheapness of her trinkets. It is rather pathetic."

"There is nothing pathetic about her. We will continue this in the morning-room and *they* can continue their lessons, which are, after all, her reason for being here."

"Oh, they are gone," said Hilary. His cheeks were pink from the cold outside.

"Why did you not stay in your bedroom as you were told?"

"I had nothing to do. I thought of my apology before I got there. It was: 'I am sorry, dear girl, that I spoke too near the point'."

"You could have spent longer and thought of a real apology."

"Look how long Papa spent and he did not even think of a punishment, which is a much easier thing."

Several times during the evening, Mr Wilson said: "But you cannot dismiss a girl because her beads break."

"There have been other things and will be more," his wife replied.

So that there should not be more that evening, he did not move from the drawing-room where he sat watching her doing her wool-work. For the same reason, Florence left the schoolroom empty. She went out and walked rather nervously in the park, feeling remorseful, astonished and upset.

"Did you mend your necklace?" Hilary asked her in the morning.

"I lost the beads."

"But, my poor girl, they must be somewhere."

She thought: There is no reason to suppose that I shall get back what I never had in the first place.

"Have you got a headache?"

"Yes. Go on with your work, Hilary."

"Is it from losing the beads?"

"No."

"Have you a great deal of jewellery I have not seen yet?"

She did not answer and he went on: "You still have your brooch with your grandmother's plaited hair in it. Was it cut off her head when she was dead?"

"Your *work*, Hilary."

"I shudder to think of chopping it off a corpse. You could have some of my hair, now, while I am living." He fingered it with admiration, regarded a sum aloofly and jotted down its answer. "Could I cut some of yours?" he asked, bringing his book to be corrected. He whistled softly, close to her, and the tendrils of hair round her ears were gently blown about.

"It is ungentlemanly to whistle," she said.

"My sums are always right. It shows how I can chatter and subtract at the same time. Any governess would be annoyed by that. I suppose your brothers never whistle."

"Never."

"Are they to be clergymen like your father?"

"It is what we hope for one of them."

"I am to be a famous judge. When you read about me will you say: 'And to think I might have been his wife if I had not been so self-willed?'"

"No, but I hope that I shall feel proud that once I taught you."

"You sound doubtful."

He took his book back to the table. "We are having a quiet morning," he remarked. "No one has visited us. Poor

119

Miss Chasty, it is a pity about the necklace," he murmured, as he took up his pencil again.

Evenings were dangerous to her. He said he would come, she told herself, and I allowed him to say so. On what compulsion did I?

Fearfully, she spent her lonely hours out in the dark garden or in her cold candlelit bedroom. He was under his wife's vigilance and Florence did not know that he dared not leave the drawing-room. But the vigilance relaxed, as it does; his carelessness returned and steady rain and bitter cold drove Florence to warm her chilblains at the schoolroom fire.

Her relationship with Mrs Wilson had changed. A wary hostility took the place of meekness and when Mrs Wilson came to the schoolroom at tea-times, Florence stood up defiantly and cast a look round the room as if to say: "Find what you can. There is nothing here." Mrs Wilson's suspicious ways increased her rebelliousness. I have done nothing wrong, she told herself. But in her bedroom at night: *I* have done nothing wrong, she would think.

"They have quite deserted us," Hilary said from time to time. "They have realized you are worth your weight in gold, dear girl; or perhaps I made it clear to my father that in this room he is an interloper."

"Hilary!"

"You want to put yourself in the right in case that door opens suddenly as it has been doing lately. There, you see! Good-evening, Mamma. I was just saying that I have scarcely seen you all day." He drew forward her chair and held the cushion behind her until she leaned back.

"I have been resting."

"Are you ill, Mamma?"

"I have a headache."

"I will stroke it for you, dear lady."

He stood behind her chair and began to smooth her forehead. "Or shall I read to you?" he asked, soon tiring of his task. "Or play the musical-box?"

"No, nothing more, thank you."

Mrs Wilson looked about her, at the tea-cups, then at Florence. Sometimes it seemed to her that her husband was right and that she was growing fanciful. The innocent appearance of the room lulled her and she closed her eyes for a while, rocking gently in her chair.

"I dozed off," she said when she awoke. The table was cleared and Florence and Hilary sat playing chess, whispering so that they should not disturb her.

"It made a domestic scene for us," said Hilary. "Often Miss Chasty and I feel that we are left too much in solitary bliss."

The two women smiled and Mrs Wilson shook her head. "You have too old a head on your shoulders," she said. "What will they say of you when you go to school?"

"What shall I say of *them*?" he asked bravely, but he lowered his eyes and kept them lowered. When his mother had gone, he asked Florence: "Did you go to school?"

"Yes."

"Were you unhappy there?"

"No. I was homesick at first."

"If I don't like it, there will be no point in my staying," he said hurriedly. "I can learn anywhere and I don't particularly want the corners knocked off, as my father once spoke of it. I shouldn't like to play cricket and all those childish games. Only to do boxing and draw blood," he added, with sudden bravado. He laughed excitedly and clenched his fists.

"You would never be good at boxing if you lost your temper."

"I suppose your brothers told you that. They don't sound

very manly to me. They would be afraid of a good fight and the sight of blood, I daresay."

"Yes, I daresay. It is bedtime."

He was whipped up by the excitement he had created from his fears.

"Chess is a woman's game," he said and upset the board. He took the cushion from the rocking-chair and kicked it inexpertly across the room. "I should have thought the door would have opened then," he said. "But as my father doesn't appear to send me to my room, I will go there of my own accord. It wouldn't have been a punishment at bedtime in any case. When I am a judge I shall be better at punishments than he is."

When he had gone, Florence picked up the cushion and the chess-board. I am no good at punishments either, she thought. She tidied the room, made up the fire, then sat down in the rocking-chair, thinking of all the lonely schoolroom evenings of her future. She bent her head over her needle-work – the beaded sachet for her mother's birthday present. When she looked up she thought the lamp was smoking and she went to the table and turned down the wick. Then she noticed that the smoke was wreathing upwards from near the fire-place, forming rings which drifted towards the ceiling and were lost in a haze. She could hear a woman's voice humming softly and the floorboards creaked as if someone were treading up and down the room impatiently. She felt in herself a sense of burning impatience and anticipation and watching the door opening found herself thinking: If it is not he, I cannot bear it.

He closed the door quietly. "She has gone to bed," he said in a lowered voice. "For days I dared not come. She has watched me at every moment. At least, this evening, she gave way to a headache. Were you expecting me?"

"Yes."

"And once I called you Miss Mouse! And you are still Miss Mouse when I see you about the garden, or at luncheon."

"In this room I can be myself. It belongs to us."

"And not to Oliver as well – ever?" he asked her in amusement.

She gave him a quick and puzzled glance.

"Let no one intrude," he said hastily. "It is our room, just as you say."

She had turned the lamp too low and it began to splutter. "Firelight is good enough for us," he said, putting the light out altogether.

When he kissed her, she felt an enormous sense of disappointment, almost as if he were the wrong person embracing her in the dark. His arch masterfulness merely bored her. A long wait for so little, she thought.

He, however, found her entirely seductive. She responded with a sensuous languor, unruffled and at ease like the most perfect hostess.

"Where did you practise this, Miss Mouse?" he asked her. But he did not wait for the reply, fancying that he heard a step on the landing. When his wife opened the door, he was trying desperately to light a taper at the fire. His hand was trembling and when at last, in the terribly silent room, the flame crept up the spill it simply served to show up Florence's disarray which like a sleep-walker, she had not noticed or put right.

She did not see Hilary again, except as a blurred little figure at the schoolroom window – blurred because of her tear-swollen eyes.

She was driven away in the carriage, although Mrs Wilson had suggested the station fly. "Let us keep her disgrace and her tearfulness to ourselves," he begged, although he was exhausted by the repetitious burden of his wife's grief.

"*Her* disgrace!"

"My mistake, I have said, was in not taking your accusations about her seriously, I see now that I was in some way bewitched – yes, bewitched is what it was – acting against my judgment; nay, my very nature. I am astonished that anyone so seemingly meek could have cast such a spell upon me."

Poor Florence turned her head aside as Williams, the coachman, came to fetch her little trunk and the basket-work hold-all. Then she put on her cloak and prepared herself to go downstairs, fearful lest she should meet anyone on the way. Yet her thoughts were even more on her journey's end; for what, she wondered, could she tell her father and how expect him to understand what she could not understand herself?

Her head was bent as she crossed the landing and she hurried past the schoolroom door. At the turn of the staircase she pressed back against the wall to allow someone to pass. She heard laughter and then up the stairs came a young woman and a little girl. The child was clinging to the woman's arm and coaxing her, as sometimes Hilary had tried to coax Florence. "After lessons," the woman said firmly, but gaily. She looked ahead, smiling at herself. Her clothes were unlike anything that Florence had ever seen. Later, when she tried to describe them to her mother, she could only remember the shortness of a tunic which scarcely covered the knees, a hat like a helmet drawn down over eyes intensely green and matching the long necklace of glass beads which swung on her flat bosom. As she came up the stairs and drew near to Florence, she was humming softly against the child's pleading; silk rustled against her silken legs and all of the staircase, as Florence quickly descended, was full of fragrance.

In the darkness of the hall a man was watching the two go round the bend of the stairs. The woman must have looked back, for Florence saw him lift his hand in a secretive gesture of understanding.

It is Hilary, not his father! she thought. But the figure turned before she could be sure and went into the library.

Outside on the drive Williams was waiting with her luggage stowed away in the carriage. When she had settled herself, she glanced up at the schoolroom window and saw Hilary standing there rather forlornly and she could almost imagine him saying: "My poor dear girl; so you were not good enough for me, after all?"

"When does the new governess arrive?" she asked Williams in a casual voice, which hoped to conceal both pride and grief.

"There's nothing fixed as far as I have heard," he said.

They drove out into the lane. When will it be *her* time? Florence wondered. I am glad that I saw her before I left.

"We are sorry to see you going, Miss." He had heard that the maids were sorry, for she had given them no trouble.

"Thank you Williams."

As they went on towards the station, she leaned back and looked at the familiar places where she had walked with Hilary. I know what I shall tell my father now, she thought, and she felt peaceful and meak as though beginning to be convalescent after a long illness.

THE GHOST DOWNSTAIRS

(BBC, 1983)
Starring: Cyril Cusack, Mike Gwilym &
Jonathan Byatt
Directed by Andrew Gosling
Story 'The Constable's Tale' by Leon Garfield

Leon Garfield is another writer like M.R. James whose ghost stories have proved ideal for adapting for Christmas viewing. Particularly memorable among his contributions to this tradition was 'The Ghost Downstairs' which Ian Keill scripted and produced for the BBC in 1982. The story of a mysterious figure named Mr Fishbane who takes up residence in the basement of a solicitor's office and there begins to conjure up ghosts from the past, the dramatization provided a unique role for Cyril Cusack as Fishbane, with Mike Gwilym as the clerk, Mr Fast, who pores over old documents by day and dreams of power and riches by night. In a feature article about the production before it was screened, the *Radio Times* commented, 'Mr Fast is a mean Victorian lawyer, skilled with small print and binding contracts – this is a Christmas ghost story that may make us think of Scrooge.' In fact, although Leon Garfield has described the Charles Dickens' classic about the old miser as one of the most influential ghost stories in the English language, he admitted that it was Faust he had in mind when inventing Mr Fast. Nonetheless, the drama which cleverly incorporated some scary illustrations by Errol Le Cain that unexpectedly came to life on the small screen, remained long in the memory of viewers and further enhanced the author's reputation in the supernatural genre.

Although Leon Garfield (1921–) is sometimes categorized as a children's writer – though not in the United States – his ghost stories have a wide following among lovers of supernatural fiction. Related to the great German poet, Heinrich Heine (who also wrote about the weird and the uncanny in several of his works), Garfield was a teacher of biochemistry for a number of years while developing his talent as a writer. It was not until 1964, however, that his mastery of the macabre was spotted when he published *Jack Holborn*, an eerie and weird adventure which revealed his fascination with myths and legends. Since then he has never looked back with his works like *Devil-in-the-Fog* (1966), *Mister Corbett's Ghost* (1969) and *The Lamplighter's Funeral* (1975) making him a household name on both sides of the Atlantic as well as earning him a Whitbread award. A number of these, including *The Ghost Downstairs* (1972), have been adapted for TV. 'The Constable's Tale', written for the special Christmas number of the *Daily Mail* in 1993, is somewhat in the mould of that book as well as being another example of Leon Garfield's admiration for the work of Charles Dickens. In it, he ingeniously retells the story of Scrooge's change of heart from the point of view of a Victorian constable who was on duty that traumatic Christmas day . . .

Christmas Eve. It was foggy: a very thick, brown fog, having something of the smotheringness of Mrs Porlock's gravy, which rendered beef, gristle, turnip, potato and trouser-button all brothers under its skin.

So thought Constable Porlock, on duty in the vicinity of Cornhill; although he might have been a policeman on the Moon for all he could distinguish of his surroundings. Nonetheless his tour of duty had been rewarding: several kindly folk had pressed silver sixpences and even shillings into his outstretched hand as he wished them a merry Christmas, and a pair of charity gentlemen had given him a cigar. He began to wave his arms vigorously to ward off the bitter chill.

"I beg your pardon, sir!" he apologised, as he fetched a hurrying gent who came out of the fog a brisk fourpenny one round the ear and sent him staggering. "Allow me, sir! A very merry Christ – Why! If it ain't Mr Cratchit!"

It was indeed Mr Scrooge's thin little clerk, in his long white muffler and very little else to keep him warm. Hastily, Constable Porlock withdrew his outstretched hand and, after fumbling in his pocket, pressed a silver sixpence into Bob Cratchit's frozen palm. "For Tiny Tim, sir," said he, referring to Bob Cratchit's youngest, a poorly child, not likely to see another Christmas.

"And the compliments of the season to Mrs Cratchit and all the family!" he called as Bob Cratchit, after thanking him, vanished, leaving for a moment the ends of his muffler flying in the foggy air, like froth blown from a tankard.

Constable Porlock sighed heavily. Poor Mr Cratchit looked scarce able to keep his own body and soul together, let alone provide for his little family in Camden

Town. His was a hard life, and there was no doubt that the hardest thing in it was his employer, Mr Ebenezer Scrooge.

There was a faint yellow glow ahead, which, as Constable Porlock approached, resolved itself into a burning brazier, the property of some workmen who had been repairing gas pipes in a neighbouring court. The sight of it put Constable Porlock in mind of his cigar. Begging the loan of a pair of tongs, he extracted a glowing coal and, becoming for a moment a fiery goblin policeman, lit up and proceeded on his way, puffing contentedly and adding little clouds of blue fog to the brown.

"A merry Christmas to you, sir!"

"Humbug!"

"Why, bless my soul if it ain't Mr Scrooge!" exclaimed Constable Porlock, withdrawing his hopeful hand from the shadowy figure that had crossed his path. "Allow me, sir," he insisted, skipping ahead of Bob Cratchit's stony-hearted employer with the charitable intention of guiding him through the fog by means of the dancing glow of his cigar.

"If I might make so bold, sir: Lead kindly light, amid the encircling gloom, lead thou me on!"

"Humbug!" shouted Scrooge in a fury, striving to escape from the poetical policeman; but Constable Porlock's cigar, like a drunken firefly, continued to jiggle and gyrate ahead of him until they reached the entrance of the yard down which Scrooge lived.

"A merry Christmas, Mr Scrooge," offered Constable Porlock for the last time, and was rewarded with three loud, sharp "Humbugs!" that went off like pistol shots as Scrooge vanished into the blackness of the yard. Constable Porlock sighed: he had done his best.

He turned away and observed, with surprise and pleasure, a public-house nearby, softly shining in the fog, like a large Christmas box in gently billowing unwrappings of brown paper.

It was the Queen's Arms. Strange, he'd thought it was on the other side of the street . . .

"A merry Christmas, Constable Porlock!" greeted the landlord, rising up, it seemed, from the arms of the Queen herself, for he wore a paper crown and an air of tipsy pride. "What is your pleasure, sir?" He gestured towards the grove of green and golden bottles that winked and gleamed on shelves behind the counter.

"A merry Christmas, landlord, and a glass of brandy and water, if you'd be so kind."

The constable appeared to be the only customer; and the landlord, who had been celebrating on his own – his lady having retired to sleep off the effects of several deep potations – was glad of the company. He joined Constable Porlock in a seat by the fire, and the pair of them sat, with their feet on the fender rail, toasting their toes and each other in brandy and port wine.

They talked of this and that, of wives and little ones, and the state of the nation; and when the port and brandy ran out, they talked of God and the devil, and passed on to rum and gin . . .

"How long," inquired the landlord, suddenly, "has he been sitting there?" and he pointed towards the door.

Constable Porlock looked and, sure enough, there was a stranger sitting on a high-backed chair – very still, very pale, very quiet. There was something about him that prevented Constable Porlock wishing him a merry Christmas. It was as if the words would have been a grave discourtesy to one in his evident discomfort. He wore a bandage round his head, as if he had a toothache:

and a dreadful look about his eyes, as if there was an ache inside beyond all hope of cure.

"Do you happen to have such a thing as a feather about you?" inquired the landlord softly, leaning towards Constable Porlock.

"No," returned the constable, with a puzzled frown. "Why?"

"To knock me down with!" muttered the landlord. "As I live and breathe, that's Ebenezer Scrooge's old partner, Jacob Marley, who's been dead these seven years!"

Instantly all the warmth that the brandy and rum had kindled in Constable Porlock's veins was extinguished; and as he peered at the spectral inhabitant of the chair, he felt distinctly chilly, with a strong tendency for his hair to stand on end.

With trembling fingers, he reached for his notebook and pencil to record the extraordinary event; but even as he did so, the parlour clock struck the hour, (which one, Constable Porlock was too distressed to observe), and the spectral one rose up, like smoke, and hovered by the door. It seemed that the clock had reminded it of an appointment and it was about to depart like, as the gentleman in the play observed, "a guilty thing upon a fearful summons". But it hesitated, passing its hands back and forth through the back of the chair, as if it were practising conjuring tricks for a Christmas party of infant ghosts.

Suddenly it spoke. Plainly it felt it owed the pair before the fire an explanation for its appearance in the Queen's Arms. "My business," it began, in a whispering voice, like dead leaves, "is not with you. It is with old Ebenezer Scrooge. I am come to warn him that, unless he repents his hard and grasping way of life, he will suffer a fate even worse than mine."

Here, the wretched ghost gave such a groan that its listeners were left in no doubt that the fate it was suffering was an exceedingly unpleasant one. "He will be visited by three spirits: first will be the Spirit of Christmas Past; then the Spirit of Christmas Present; and last of all, the Spirit of Christmas Yet To Come."

Then, with a final flourish of its wispy hands through the chair, it vanished.

Constable Porlock and the landlord gazed at one another, then at the chair, then at the door.

At length, Constable Porlock spoke. "As I see it, landlord, Mr Scrooge is a gentleman very set in his ways. I can't see three spirits making much of an impression on him. Six months' hard labour might be more to the purpose."

"Or a dozen of the birch," suggested the landlord.

"Cat o'nine tails, more likely," improved Constable Porlock, who, like all Englishmen, was a sailor at heart.

"In the good old days," sighed the landlord, "there'd have been the thumb-screw".

"And the rack!"

"And red-hot irons . . ."

So they went on, devising sterner and sterner punishments to bring Scrooge to repentance. "But three spirits will never make a mark on a granite gent like Ebenezer Scrooge," concluded Constable Porlock, with a sad shake of his head. "Waste of time."

The mention of time caused him to look up at the clock; but he did not properly take in the situation of the hands. He stood up.

"Going home to Mrs Porlock and roast goose?" inquired the landlord.

Constable Porlock shook his head. "Beef stew, more likely," he said, "and anyway, it's too foggy. I'm just stepping out to clear my head."

He was gone for just sufficient time for the landlord to replenish the rum and gin. "Why, what's amiss, Constable Porlock?" he cried as the constable returned. "You look as if you've seen another ghost!"

Constable Porlock sat down heavily in his place by the fire. He wiped his brow and stared at the landlord. "It's begun!" he whispered. "They're at it even now!" He took out his notebook and, moistening the tip of his pencil with a large, thirsty tongue, began to write.

When he had finished, he passed the book to the landlord in evidence of what he had seen.

'Christmas Morning. One o'clock. Fog lifting a little. Observed Mr Scrooge's residence. Light showing in first-floor front. Observed Mr Scrooge, in the company of small, white-clad personage whose head appeared to be lit up like a candle, emerging from the said window and proceeding in an easterly direction, some 20ft above the chimney-pots. From information received, it would appear that the small personage was a spirit, known as the Spirit of Christmas Past.'

The landlord returned the notebook, and he and Constable Porlock sat staring into the fire. "Christmas past," he murmured, and Constable Porlock nodded and sighed. His thoughts, as swift and airy as Scrooge's strange journey, were revisiting a Christmas morning long ago, when he was first courting Mrs Porlock, and he'd walked five miles through the snow just for the chance of a mistletoe kiss.

He smiled as he remembered putting his arm round her waist and discovering how slender she was, slender enough "to have crept into any alderman's thumb-ring", as the gentleman said in the play.

Then he thought of those first Christmases when they were married, and everything she cooked for him was spiced and sauced and flavoured with laughter and love . . .

"Listen!" muttered the landlord, laying his hand on Constable Porlock's sleeve. "He's coming back!" Constable Porlock listened; and there was indeed a strange wailing sound in the air, the sound of a soul in distress.

He rose to his feet and, taking his notebook, went outside into the night. Impatiently the landlord waited. At last Constable Porlock returned. "Well?" demanded the landlord. "Was it them?"

Constable Porlock held up his hand for silence. He resumed his seat by the fire and, as if unwilling to entrust what he had witnessed to anything so ephemeral as the spoken word, opened his notebook and began to write. When he had finished, as before, he passed his notebook to the landlord, who read:

'Christmas Morning. Still one o'clock. Fog much improved. Snow beginning to fall. Observed Mr Scrooge, in the company of the small white personage, approaching across the chimney tops.

'Mr Scrooge appeared to be greatly distressed. Observed them enter Mr Scrooge's residence through the window of the first floor front. Shortly after, observed Mr Scrooge again emerge, this time in the company of an altogether larger person, in seasonable attire, being clad in a long green robe, edged with fur, and sporting a chaplet of holly. As before, Mr Scrooge and companion proceeded, some 20ft above the chimney pots, this time in the direction of Camden Town. From information received, it is presumed that this second companion was the Spirit of Christmas Present.'

"Christmas Present!" sighed the landlord. "You and Mrs Porlock will be celebrating in style, I expect!"

Constable Porlock did not answer. He was thinking of his little house in the Pentonville Road, where Mrs Porlock would be waiting for him, alone. Their children had long since flown the nest: two to Australia, one to Canada, and one, the youngest, to the grave.

Mrs Porlock, somewhat stouter than of old, would have done her best; but, Lord love us! she was a terrible cook with a mania for gravy as thick and sour as the fog. Sadly he wondered what had become of the lovely girl he had known, whose every dish was as savoury sweet as her lips.

"Landlord . . ." he began, when there was a violent blast of wind and the door of the Queen's Arms flew open! A tremendous gust of snow rushed in, and when it subsided they saw Ebenezer Scrooge outside! He was on his knees before a dreadful hooded figure, all in black.

It needed no great power of divination to know that the grim figure before whom Scrooge knelt, was the Spirit of Christmas Yet to Come.

The landlord rose up and went to shut the door. "Ain't you going to write it down?" he asked Constable Porlock.

The constable shook his head. He was feeling weary, wearier than he'd ever felt in his life before. He closed his eyes.

"The Spirit of Christmas Yet To Come," he whispered; and suddenly he was in the parlour of his house in Pentonville Road, and gazing up at the ceiling.

He was lying in his coffin, and Mrs Porlock was

laying a little bunch of lilies of the valley on his chest. She did not look very sad. But why should she?

The Porlock she had known and loved had died many years ago; and all she had to live and cook for had been an empty shell. He had died of the commonest curse of all – forgetfulness. Having paid her floral tribute, she went away, and the undertaker's men came with the coffin lid. "No! No!" he cried. "Let me have one last look!"

Then he awoke.

"A merry Christmas!" said the landlord. "It's eight o'clock of a fine Christmas morning!"

Constable Porlock sat up. He went to the door and looked out. The sun was shining brightly and the world was white with snow. Somebody was shouting. It was Mr Scrooge from his bedroom window.

He was shouting to a boy below to go to the poulterers and buy the largest turkey in the world and take it to Bob Cratchit's! He was a man transformed with joy, as if he had been given a second chance to live his life!

"Boy!" called out Constable Porlock when Mr Scrooge had done with him. "Do you know the flower shop next to the poulterer's?"

"I'll say I do," said the boy.

"Do they still have their hot-house flowers?

"I'll say they do!"

"Then tell 'em to send a dozen red roses to Mrs Porlock of 27 Pentonville Road, and tell 'em to put in a card saying, 'A Merry Christmas, darling, and don't forget the mistletoe'!"

"I'll say I will!" said the boy, and, pocketing the money, shot off in a flurry of snow.

"Well," said the landlord, as Constable Porlock prepared to go home, "it looks like old Jacob Marley was no fool. I doubt if the rack and thumb-screw would have done half so well!"

TALES FROM THE DARKSIDE

(Laurel TV, 1985)
Starring: Fritz Weaver, Jean Marsh &
Keenan Wynn
Directed by Tom Savini
Story 'Clay' by George A Romero

Tales From The Darkside has been perhaps the most popular and widely appreciated supernatural series on American television in the past decade – thanks in no small degree to the work of the producer, George A Romero, and the contributions he has secured from a number of the leading genre writers including Robert Bloch, Stephen King and Clive Barker. Romero, internationally famous for his small-budget zombie movie, *The Night of the Living Dead* (1968) which became a box-office sensation all over the world and inspired several sequels, had been an admirer of the TV anthology series ever since the days of *Twilight Zone*. The success of the *Living Dead* movies gave him the clout to launch his own programme in which he made a point of featuring stories with trick endings in the style of the great American writer, O.Henry: another of Romero's formulative influences. Among the highlights of the series – which one reviewer admiringly referred to as 'a macabre *Twilight Zone*' – have been 'Sorry, Right Number' from a story by Stephen King and an excellent ghost tale 'Everybody Needs A Little Love' by Robert Bloch.

George A Romero (1939–) was born in New York, the son of an artist who designed posters for the Broadway theatres and movie houses which gave the youngster his interest in the entertainment business. At 14, George made his first film, *Man From The Meteor* which got him into trouble with the authorities during shooting when he threw a burning dummy from a building – but the experience did nothing to deter his intention of getting into the movies. After college, he worked in a production company for several years while raising the finances to make *Night of the Living Dead* which, when finally released, changed his life forever. Despite the success of these pictures, George has resisted becoming part of the Hollywood establishment, though his commercial success has continued as a result of working with Stephen King on various projects including the *Creepshow* series and the film version of *Pet Sematary*. He has also written a number of screenplays and a handful of short stories like this next item, 'Clay' which was adapted for the first series of *Tales of the Darkside*.

Nobody knew who he was. People knew him to see him. He'd been around the neighborhood for as long as it could be called a neighborhood, but nobody knew exactly who he was. The few who came in contact with him, store owners and clerks, people at the church, the old Monsignor himself, recognized him as Tippy. That was it. He wasn't known, he was simply recognized, and only by the ones who had been around Castle Hill Avenue long enough. Recognized, like an old piece of furniture one periodically rediscovers in an attic.

For that matter the old Monsignor was merely recognized, not really known anymore. He, too, was a remnant from the past, soon to be swallowed and lost forever in the huge digestive tract of the city. He was all but forgotten already, even though he still rattled about in the massive stone church he'd caused to exist. When only the stone was left would he be remembered at all? When he was a boy his father had walked him through a cemetery, pointing out, "The bigger the tombstone, the harder to find the name of the deceased." It was meant to be a lesson in humility.

The Monsignor was closer to Tippy than anyone in the world, although it was unknown to either man. He was the closest because he was the only person whose life was touched by the tattered Irishman. The priest felt guilt whenever he saw Tippy. It was a feeling he'd carried privately since 1942. It would bite at him like an angina and drive him to penance in the middle of a stormy night, usually a night after he'd run into Tippy on the street, or seen him at Mass, or heard one of his strange confessions. The penance would make things worse: He'd say the words by rote, and feel guiltier for saying them, hypocritical. "I detest all my sins because of Thy just punishment, but most of all because they offend Thee, my God, Who art all good and deserving of all my love." The priest knew there could no longer be a true Act of Contrition when there was no longer faith.

What that old man felt inside him was not repentance, but self-pity and fear. Not fear of eternal reprisal, but of there being no eternity at all. Fear that his body was clay and clay alone, not containing the soul he'd been promised. The soul he'd promised in turn to Tippy when Tippy was a boy in 1942.

The old Monsignor was a shepherd who'd come to loathe the sheep. He hated their smell and their complaining sound. He hated everything about them that made them animal. Growing up in farm country upstate, he'd seen a wild look in the eyes of sheep as they let themselves be led from mud pit to shearing to slaughter. In the city he'd seen that same wild stare just above a toothless grin or an outstretched hand reaching up from the gutter. "Father, can ya do me any good?" Too often he'd thought as he stared back at the writhing beast, No, but you can do me evil.

He'd retreated from any association with the creatures around him. How could he hold himself up as holy, hold himself up as one of God's chosen, if he admitted to being one of *them*? To survive, he'd convinced himself that he was separate from the rest; he'd come to view that separateness not as sin, but somehow as making him less of a sinner. He'd buried his abandonment of the flock behind the books and ledgers of the orderly parish he'd managed. He'd built the church, then the school. He'd stayed. He'd kept St Matthew's alive and flourishing just eight miles from the cesspool that was Manhattan: a feat, in his mind, not unlike keeping a sand castle intact in a pounding surf.

But despite his diocesan accomplishments, he'd come to old age and arthritic exhaustion in mortal fear. He'd stare at his body, wrinkled and pale blue in a night's lightning flash, and think of the clay, of the wounded eyes of Tippy as a boy. He'd held those eyes in attention for a moment, then let them go. Disembodied, they stared at him, out of dreams, out of shadowy corners of his room. There was faith in those eyes, and on their surface, wet with tears, the priest saw a reflection of his old self, a reflection growing dimmer with the years, as it might on a tarnishing piece of silver.

Now those eyes stared up from the pews each Sunday, out of the face of a poor, retarded nonentity beasts of the city had puked into life. Damn those eyes! They had faith in them still. Was it too late to reach out, to break the silence? Yes. What about all the others he'd ignored since he started ignoring Tippy? The priest could never open that floodgate for fear of the thousand lost beings that might enter to haunt him. One pair of eyes was enough. And, after all, Tippy was at Mass every week. He made his confession regularly. If there were such things as souls then his was clean enough. His sins were grotesque but childish. The tragic aberrations of a lonely damaged mind, of no apparent harm to anyone but the sinner himself. Tippy was mad, and nothing the priest could have done would ever have prevented that. Perhaps it was the madness that enabled him to keep the faith.

God, what was the last name? O'Malley? O'Meara? O'Something.

Tippy O'Something's father had been one of New York's finest when New York was at its finest, if there ever was a fine New York. He had walked the beat before Metropolitan Life had created Parkchester, before the parish had a church, before the old Monsignor had even become a novice.

Tippy's life was all emotion without intellect, sensation without reason. The good taste of a stew, the pain of a paddle, a strap, a fist or a boot heel, the cold of a winter without heat: all were things that simply were. There was no affection, but there was no hatred either, just reaction in kind to the cruelties of the world.

In the first ten years of his life, before 1942, a number of things made impressions on Tippy that he would carry in memory as the priest carried a memory of him. He remembered his dad's police jacket and his mother's breasts, which he once saw when she came chasing after one of her men friends who was chasing after Tippy. His mother never brought men friends around when Tippy's brothers were home, but Tippy promised not to tell Dad, so she brought them when he was home.

He knew what they did in her bedroom because he'd asked once and she'd shown him with a banana. That time he'd seen her bottom part. It hadn't seemed nearly as impressive as her breasts. He thought his own bottom part was much more important looking. His mother had said she needed her men friends because, while Dad was good enough, she had to have an Italian or a Jew once in a while to remind her she was a woman. Tippy had supposed that meant dad never did the banana trick with his thing in mom's bottom part.

He didn't remember any of the men friends, just that he didn't like most of them. He didn't even remember the one who chased him, just that the man came into his room with no clothes on. He smelled of whiskey and he wanted to put his thing in Tippy's mouth.

Tippy ran through the house. The naked man chased him and his mother came screaming from the bedroom, her breasts bouncing. She was bruised on her face and a cut over her eye ran red. She broke a lamp over the man's head. It was the last thing Tippy saw before he fell out the window.

The blackness outside came with a rush of cold air. Tippy couldn't tell if he was right side up or upside down. Then he hit. He knew he hit because he heard the sound and his breath stopped and he felt even colder. But there wasn't pain, not right away. He just felt like he was made of clay, and it seemed as though part of him was breaking off. He couldn't tell which part – his chest, his neck, the top of his head – but something on him or in him was breaking away and leaving the rest of his body behind. Could it be stuck back and molded in the way he molded the clay he played with?

Then came the pain.

Then came . . . nothing.

"You damn near died." He remembered his dad saying that. But was that about the time he fell or the time he was so sick? The time he had a hundred and six. "A hundred and six? Why, ya should be proud of that. The hottest New York gets is only a hundred." He remembered his dad saying that, too, and he remembered his dad laughing. He didn't feel like he was breaking apart that time, but he did feel like he was made of clay again. When his mom pushed the big glass onto his chest he expected it to squish in deeper than it did. Under the glass, candle wax dripped. He expected it to burn but it wasn't much hotter than his feverish skin.

That night his father took the candle and glass away and put leeches on Tippy's chest and his mother argued and his father screamed. Then his father started to drink and he screamed louder. "Don't you tell me you know what's good for 'im, woman, you that don't care but ta let 'im see ya runnin' naked with a man ain't 'is father. You're a slut, and if I didn't need ya in this house I'd not even let ya near my children. Ya need ta feel like a woman, is it? Well don't I need ta feel like a man? And all the while I'm payin' the mortgage on this mausoleum you're here takin' pleasure up yer nasty little twat! Ain't it enough I'm in the streets dealin' with hoodlums and whores? Do I hafta have them in ma home?"

After that Tippy just heard a lot of punching and crashing and screaming and crying. Then one of his brothers came in and asked if Tippy died could he have his toys.

After his brother left his dad came in with his bottle of whiskey and sat in a chair. His mom tried to come in as well, but Dad jumped up and slammed the door in her face. She went off crying and Dad flopped back into his chair. Tippy closed his eyes. The feeling that he was made of clay came over him again. Once in a while a leech would move and it felt like a thumb in the clay's surface. Once in a while he could hear his dad swallowing.

When he was well his brothers just took his toys, what few there were, without asking. They never took his clay, though. They didn't like it the way he did. He had five boxes of it, three from three Christmases and two from birthdays in between, only he didn't keep the boxes, just the clay, in a lump in a drawer. He'd worked it so much the individual colors were almost gone: The greens, reds and yellows had turned to a kind of gray. It still felt the same, though. He'd take it out at night and try to make things. He tried to make breasts once, and to stick them onto his chest which still had marks from the leeches. He was so glad he had his own room. Other poor people had to live in rooms together. He was glad his dad was paying for the . . . mor . . . morgasoleum.

"It ain't right a cop should be a poor man." His father only talked to Tippy when he was drunk. He screamed at him and beat him up other times, but he only talked properly when he was drunk. Not that he wouldn't ever rage with the whiskey – he would sometimes, and he'd scream louder and hit harder than normal – but sometimes the whiskey would seem to make him sad and those were the times he talked.

"But I've got the four of yas and the liquor ta pay for and the place here. But I will not go to a desk job, never. Not that they'd have me, wi' me not knowin' me r's as good as some. Oh, Tip. This old New York's no place fer the children of God." Then he blessed himself and kissed the little crucifix he wore on his neck chain.

"Caught a man robbin' a Chinese laundry today. He run and I chased 'im and I got 'im in the gutter and beat 'im 'til he was a lump looked like yer famous clay there. Then I found I knew the man. Feller I used ta drink with over at Pelham Bay. He didn't know me. He'd gone from drink ta morphine and he didn't know me at all."

Tippy picked his dad's police jacket off the back of a chair and put it on as he listened. It was a wonderful jacket, with gold stripes on the sleeves and brass buttons up the front. The sleeves were way too long on the boy and the bottom hung at his shins. If he were made of clay, he thought, he could stretch himself out and make the jacket fit.

"They say that in less than ten years, Tip, there'll be eight million people in New York. How many of 'em'll know me then? Know me name. Me own old dad told me when he put me on the boat, he said, 'Just don't let 'em forget yer name. When they know who ya are it's harder for them ta do ya harm.' Well, they know me name around here all right. Just let 'em try ta forget it. I'll kick it down their throats if I have to. They'll hate me, and many of 'em already do, 'cause I won't let 'em do their dirt. They'll hate me but they'll damn well know who I am."

Tippy wasn't allowed to go far on his own. He had to

stay in sight of the front window, under the shadow of the elevated trains. He had a few pals. They beat him up, mostly, and made fun of him, but they used him when they needed another player for potsy or stickball, and that was often enough so that he got some recreation. He was never sent to school. His mother and dad argued about that, too, and wound up throwing things at each other again. If he went to school he couldn't go to work and they needed the money. His brothers already worked. His father said, "A man has a right ta work his children if he needs. I'm not a truant officer, I'm a cop on the street."

Tippy knew he'd have to go to work soon and that would mean less time to play, so when his mother fell bed-sick he took advantage of it and stayed outside longer. He even walked out of sight of the front window three different times. That's how he met his friend Lucille. They would sit and talk and she would tell him what was uptown and downtown in places she was allowed to go. She was even allowed to ride the train by herself. And she was allowed to go to movies. Tippy imagined that was how it was if you had money. She told him about a giant ape she'd seen in a movie, and about how the ape had destroyed an elevated train just like the one over their heads as they spoke. She told him things that were going on around the neighborhood, some of them having to do with Tip's dad. How he'd arrested one of his best friends and informed on another. How he would take a bit of money from stores while promising to keep them protected, and how he beat up a man in a candy store when he wouldn't pay the bit of money. Tippy didn't care about those things. He felt it all had to do with his dad being more important than the others on Castle Hill. Because his dad had a name, and a uniform. Tippy loved uniforms. Uniforms made anyone important: a copper, a solider, a priest. He wasn't sure you even needed a name if you had a uniform because the uniform said who you were.

Lucille always wanted to play house. She said Tippy was the only boy who'd ever play it with her. She'd be the mum, him the dad. They'd eat supper on her toy plates with Tippy's clay as the food. Then they'd scream at each other in some invented argument, and sometimes they'd even hit each other. Once Tippy tried to tell Lucille about the banana trick and about how their bottom parts were different. Lucille said she knew that already and that she'd like to try and play it with Tip. They were afraid to go to either's house, though, and they couldn't do it in the street, so they just sat there where the sun couldn't reach them for the great tracks overhead.

The night his mother died she wanted to give Tippy the funny-shaped star she wore on her neck chain. His father snatched it away before she could unclip it with her shaking fingers.

"That'll be the day," his father said. Those were the last words ever spoken between Tippy's mom and dad and it was the last time they ever touched. The woman turned to Tippy, who was sitting closer than his brothers. She cried for a while. Then that stopped. Then she just said good-bye and closed her eyes.

Later his father came into Tippy's room smelling of whiskey. "There's only one God anyway, for all of us. For the nigger, the Jew or me or you. And He'll always forgive ya yer trespasses. He's forgiven her, yer mum. He's forgiven me. I beat her about. I beat you about. I beat about a hundred others on the street. I've killed four men so far and still I'm forgiven. And so is she, yer mum. Ya get angry, that's all. Ya get angry and ya hafta beat things about now and again. Ya hafta beat things about a bit just ta show yer here. Just ta show yer here! Anyway, don't ever forget there's a God. She's gone. Someday I'll be gone. Yer brothers'll not look after ya. Yer God will."

The priest, too, had been raised without much affection, but with intelligence and gentility, with books to read and hymns to sing and lessons after supper. His father was an accountant and his mother volunteered at the library. He was the only child, and the three lived together with privacy and propriety, the way people should. Issues were discussed, not argued.

He had plenty of sky, and the fresh green hills around him, and a bicycle, bat and glove. The only violence in his life was at sport and the only hard labor was pedaling uphill to home; they lived halfway up a small mountain. Below them, in the valley, grew the wine grapes, and above them, at the summit, stood the seminary. Both were in view from the front window.

He had an unemotional youth, which made it easy for him to accept a simplistic preordination for mankind, and therefore for himself. Without passions, one can resist temptations easily, but one can mistake order for goodness. He wasn't prepared at all for the disorder of the city. A disorder that seemed to make lies of his beliefs.

He came to the neighborhood when the diocese was funding new construction to keep up with the population. While St Matthew's was being built he served Mass every Sunday at Roone's, an old tavern under the el. The regulars at the bar didn't mind the weekly intrusions. They would set aside their schnapps and even genuflect at the Offertory. There was a pride in the parish come to Castle Hill. The importance of it cut through the smoke and the smell of beer on varnish, cut through the malarkey about Roosevelt, the unions and the new Irish fighter. The boys at Roone's allowed the parish as a good thing, progress for the neighborhood. And it was only a wee sacrifice to shut off the taps for an hour or two on Sunday. Many of the men hadn't been to Mass since before the boats that brought them to New York.

During the week an occasional wedding, or a funeral – and the bar just a few yards from the casket – would be just another reason to drink. In the autumn of 1942, it was Mrs O'Something's casket. The priest spoke the service and old man O'Something had to recruit from among the boys at the bar to carry his dead woman's coffin out to its hearse. No other family attended. Just Officer O'Something and his three young children, him in his dress uniform, digging in a torn and stitched cloth change purse for silver to buy rounds for volunteers.

"I know yas hate me, boys," he said. He'd been drinking before, at home. His stern face was red and resolute as if he were making a pinch in an alley. "And I hate yas back. But I ask yas ta tip one wi' me and then help me carry me . . ." Margaret? Mary? Mathilda? ". . . out ta the only car she's ever rid in."

"That's me name." A child's voice spoke softly up at the priest who'd been carefully folding his vestments on top of the coffin. The youngest of the policeman's children plopped something down on the lid of the great box near the priest's linens. It was a lump of modeling clay, half molded into some indiscernible shape, soft and drooping from the warmth of the boy's hands.

"Me dad said, 'Tip one wi' me.' That's me name. Tip."

"Is it now," the priest said.

"Will ya not even do me this favor in me hour o' grief?" Tip's father was staring them down and the boys at the bar looked at each other, then they looked at Roone, the proprietor. They all knew the dead woman's reputation;

stories got around in bars. Fact is, one of them there had actually slept with her, but that was known only to himself and to young Tip.

Roone looked over at the policeman's children. Then he said, "Sure we'll drink with ya if that's what ya want." And the whiskey started to flow. The priest declined, forgiven only because of his collar. Tip wasn't allowed a drink but his brothers, only two and four years older than he, were actually forced to swallow glassfuls of the burning stuff. After the change purse was empty, but for carfare home from the cemetery, Roone kept pouring on the house, with Officer O'Something careful to point out that there were no favors to be expected in return for the gesture. [Favors of the semiofficial kind.]

During that October drunk young Tip sat waiting near his dead mother, and he and the priest talked. "Is me mum really in the box, then?"

"No. She's long gone, Tip."

"Gone where, is it?"

"If she was good, to Heaven. Pray to the Lord that's so. If she was bad, to the other place."

"There's nothin' in the box then?"

"Oh yes. The poor stuff she was made of. The stuff you saw walkin' about. Her body, which means nothin' at all to you, me or the Lord."

She was long gone from her body. The part of her that was really her had broken away and left. That made sense to Tip. It had almost happened to him. He knew what it felt like. And here was a man in a priest's uniform tellin' it after all.

Then the priest picked up the lump of clay from the inexpensive coffin. Little fragments of green, yellow and red stuck to the crevices of the simple carving on the lid.

The boy picked them off with his fingernails, rolling them into a colorless ball as he listened.

"We're made of clay like this, Tip, while we're here on Earth, that is. It's a mystery, Tip. So don't worry if you don't understand it. Just believe it as the truth. What's this you've made here with this clay?"

"It's King Kong."

"And what on Earth is King Kong?"

"It's a giant great ape what destroyed New York, and even the el, when they brought him here from the jungle. It's in a movie. I didn't see it, but me pal told me the story."

"Oh, it's a monkey then."

"An ape."

"Well. You or I or anyone can take this clay and make it into the body of an ape – a donkey, a flower, a person – and it still wouldn't be alive, would it? Only God can take this clay and shape it and then make it alive. Because only God knows how to put a soul inside the thing he's made. Not that apes or donkeys have souls, mind you."

"Do Italians and Jews have souls?"

"Hah . . . some say not." Oh, why did he let himself say that? Why did he let himself sink to that nasty little joke? A city joke, it was. A good laugh for a city brute. Not for him.

"Me mother was a Jew," Tippy said, and before the priest could speak again the boy's father came snorting out of the smoke at the bar.

"*Turned Catholic and gone to her salvation!*" The red-faced policeman bellowed. Contorted with rage, he looked vengeful, "*Gone to Heaven is me . . .*" Mary? Margaret? Or was it Ethel? Or Ruth?

"If she was good," the boy said. "If not, she's gone to the other place."

And the great drunken oaf of a 'man in blue' lifted young Tip clean off the floor, bringing fist after fist into the boy's face, knocking loose some teeth in a sea of blood. It was then that Tip's eyes found the priest where he sat dumbstruck: sad, pleading eyes that flashed forgiveness; understanding, even as they were being puffed shut by the brutal pounding.

Some of the barflies rushed to stop him, but old O'Something held young Tip's lapels with his left hand while his right fell like a sledge again and again. The vengeance the priest had read on his face had erupted over the limp boy like pus from a seething boil. The priest jumped up but was ineffectual; he didn't know how to face such violence. Like cattle the group stampeded into him, over him. He could smell the whiskey in their expelled gasses, he could feel the sweat in their gritty clothing, he could see the filth in the pores of their skin. It all made him want to vomit.

In the struggle the coffin was knocked from the bar tables holding it and the priest's vestments were ground into the dust and sawdust on the floor as the drunks at Roone's lapsed into Gaelic with their reproaches. The raging old O'Something had to be knocked unconscious before he let go of his unconscious son, who fell into a corner still clutching his lump of clay.

The priest saw the boy on the street the following week. His face was still puffed, with running sores in two places. There were no bandages. The boy said, "Hello, Father," and the priest said "hello" back at him. The boy stood a moment, looking up, and at that moment the priest might have saved himself years of agony by simply saying a few words. But the words never came and the boy walked away.

*   *   *

153

And that's how it was week after week, under the el, at the grocer's and at Mass, with nothing but hello and good-bye. Oh, what cruel punishment for the priest to have to face it so often, what bitter fate that the two should have stayed so long in the neighborhood together. What damning things were those hellos and good-byes with no conversation in between, while St Matthew's became a magnificent stone work, half a block long and with spires taller than the neighboring tracks.

In 1947 one of Tippy's brothers was crushed by a truck carrying steel girders. Three years later his other brother died in a street fight with several other union organizers. His father, the old policeman, died in '54 of liver cancer. The priest was at all three funerals and so was Tippy.

Someone from the Police Department made all the arrangements for O'Something's burial so conversation with the son wasn't necessary even in an official sense. Tip just stood about, half smiling, his nose running a bit. He had a lump of clay in his pocket but nobody could see it. The sun rays fell on him through the stained glass of the window that showed Jesus resurrecting; the light made Tip's face go all green and yellow and red. "Hello," he said to the priest. It was the singsong, overzealous hello of a retard. The priest had never noticed before. Cities conceal such characteristics – the mob makes madmen less visible, along with good men – but there, in the nave of the church, standing close to his old dad's coffin, Tippy, at twenty-two years, was clearly feebleminded. The realization washed over the priest even as the sound of Tip's enthusiastic hello echoed off the great stone walls of the basilica – and still the priest kept silent. The silence seemed to echo as well.

In the days that followed, the priest drummed up the resolve to go visit Tip. But before it happened someone brought the news that old man O'Something had left an old brownstone and a bit of money he'd been misering away, and that Tip's actually gotten a job hefting crates at the new Parkchester Gristede's. The priest never made his visit.

So time marched, and the priest was forced, by the walls of the city that locked them together, to watch Tip progress, or regress, until eventually the two became the old Monsignor and the withered derelict people ignored. Old things that waddled through the neighborhood, bearing no resemblance to their former selves, except to one another's eyes.

The old Monsignor reasoned that it was the fate of people in cities to go about banging off the walls until their brains were pulp, with no air to breathe, no earth to touch, no feeling of contact, no matter that they lived above, below, beside, within inches of one another. He used to think cities were the Devil's swamps, with the Demon himself in residence. Now that he'd seen the brutes of New York at work he knew they'd be sinners even if the Devil didn't prompt them. Did the Devil even exist? And if not, did the Other exist? Were we here alone? Beasts prowling on a spinning rock in the nothingness of space. We no longer even knew each other's names.

Damn! Was it O'Malley? O'Meara? He'd have to check the funeral records.

Over the years four dying men had staggered bleeding into the church to make their last confessions. Burglers had seven times stolen ornaments from the altar. There'd been countless desecrations; the graffiti on the stone walls outdid the elaborate paintings on the trains that rumbled overhead. The priest had found marijuana in the poor box, and bags of shit and, in one case, a bloody fetus on the rectory doorstep. It all went to justify his fear.

So he carried out what he felt more and more to be a charade. He'd baptize them, marry them and extreme unct them, but he'd never get closer than that for fear of being contaminated.

Once in a sermon he spoke of an ape that came from the jungle and destroyed New York. The ape, in the sermon, was man. That night he felt the guilt. It came with the undulating shadows of an electrical storm. He'd lived quite properly. He'd never known, had even shunned, animal passion, and that had brought him to lie alone in the dark with his intellect. His faith had disintegrated; his guilt could never be absolved.

Old Tippy loved to do penance, to feel forgiven as he knelt at the altar rail among a hundred glowing candles, bathed in the smell of incense, surrounded by the figures of saints and angels, and looking up at the body of God Himself, arms outstretched, bleeding wounds gaping in hands and feet and side. God was long gone from His body just as Tippy's mother was long gone from hers. Just as Tippy and all other people would be long gone after they died. He was so glad the priest had told him how it worked. He couldn't wait until it was his turn to go to Heaven. He knew he'd go there and not to the other place because he knew he was basically good. And even when he was bad he told it in confession and the penance made him good again.

Tippy always went to the old Monsignor to confess his sins. He didn't like the new young priest who smelled of cologne and used modern talk. He didn't need talk. Only forgiveness. The musty little confessional, the one closest to the altar, was a dark wood and purple velvet womb that Tippy'd been returning to for some thirty-five years. The even tone of the old Monsignor's voice, never shocked, never angry, was like a warm blanket used by the hand of God to tuck the absolved Tippy back into his proper place in a frightening world while he waited for the world after. Tippy loved to go to confession. He loved and believed fully in God.

The Monsignor had only recently associated the hesitant voice with old Tip. One day, hearing the middle-aged whisper tell of the sins of a child, he peeked out the door as the sinner waddled away toward his penance at the altar rail. Tippy was wearing his old dad's police jacket, and there were holes in his soles, visible as he knelt in the smoke from the candles.

They'd stopped selling the clay a while back. At least Tippy could never find it anymore. Not the good kind. He'd tried the new kinds and they were no good at all. The colors weren't right. He couldn't smooth them and blend them together. They didn't feel good against his skin. The old kind was the best. Green, yellow and red. Hard in the cold air, soft in the hand. Over time Tippy'd bought hundreds and hundreds of boxes of the stuff. It stayed good forever.

If the priest had ever visited Tippy's brownstone under the el, if he'd ever gone up to the third floor, he would have seen the beast of the city at its most dissolute. The priest, in his most frenzied conjurations of the depths man plumbed, could never have imagined the profound horror of those dimly lit rooms where sat the life-sized lumps of putty that were Tippy's friends. Tippy's lovers. Some were in chairs, some on the floor. Two were propped at the dinner table. In a back room one lay on the bed, and in the bathroom one was twisted into the tub. They were crudely shaped to resemble human figures; their features were grotesque and clumsily crafted. They bore lumpy noses and had great gaping holes for mouths, their arms and legs were too long or too short and their torsos were bent and sagging from their own weight. They had all the proper sexual parts under their clothing. They were dressed in things that had belonged to Tippy's brothers, his dad and his mom.

The rooms on that floor had been the brothers', so Tippy had had to do a little converting. He'd brought up his own bed, because he liked it better than either of the ones up there. And he'd brought up the dining table and chairs to use both as work space and as a place for family supper. Everything else was as it had always been as long as the O'Somethings lived there. Oh, except for the two good stuffed chairs with embroidered cushions – these Tippy had covered with bed sheets so the clay wouldn't rub into the fabric. The clay rubbed into everything. The cracks in the floor, the pattern on the silverware, the carving on the headboard of Tippy's bed.

Tippy was quite content upstairs with his pals. He'd play with them and mold them differently to suit his moods and purposes. He'd sit them at table and push food into the openings that were their mouths. At night he'd sit with them and hold them and comfort them and tell them stories of the things he'd done when he'd gone beyond where the front window could see. Other times, he'd pretend to be drunk and angry, and he'd throw things about the room and scream and pull the figures apart brutally.

He hated to go to work because he needed the days for repair and for thinking up new tricks. He kept his job, though, at Gristede's, because he needed money to support his family. Saturdays and Sundays he spent at home, except for going to Mass. He was constantly making improvements on his brood. He'd saved enough money so that they all had wigs now, and recently he'd given them all steelie kabolas for eyes: He'd found them in his brother's marble box, painted on irises, and shoved them into the clay heads. Then he gave the females eyebrows that he clipped from his own pubic hair, which was just growing back in so it was the right length for eyebrows. He'd cut it off a few months ago for another purpose.

He made little clay leeches for when his family was sick. He put tubes of toothpaste inside the male penises. It made them permanently erect but it made them able to squirt something that looked like what Tippy squirted, and it tasted good. Tippy'd tried other things – shampoo, hair conditioner, mayonnaise – but none of them tasted as good as toothpaste. He wanted to make a tongue for a female out of a piece of liver from Gristede's, but the mouth broke apart at the jaw as he tried to secure the piece of raw meat. So he molded the clay back together and put lipstick on the mouth inside. He found that the liver worked well in the vaginal orifice, though. It felt even warmer and smoother than the clay.

He would fish his own stools out of the toilet and mold them into the figures' buttocks. He would shove his fingernail clippings into the ends of their fingers. He would shove his snot into their nostrils. He would open cavities in their clay chests and fill them with chicken innards, or with tomato juice, so they would seem to bleed when he stabbed them.

He used baby bottles and milk in the breasts of the female he liked best. Lucille. She was his favorite. He slept only with her at night. He constantly worked on her with loving hands, trying to refine her features. He even gave her eyelashes and toes. None of the others had toes. He gave her teeth, which he broke, one at a time, off one of those chatter-mouth toys, and inserted individually in her clay mouth. Between her legs was the pubic hair shaved from Tippy's own groin. In the clay beneath the hair was a hole made by a banana.

The problem was moving her. Lucille was very heavy, and she broke apart easily. He had run a strip of wood from her torso through her neck and up into her head. That kept the neck joint from breaking, though it added to the weight, but Tippy didn't like the idea of that hard piece of wood inside Lucille. He thought her inside should be just as soft as her outside, and anyway the wood strip didn't solve the problem of the arms and legs. They were impossible. Whenever he moved her they would break, and he would have to reattach them and mold them back in. One morning he awoke in only one of Lucille's arms; the other was on the floor where it had fallen in the night. The fingers were damaged and the wrist was bent. Somehow that was the last straw. That morning Tippy knew he had to do something about the problem.

Maria Esposito walked hurriedly home through the shadows under the el. The train she had just ridden from her job downtown was rolling off into the dark, and the loud roar scared her as it did every night. She tried to think of bright things: of breakfast, of birthday presents, of store windows with dancing mannequins wearing the jeans she was saving to buy. Every night the same thoughts fought against the dark and every night she survived the imagined perils lurking in the shadows. She was becoming experienced at the ritual. She was becoming a seasoned city dweller.

Tippy didn't know Maria Esposito's name, but he knew she was exactly the right size. He'd been watching her recently. She was exactly the right size to put inside Lucille.

The train's wheels screamed a piercing metallic scream as it rounded a curve in the elevated rails. Beneath that noise nobody heard Maria Esposito's last words, even though she shouted them as loudly as she could, and in the darkness of the alley, on the other side of the building from the el, nobody saw old Tippy carry her unconscious body in through the back entrance of the old O'Something brownstone.

Tippy stabbed Maria Esposito on his dining room table, carefully and slowly through the heart, with a wire coat hanger he'd straightened. He caught as much of the blood as he could, in pots, for later use. The girl came around to semiconsciousness before she died. She felt the burning pain in her chest. She tried to speak, to scream, but she was too weak. She saw Tippy smiling down at her. At first she thought she was in a hospital, that Tippy was some sort of orderly who would tell her she was all right. There'd been an accident, but she was all right. Then she realized she was in somebody's house. An old house with little-flower-patterned wallpaper, and sheets over the furniture. Even through her excruciating pain she could smell the foul stench of the place, the stench of rotting food and month-old milk and human waste that hadn't been flushed away. Then she knew she was dying. She was in the clutches of a madman and he had stabbed her and she was dying. Her only hope was that it was all a dream. It was fuzzy like a dream, somehow unreal around the edges, out of focus, impossible. Those shapes. What were they? There, in the corners, at the edges of sight, just that much darker than the shadows that they could be seen at all. Her head turned toward one of them. Her eyes brought it into sharpness. It was a thing that looked like a woman. It had a hairdo and was dressed like a woman, but where its face should be there was just a grayish grotesque lump, a distorted mass of what looked like clay.

Then she felt something and she looked toward the sensation. She saw what seemed to be a policeman. He was using his billy club to mold some substance onto her legs. The substance was green and yellow and red.

"Bless me, Father, for I have sinned. It's a week since me last confession."

"Yes, my son."

"Well . . . I was bad to George."

"George this time."

"Yes, Father. I pulled his fingers off 'cause I was angry with him."

"Mmmmm hmmmm. Anything else?"

"I didn't feed Henry this whole week. I was angry with him, too."

"What else?"

"Well," Tippy hesitated in the dark before the deep smell of incense made him secure enough to go on. "I put my thing into Lucille again."

"Once?"

"No."

"How many times?"

"Nine."

"Mmmmm hmmmm. Anything else?"

Another hesitation. Then, "No, Father."

"Well. You know your sins with . . . Lucille . . . are your worst sins. You mustn't think impurely anymore or next you'll go from toy people to real ones. You've never done anything impure with a real woman, have you?"

Yet another hesitation. "No, Father."

"No. No, I'm sure you haven't. How could you? How

could you get close enough, you poor . . ." The old Monsignor caught himself. He made the sign of the cross with a shivering hand. "Three Our Fathers and three Hail Marys for your penance."

Then the priest shut the sliding screen that separated him from his nemesis. After a moment he heard Tippy shuffle out of the confessional. He saw a shadow pass by the little crucifix-shaped hole carved in his door as the derelict moved of toward the altar. He imagined the unshaven wretch huddled in a dark bedroom with a little grouping of clay figures. George. Henry. Lucille. In his mind the figures were small and impossibly misshapen, like the ape on the coffin lid at Roone's. He imagined the poor madman poking a hole in one of the vile things and sliding it up and down on his penis in the shadows. The vision made him gag. He didn't even hear the voice of the old woman who'd taken Tippy's place and who'd already begun to pour her sorrows at him through the screen. He only hoped he could sleep that night.

Tippy lit a candle at the altar rail. He hadn't told the old Monsignor about the girl. His dad had killed four, he said, and he was still forgiven. The girl was Tip's first. And besides, he hadn't done anything impure with the girl. He hadn't. She was long gone when he'd done the impure things. Long gone like his mum. He'd even waited to make sure. He'd given her plenty of time to get gone, and now, if she was good, she was in heaven. The part of her that was left was clay, clay he was using just to keep the other clay that was Lucille together.

He said his Our Fathers and his Hail Marys and then he knelt a while before leaving the church. He couldn't wait 'til next week when he could come back again. The place made him feel so safe.

163

TERROR AT LONDON BRIDGE

(NBC Movie-of-the-Week, 1985)
Starring: David Hasselhoff, Stefanie Kramer &
Randy Mantooth
Directed by E.W. Swackhamer
Story 'A Final Stone' by William F. Nolan

The Turn of the Screw by Henry James is among the half-dozen or so most famous ghost stories in the world. The novel, first published in 1898, has been filmed several times and also adapted for television – notably in 1974 by the next contributor, William F. Nolan (1928-), an American scriptwriter, novelist and short story writer whose contributions to the ghost story on TV tradition makes his appearance in this collection essential. His two-part miniseries version was filmed in London by director Dan Curtis with Lynn Redgrave, Jasper Jacob and Eva Griffith. This was Bill's second ghost story project with Dan Curtis: a year earlier he had written the script for *The Norliss Tapes* about an investigator of the supernatural who looks into the case of a woman whose diabolist husband has risen from the dead as a ravening monster. The drama, with Angie Dickinson, Roy Thinnes and Claude Atkins, was hailed by British TV critic Leslie Halliwell as 'a genuinely frightening horror movie and an example of what can be done on a low budget.' In 1976, Bill adapted Robert Marasco's novel about

164

A Final Stone

an evil house, *Burnt Offerings*, which starred Bette Davis, Karen Black and Oliver Reed and was once again directed by Dan Curtis.

'Terror at London Bridge' which Bill wrote in 1985 was, however, based on a short story of his own, 'A Final Stone'. This brought together two of the English capital's most enduring legends, the famous old Thames bridge and the infamous Victorian serial killer, Jack the Ripper, but in the unexpected location of Arizona, USA. It was one more ingenious storyline from the Californian writer who became famous in the Sixties for his co-writing role in the creation of the book, film and TV series, *Logan's Run* (1967), and is now ranked among the most versatile and prolific contributors to the supernatural and mystery genres in America. The movie was filmed entirely on location at Lake Havasu in Arizona where the the bridge which once crossed the River Thames was transported and reconstructed some years ago. A model of 'London Village' in the shadow of the bridge was also used for the shoot as well as the nearby city. Broadcast by NBC on November 22, 1985, 'Terror at London Bridge' has also been seen in Europe on cinema release, but this marks the first anthology appearance of the unnerving story on which the unique TV show was based . . .

They were from Indianapolis. Newly married. Dave and *stirring, flexing muscle, feeling power now . . . anger . . . a sudden driving thirst for* Alice Williamson, both in their late twenties, both excited about their trip to the West Coast. This would be their last night in Arizona. Tomorrow they planned to be in Palm Springs. To visit Dave's sister. But only one of them would make it to California. Dave, not Alice, *with the scalpel glittering*

Alice would die before midnight, her throat slashed cleanly across, *glittering, raised against the moon*

"Wait till you see what's here," Dave told her. "Gonna just be fantastic."

They were pulling their used Camaro into the parking lot at a tourist site in Lake Havasu City, Arizona. He wouldn't tell her where they were. It was late. The lot was wide and dark, with only two other cars parked there, one a service vehicle.

"What *is* this place?" Alice was tired and hungry. *hungry*

"You'll find out. Once you see it, you'll never forget it. That's what they say."

"I just want to eat," she said. *the blade eating flesh, drinking*

"First we'll have a look at it, then we'll eat," said Dave, *then getting out of the car, walking toward the gate* smiling at her, giving her a hug.

The tall gate, black pebbled iron, led into a picture-perfect Tudor Village. A bit of Olde England rising up from raw Arizona desert. A winged dragon looked down at them from the top of the gate.

"That's ugly," said Alice.

"It's historic," Dave told her. "That's the official Heraldic Dragon from the City of London."

"Is *that* what all this is – some sort of replica of London?"

"Much more than that. Heck, Ally, this was all built *around* it, to give it the proper atmosphere."

"I'm in no mood for atmosphere," she said. "We've been driving all day and I don't feel like playing games. I want to know what you —"

A Final Stone

Dave cut into the flow of her words: "There it is!"

They both stared at it. Ten thousand tons of fitted stone. Over nine hundred feet of arched granite spanning the dark waters of the Colorado River. Tall and massive and magnificent.

"Christ!" murmured Dave. "Doesn't it just knock you out? Imagine – all the way from England, from the Thames River . . . the by-God-for-real London Bridge!"

"It *is* amazing," Alice admitted. She smiled, kissed him on the cheek. "And I'm glad you didn't tell me . . . that you kept it for a surprise."

glittering cold steel

They moved along the concrete walkway beneath the Bridge, staring upward at the giant gray-black structure. Dave said: "When the British tore it down they numbered all the stones so our people would know where each one went. Thousands of stones. Like a jigsaw puzzle. Took three years to build it all over again here in Arizona." He gestured around them. "All this was just open desert when they started. After the Bridge was finished they diverted a section of the Colorado River to run under it. And built the Village."

"Why did the British give us their bridge?"

"They were putting up a better one," said Dave. "But, hey, they didn't *give* this one to us. The guy that had it built here paid nearly two and a half million for it. Plus the cost of shipping all the stones over. Some rich guy named McCulloch. Died since then, I think."

dead death dead dead death

"Well, we've seen it," said Alice. "Let's eat now. C'mon, I'm really starving."

"You don't want to *walk* on it?"

"Maybe after we eat," said Alice, *going inside the restaurant now . . . will wait . . . she's perfect . . . white*

167

throat, blue vein pulsing under the chin . . . long graceful neck . . .

They ate at the City of London Arms in the Village. Late. Last couple in for dinner that evening. Last meal served.

"You folks should have come earlier," the waitress told them. "Lots of excitement here today, putting in the final stone. I mean, with the Bridge dedication and all."

"I thought it was dedicated in 1971," said Dave.

"Oh, it was. But there was this *one* stone missing. Everyone figured it had been lost on the trip over. But they found it last month in London. Had fallen into the water when they were taking the Bridge apart. Today, it got fitted back where it belonged." She smiled brightly. "So London Bridge is *really* complete now!"

Alice set her empty wineglass on the tablecloth. "All this Bridge talk is beginning to *bore* me," she said. "I need another drink."

"You've had enough," said Dave.

"Hell I have!" To the waitress: "Bring us another bottle of wine."

"Sorry, but we're closing. I'm not allowed to —"

"I *said* bring another!"

"And she said they're closing," snapped Dave. "Let's go."

They paid the check, left. The doors were locked behind them.

The City of London Arms sign blinked off as they moved down the restaurant steps. *to me to me*

"You'll feel better when we get back to the motel," Dave said.

"I feel fine. Let's go walk on London Bridge. That's what you wanted, isn't it?"

"Now now, Alley," he said. "We can do that tomorrow, before we leave. Drive over from the motel."

"*You* go to the damn motel," she said tightly. "*I'm* walking on the damn Bridge!"

He stared at her. "You're *drunk!*"

She giggled. "So what? Can't drunk people walk on the damn Bridge?"

"Come on," said Dave, taking her arm. "We're going to the car."

"You go to the car," she snapped, pulling away. "I'm gonna walk on the damn Bridge."

"Fine," said Dave. "Then you can get a *taxi* to the motel."

And, dark-faced with anger, he walked away from her, back to their car. Got in. Drove off.

alone now for me . . . just for me

Alice Williamson walked toward London Bridge through the massed tree shadows along the dark river pathway. She reached the foot of the wide gray-granite Bridge steps, looked up.

At a tall figure in black. Slouch hat, dark cloak, boots.

She was looking at death.

She stumbled back, turned, poised to run – but the figure moved, glided, flowed *mine now mine* down the granite steps with horrific speed.

And the scalpel glitter-danced against the moon.

Two days later.

Evening, with the tour boat empty, heading for its home dock, Angie Shepherd at the wheel. Angie was the boat's owner. She lived beside the river, had all her life. Knew its currents, its moods, under moon and sun, knew it intimately. Thompson Bay . . . Copper Canyon

. . . Cattail Cove . . . Red Rock . . . Black Meadow . . .
Topock Gorge. Knew its eagles and hawks and mallards,
its mud turtles and great horned owls. Knew the sound of
its waters in calm and in storm.

Her home was a tall, weathered-wood building that
once served as a general store. She lived alone here.
Made a living with her boat, running scenic tours along
the Colorado. Age twenty-eight. Never married, and no
plans in that area.

Angie docked the boat, secured it, entered the tall
wooden building she called Riverhouse. She fussed in
the small kitchen, taking some wine, bread, and cheese
out to the dock. It was late; the night was ripe with river
sounds and the heart-pulse of crickets.

She sat at the dock's edge, legs dangling in the cool
water. Nibbled cheese. Listened to a night bird crying
over the river.

Something bumped her foot in the dark water. Something heavy, sodden. Drifting in the slow night current.

Something called Alice Williamson.

Dan Gregory had no clues to the murder. The husband was
a logical suspect (most murders are family-connected),
but Gregory knew that Dave Williamson was not guilty.
You develop an instinct about people, and he knew
Williamson was no wife-killer. For one thing, the man's
grief was deep and genuine; he seemed totally shattered
by the murder – blamed himself, bitterly, for deserting
Alice in the Village.

Gregory was tipped back in his desk chair, an unlit
Marlboro in his mouth. (He was trying to give up
smoking.) Williamson slouched in the office chair in
front of him, looking broken and defeated. "Your wife
was drunk, you had an argument. You got pissed and

170

drove off. Happens to people all the time. Don't blame yourself for this."

"But if I'd stayed there, been there when —"

"Then you'd probably *both* be dead," said Gregory. "You go back to the motel, take those pills the doc gave you and get some sleep. Then head for Palm Springs. We'll contact you at your sister's if we come up with anything."

Williamson left the office. Gregory talked to Angie Shepherd next, about finding the body. She was shaken, but cooperative.

"I've never seen anyone dead before," she told him.

"No family funerals?"

"Sure. A couple. But I'd never walk past the open caskets. I didn't want to have to see people I'd loved . . . *that* way." She shrugged. "In your business I guess you see a lot of death."

"Not actually," said Gregory. "Your average Highway Patrol officer sees more of it in a month than I have in ten years. You don't get many murders in a town this size."

"That how long you've been Chief of Police here, ten years?"

"Nope. Just over a year. Used to be a police lieutenant in Phoenix. Moved up to this job." He raised an eyebrow at her. "How come, you being a local, you don't know how long I've been Chief?"

"I never follow politics – *especially* small-town politics. Sorry about that." And she smiled.

Gregory was a square-faced man in his thirties with hard, iced-blue eyes, offset by a quick, warm way of grinning. Had never married; most women bored him. But he liked Angie. And the attraction was mutual.

Alice Williamson's death had launched a relationship.

*   *   *

In August, four months after the first murder, there were two more. Both women. Both with their throats cut. Both found along the banks of the Colorado. One at Pilot Rock, the other near Whipple Bay.

Dan Gregory had no reason to believe the two August 'River Killings' (as the local paper had dubbed them) had been committed near London Bridge. He told a reporter that the killer might be a transient, passing through the area, killing at random. The murders lacked motive; the three victims had nothing in common beyond being female. Maybe the murderer, suggested Gregory, was just someone who hates women.

The press had a field day. 'Madman on Loose' . . . 'Woman-Hating Killer Haunts Area' . . . 'Chief of Police Admits No Clues to River Killings.'

Reading the stories, Gregory muttered softly: "Assholes!"

Early September. A classroom at Lake Havasu City High School. Senior English. Lyn Esterly was finishing a lecture on William Faulkner's *Light in August*.

". . . therefore, Joe Christmas became the victim of his own twisted personality. He truly believed he was cursed by an outlaw strain of blood, a white man branded black by a racially bigoted society. Your assignment is to write a five-hundred-word essay on his inner conflicts."

After she'd dismissed the class, Lyn phoned her best friend, Angie Shepherd, for lunch. They had met when Lyn had almost drowned swimming near Castle Rock. Angie had saved her life.

"You're not running the boat today, and I need to talk to you, okay?"

"Sure . . . okay," agreed Angie. "Meet you in town. Tom's all right?"

"Tom's it is."

Trader Tom's was a seafood restaurant, specializing in fresh shrimp, an improbable business establishment in the middle of the Arizona desert. Angie, 'the primitive,' adored fresh shrimp, which had been introduced to her by Lyn, the 'city animal,' their joke names for one another.

Over broiled shrimp and sole amandine they relaxed into a familiar discussion: "I'll never be able to understand how you can live out there all alone on the river," said Lyn. "It's positively *eerie* – especially with a killer running loose. Aren't you afraid?"

"No. I keep a gun with me in the house, and I know how to use it."

"*I'd* be terrified."

"That's because you're a victim of your own imagination," said Angie, dipping a huge shrimp into Tom's special Cajun sauce. "You and your fascination with murder."

"Lots of people are true-crime buffs," said Lyn. "In fact, that's why I wanted to talk to you today. It's about the River Killings."

"You've got a theory about 'em, right?"

"This one's pretty wild."

"Aren't they all?" Angie smiled, unpeeling another shrimp. "I'm listening."

"The first murder, the Williamson woman, that one took place on the third of April."

"So?"

"The second murder was on the seventh of August, the third on the thirty-first. All three dates are a perfect match."

"For what?"

"For a series of killings, seven in all, committed in 1888 by Jack the Ripper. His first three were on exact matching dates."

Angie paused, a shrimp halfway to her mouth. "Wow! Okay . . . you *did* say wild."

"And there's more. Alice Williamson, we know, was attacked near London Bridge – which is where the Ripper finally disappeared in 1888. They had him trapped there, but the fog was really thick that night and when they closed in on him from both ends of the Bridge he just . . . vanished. And he was never seen or heard of again."

"Are you telling me that some nut is out there in the dark near London Bridge trying to duplicate the original Ripper murders? Is that your theory?"

"That's it."

"But why *now?* What triggered the pattern?"

"I'm working on that angle." Lyn's eyes were intense. "I'm telling you this today for a vitally important reason."

"I'm still listening."

"You've become very friendly with Chief Gregory. He'll listen to you. He must be told that the fourth murder will take place *tonight*, the eighth of September, before midnight."

"But I . . ."

"You've got to warn him to post extra men near the Bridge tonight. And he should be there himself."

"Because of your theory?"

"Of course! Because of my theory."

Angie slowly shook her head. "Dan would think I was around the bend. He's a realist. He'd laugh at me."

"Isn't it *worth* being laughed at to save a life?" Lyn's eyes burned at her. "Honest, Angie, if you don't convince Gregory that I'm making sense, that I'm onto a real pattern here, then another woman is going to get her throat slashed near London Bridge tonight."

Angie pushed her plate away. "You sure do know how to spoil a terrific lunch."

*   *   *

That afternoon, back at Riverhouse, Angie tried to make sense of Lyn's theory. The fact that these murders had fallen on the same dates as three murders a century earlier was interesting and curious, but not enough to set a hard-minded man like Gregory in motion.

It was crazy, but still Lyn *might* be onto something.

At least she could phone Dan and suggest dinner in the Village. She could tell him what Lyn said – and then he *would* be there in the area, just in case something happened.

Dan said yes, they'd meet at the City of London Arms.

When Angie left for the Village that night she carried a pearl-handled .32-caliber automatic in her purse.

If. Just if.

Dan was late. On the phone he'd mentioned a meeting with the City Council, so maybe that was it. The Village was quiet, nearly empty of tourists.

Angie waited, seated on a park bench near the restaurant, nervous in spite of herself, thinking that *alone, her back to the trees, thick shadow trees, vulnerable* maybe she should wait inside, at the bar.

A tall figure, moving toward her. Behind her.

A thick-fingered hand reaching out for her. She flinched back, eyes wide, fingers closing on the automatic inside her open purse.

"Didn't mean to scare you."

It was Dan. His grin made her relax. "I've . . . been a little nervous today."

"Over what?"

"Something Lyn Esterly told me." She took his arm. "I'll tell you all about it at dinner."

lost her . . . can't with him
And they went inside.

". . . so what do you think?" Angie asked. They were having an after-dinner drink. The booths around them were silent, unoccupied.

"I think your friend's imagination is working over-time."

Angie frowned. "I knew you'd say something like that."

Dan leaned forward, taking her hand. "You don't really believe there's going to be another murder in this area tonight just because *she* says so, do you?"

"No, I guess I don't really believe that."

And she guessed she didn't.

But . . .

There! Walking idly on the Bridge, looking down at the water, alone, young woman alone . . . her throat naked, skin naked and long-necked . . . open to me . . . blade sharp sharp . . . soft throat

A dark pulsing glide onto the Bridge, a swift reaching out, a small choked cry of shocked horror, a sudden drawn-across half-moon of bright crimson – and the body falling . . . falling into deep Colorado waters.

Although Dan Gregory was a skeptic, he was not a fool. He ordered the entire Village area closed to tourists and began a thorough search.

Which proved rewarding.

An object was found on the Bridge, wedged into an aperture between two stones below one of the main arches: a surgeon's scalpel with fresh blood on it. And with blackened stains on the handle and blade.

It was confirmed that the fresh blood matched that of the latest victim. The dark stains proved to be dried blood. But they did not match the blood types of the other three murder victims. It was old blood. Very old.

Lab tests revealed that the bloodstains had remained on the scalpel for approximately one hundred years.

Dating back to the 1880s.

"Are you Angela Shepherd?"

A quiet Sunday morning along the river. Angie was repairing a water-damaged section of dock, briskly hammering in fresh nails, and had not heard the woman walk up behind her. She put down the claw hammer, stood, pushing back her hair. "Yes, I'm Angie Shepherd. Who are you?"

"Lenore Harper. I'm a journalist."

"What paper?"

"Freelance. Could we talk?"

Angie gestured toward the house. Lenore was tall, trim-bodied, with penetrating green eyes.

"Want a Coke?" asked Angie. "Afraid it's all I've got. I wasn't expecting company."

"No, I'm fine," said Lenore, seating herself on the living-room couch and removing a small notepad from her purse.

"You're doing a story on the River Killings, right?"

Lenore nodded. "But I'm going after something different. That's why I came to you."

"Why me?"

"Well . . . you discovered the first body."

Angie sat down in a chair opposite the couch, ran a hand through her hair. "I didn't *discover* anything. When the body drifted downriver against the dock I happened to be there. That's all there is to it."

"Where you shocked . . . frightened?"

"Sickened is a better word. I don't enjoy seeing people with their throats cut."

"Of course. I understand, but . . ."

Angie stood up. "Look, there's really nothing more I can tell you. If you want facts on the case, talk to Chief Gregory at the police department."

"I'm more interested in ideas, emotions – in personal reactions to these killings. I'd like to know *your* ideas. *Your* theories."

"If you want to talk theory, go see Lyn Esterly. She's got some original ideas on the case. Lyn's a true-crime buff. She'll probably be anxious to help you."

"Sounds like a good lead. Where can I find her?"

"Lake Havasu High. She teaches English there."

"Great." Lenore put away her notepad, then shook Angie's hand. "You've been very kind. Appreciate your talking to me."

"No problem."

Angie looked deeply into Lenore Harper's green eyes. Something about her I like, she thought. Maybe I've made a new friend. Well . . . "Good luck with your story," she said.

Lenore's talk with Lyn Esterly bore colorful results. The following day's paper carried 'an exclusive feature interview' by Lenore Harper:

'Is River Killer Another Jack the Ripper?' the headline asked. Then, below it, a subheading: 'Havasu High Teacher Traces Century-Old Murder Pattern.'

According to the story, if the killer continued to follow the original Ripper's pattern, he would strike again on the thirtieth of September. And not once, but twice. On the night of September 30, 1888, Jack the Ripper butchered *two* women in London's Whitechapel district – victims #5 and #6. Would these gruesome double murders be repeated here in Lake Havasu?

The story ended with a large question mark.

Angie, on the phone to Lyn: "Maybe I did the wrong thing, sending her to see you."

"Why? I like her. She really *listened* to me."

"I just get the feeling that her story makes you . . . well, a kind of target."

"I doubt that."

"The killer knows all about you now. Even your picture was there in the paper. He knows that you're doing all this special research, that you worked out the whole copycat-Ripper idea . . ."

"So what? I can't catch him. That's up to the police. He's not going to bother with me. Getting my theory into print was important. Now that his sick little game has been exposed, maybe he'll quit. Might not be fun for him anymore. These weirdos are like that. Angie, it could all be over."

"So you're not sore at me for sending her to you?"

"Are you kidding? For once, someone has taken a theory of mine seriously enough to print it. Makes all this work mean something. Hell, I'm a celebrity now."

"That's what worries me."

And their conversation ended.

Angie had been correct in her hunch regarding Lenore Harper: the two women *did* become friends. As a freelance journalist, Lenore had roved the world, while Angie had spent her entire life in Arizona. Europe seemed, to her, exotic and impossibly far away. She was fascinated with Lenore's tales of global travel and of her childhood and early schooling in London.

On the night of September 30, Lyn Esterly turned down Angie's invitation to spend the evening at Riverhouse.

"I'm into something *new*, something really exciting on this Ripper thing," Lyn told her. "But I need to do more research. If what I think is true, then a lot of people are going to be surprised."

"God," sighed Angie, "how you love being mysterious!"

"Guilty as charged," admitted Lyn. "Anyhow, I'll feel a lot safer working at the library in the middle of town than being out there on that desolate river with you."

"Dan's taking your ideas seriously," Angie told her. "He's still got the Village closed to tourists – and he's bringing in extra men tonight in case you're right about the possibility of a double murder."

"I *want* to be wrong, Angie, honest to God I do. Maybe this creep has been scared off by all the publicity. Maybe tonight will prove that – but to be on the safe side, if I were you, I'd spend the night in town . . . not alone out there in that damn haunted castle of yours!"

"Okay, you've made your point. I'll take in a movie, then meet Dan later. Ought to be safe enough with the Chief of Police, eh?"

"Absolutely. And by tomorrow I may have a big surprise for you. This is like a puzzle that's finally coming together. It's exciting!"

"Call me in the morning?"

"That's a promise."

And they rang off.

Ten P.M. Lyn working alone in the reference room on the

second floor of the city library. The building had been closed to the public for two hours. Even the staff had gone. But, as a teacher, Lyn had special privileges. And her own key.

A heavy night silence. Just the shuffling sound of her books, the faint scratch of her ballpoint pen, her own soft breathing.

When the outside door to the parking lot clicked open on the floor below her, Lyn didn't hear it.

The Ripper glided upward, a dark spider-shape on the stairs, *and she's there waiting to meet me, heart pumping blood for the blade* reached the second floor, moved down the silent hallway to the reference room, *pumping crimson* pushed open the door. *pumping*

To her. Behind her. Soundless.

Lyn's head was jerked violently back.

Death in her eyes – and the blade at her throat.

A single, swift movement. *pumping*

And after this one, another before midnight.

Sherry, twenty-three, a graduate student from Chicago on vacation. Staying with a girlfriend. Out for a six-pack of Heineken, a quart of nonfat, and a Hershey's Big Bar.

She left the 7-Eleven with her bag of groceries, walked to her car parked behind the building. Somebody was in the back seat, but Sherry didn't know that.

She got in, fished for the ignition key in her purse, and heard a sliding, rustling sound behind her. Twisted in sudden, breathless panic.

Ripper.

Angie did not attend Lyn Esterly's funeral. She refused to see Dan or Lenore; canceled her tours, stocked her boat with food, and took it far upriver, living like a wounded animal. She allowed the river itself to soothe and comfort her, not speaking to anyone, drifting into tiny coves and inlets . . .

Until the wounds began to heal. Until she had regained sufficient emotional strength to return to Lake Havasu City.

She phoned Dan: "I'm back."

"I've been trying to trace you. Even ran a copter upriver, but I guess you didn't want to be found."

"I was all right."

"I *know* that, Angie. I wasn't worried about you. Especially after we caught him. That was what I wanted to find you for, to tell you the news. We *got* the bastard!"

"The River Killer?"

"Yeah. Calls himself 'Bloody Jack.' Says that he's the ghost of the Ripper."

"But how did you . . . ?"

"We spotted this guy prowling near the Bridge. 'Bout a week ago. He'd been living in a shack by the river, up near Mesquite Campground. One of my men followed him there. Walked right in and made the arrest."

"And he admitted he was the killer?"

"Bragged about it! Couldn't wait to get his picture in the papers."

"Dan . . . are you *sure* he's the right man?"

"Hell, we've got a ton of evidence. We found several weapons in the shack, including surgical knives. *Three* scalpels. And he had the newspaper stories on each of his murders tacked to the wall. He'd slashed the faces of all the women, their pictures, I mean. Deep knife cuts in each news photo."

"That's . . . *sick*," said Angie.

"And we have a witness who saw him go into that

7-Eleven on the night of the double murder – where the college girl was killed. He's the one, all right. A real psycho."

"Can I see you tonight? I *need* to be with you, Dan."

"I need you just as much. Meet you soon as I've finished here at the office. And, hey . . ."

"Yes?"

"I've *missed* you."

That night they made love in the moonlight, with the silken whisper of the river as erotic accompaniment. Lying naked in bed, side by side, they listened to the night crickets and touched each other gently, as if to make certain all of this was real for both of them.

"Murder is an awful way to meet somebody," said Angie, leaning close to him, her eyes shining in the darkness. "But I'm glad I met you. I never thought I could."

"Could what?"

"Find someone to love. To *really* love."

"Well, you've found me," he said quietly. "And *I've* found you." She giggled. "You're . . ."

"I know." He grinned. "You do that to me."

And they made love again.

And the Colorado rippled its languorous night waters.

And from the dark woods a tall figure watched them.

It wasn't over.

Another month passed.

With the self-confessed killer in jail, the English Village and Bridge site were once again open to tourists.

Angie had not seen Lenore for several weeks and was anxious to tell her about the marriage plans she and Dan had made. She wanted Lenore to be her maid of honor at the wedding.

They met for a celebration dinner at the City of London Arms in the Village. But the mood was all wrong.

Angie noticed that Lenore's responses were brief, muted. She ate slowly, picking at her food.

"You don't seem all that thrilled to see me getting married," said Angie.

"Oh, but I *am*. Truly. And I know I've been a wet blanket. I'm sorry."

"What's wrong?"

"I just . . . don't think it's over."

"What are you talking about?"

"The Ripper thing. The killings."

Angie stared at her. "But they've *got* him. He's in jail right now. Dan is convinced that he . . ."

"He's not the one." Lenore said it flatly, softly. "I just *know* he's not the one."

"You're nuts! All the evidence . . ."

". . . is circumstantial. Oh, I'm sure this kook *thinks* he's the Ripper – but where is the *real* proof: blood samples . . . fingerprints . . . the actual murder weapons?"

"You're paranoid, Lenore! I had some doubts too, in the beginning, but Dan's a good cop. He's done his job. The killer's locked up."

Lenore's green eyes flashed. "Look, I asked you to meet me down here in the Village tonight for a reason – and it had nothing to do with your wedding." She drew in her breath. "I just didn't want to face this alone."

"Face what?"

"The fear. It's November the ninth. *Tonight* is the ninth!"

"So?"

"The date of the Ripper's seventh murder – back in 1888." Her tone was strained. "If that man in jail really *is* the Ripper, then nothing will happen here tonight. But . . . if he *isn't* . . ."

"My God, you're really scared!" And she gripped Lenore's hand, pressing it tightly.

"Damn right I'm scared. One of *us* could become his seventh victim."

"Look," said Angie. "It's like they say to pilots after a crash. You've got to go right back up or you'll never fly again. Well, it's time for you to do some flying tonight."

"I don't understand."

"You can't let yourself get spooked by what isn't real. And this fear of yours just isn't *real*, Lenore. There's no killer in the Village tonight. And, to prove it, I'm going to walk you to that damn Bridge."

Lenore grew visibly pale. "No . . . no, that's . . . No, I won't go."

"Yes, you will." Angie nodded. She motioned for the check.

Lenore stared at her numbly.

Outside, in the late night darkness, the Village was once more empty of tourists. The last of them had gone – and the wide parking lot was quiet and deserted beyond the gate.

"We're insane to be doing this," Lenore said. Her mouth was tightly set. "Why should *I* do this?"

"To prove that irrational fear must be faced and overcome. You're my friend now – my best friend – and I won't let you give in to irrationality."

"Okay, okay . . . if I agree to walk to the Bridge, then can we get the hell out of here?"

"Agreed."

And they began to walk.

moving toward the Bridge . . . mine now, mine

"I've been poking through Lyn's research papers," Lenore said, "and I think I know what her big surprise would have been."

"Tell me."

"Most scholars now agree on the true identity of the Ripper."

"Yes. A London doctor, a surgeon. Jonathan Bascum."

"Well, Lyn Esterly didn't believe he was the Ripper. And after what I've seen of her research, neither do I."

"Then who *was* he?" asked Angie.

"Jonathan had a twin sister, Jessica. She helped the poor in that area. They practically sainted her – called her 'the Angel of Whitechapel.'"

"I've heard of her."

"Did you know she was as medically skilled as her brother? . . . That Jonathan allowed her to use his medical books? Taught her. Jessica turned out to be a better surgeon than he was. And she *used* her medical knowledge in Whitechapel."

The stimulation of what she was revealing to Angie seemed to quell much of the fear in Lenore. Her voice was animated.

keep moving . . . closer

"No *licensed* doctors would practice among the poor in that area. No money to be made. So she doctored these people. All illegal, of course. And, at first, it seemed she *was* a kind of saint, working among the destitute. Until her compulsion asserted itself."

"Compulsion?"

"To kill. Between April third and November ninth, 1888, she butchered seven women – and yet, to this day, historians claim her *brother* was responsible for the murders."

Angie was amazed. "Are you telling me that the Angel of Whitechapel was really Jack the Ripper?"

"That was Lyn's conclusion," said Lenore. "And, when you think of it, why not? It explains how the Ripper always seemed to *vanish* after a kill. Why was it that no one ever *saw* him leave Whitechapel? Because 'he' was Jessica Bascum. She could move freely through the area without arousing suspicion. No one ever saw the Ripper's face . . . no one who *lived*, that is. To throw off the police, she sent notes to them signed 'Jack.' It was a *woman* they chased onto the Bridge that night in 1888."

Lenore seemed unaware that they were approaching the Bridge now. It loomed ahead of them, a dark, stretched mass of waiting stone.

closer

"Lyn had been tracing the Bascum family history," explained Lenore. "Jessica gave birth to a daughter in 1888, the same year she vanished on the Bridge. The line continued through her granddaughter, born in 1915, and her great-granddaughter, born in 1940. The last Bascum daughter was born in 1960."

"Which means she'd be in her mid-twenties today," said Angie.

"That's right." Lenore nodded. "Like you. *You're* in your mid-twenties, Angie."

Angie's eyes flashed. She stopped walking. The line of her jaw tightened.

Bitch!

"Suppose she was drawn here," said Lenore, "to London Bridge. Where her great-great-grandmother vanished a century ago. And suppose that, with the completion of the Bridge, with the placement of that final missing stone in April, Jessica's spirit entered her great-great-granddaughter. Suppose the six killings in the Lake

187

Havasu area were done by *her* – that it was her cosmic destiny to commit them."

"Are you saying that you think *I* am a Bascum?" Angie asked softly. They continued to walk toward the Bridge.

"I don't *think* anything. I have the facts."

"And just what might those be?" Angie's voice was tense.

"Lyn was very close to solving the Ripper case. When she researched the Bascum family history in England she traced some of the descendants here to America. She *knew*."

"Knew what, Lenore?" Her eyes glittered. "You *do* believe that I'm a Bascum." Harshly: *"Don't you?"*

"No." Lenore shook her head. "I know you're not." She looked intently at Angie. "Because *I* am."

They had reached the steps leading up to the main part of the Bridge. In numb horror, Angie watched Lenore slide back a panel in one of the large granite blocks and remove the Ripper's hat, greatcoat, and cape. And the medical bag.

"This came down to me from the family. It was *her* surgical bag – the same one she used in Whitechapel. I'd put it away – until April, when they placed the final stone." Her eyes sparked. "When I touched the stone I felt *her* . . . Jessica's soul flowed into *me*, became part of me. And I knew what I had to do."

She removed a glittering scalpel, held it up. The blade flashed in the reflected light of the lamps on the Bridge. Lenore's smile was satanic. "This is for you!"

Angie's heart trip-hammered; she was staring, trance-like, into the eyes of the killer. Suddenly she pivoted, began running.

Down the lonely, shadow-haunted, brick-and-cobblestone streets, under the tall antique lamps, past the clustered Tudor buildings of Old London.

And the Ripper followed. Relentlessly. Confident of a seventh kill.

she'll taste the blade

Angie circled the main square, ran between buildings to find a narrow, dimly lit alleyway that led her to the rear section of the City of London Arms. Phone inside. Call Dan!

Picking up a rock from the alley, she smashed a rear window, climbed inside, began running through the dark interior, searching for a phone. One here somewhere . . . somewhere . . .

The Ripper followed her inside.

Phone! Angie fumbled in her purse, finding change for the call. She also found . . .

The pearl-handled .32 automatic – the weapon she'd been carrying for months, totally forgotten in her panic.

Now she could fight back. She knew how to use a gun.

She inserted the coins, got Dan's number at headquarters. Ringing . . . ringing . . . "Lake Havasu City Police Department."

"Dan . . . Chief Gregory . . . Emergency!"

"I'll get him on the line."

"Hurry!"

A pause. Angie's heart, hammering.

"This is Gregory. Who's . . .?"

"Dan!" she broke in. "It's Angie. The Ripper's *here*, trying to kill me!"

"Where are you?"

A dry buzzing. The line was dead.

A clean, down-slicing move with the scalpel had severed the phone cord.

die now . . . time to die
Angie turned to face the killer.
And triggered the automatic.

At close range, a .32-caliber bullet smashed into Lenore Bascum's flesh. She staggered back, falling to one knee on the polished wood floor of the restaurant, blood flowing from the wound.

Angie ran back to the smashed window, crawled through it, moved quickly down the alley. A rise of ground led up to the parking lot. Her car was there.

She reached it, sobbing to herself, inserted the key.

A shadow flowed across the shining car body. Two blood-spattered hands closed around Angie's throat.

The Ripper's eyes were coals of green fire, burning into Angie. She tore at the clawed fingers, pounded her right fist into the demented face. But the hands tightened. Darkness swept through Angie's brain; she was blacking out.

die, bitch!
She was dying.
Did she hear a siren? Was it real, or in her mind?
A second siren joined the first. Filling the night darkness.

bleeding . . . my blood . . . wrong, all wrong . . .

A dozen police cars roared into the lot, tires sliding on the nightdamp tarmac.

Dan!

The Ripper's hands dropped away from Angie's throat. The tall figure turned, ran for the Bridge.

And was trapped there.

Police were closing in from both sides of the vast structure.

Angie and Dan were at the Bridge. "How did you know where to find me?"

A Final Stone

"Silent alarm. Feeds right into headquarters. When you broke the window, the alarm was set off. I figured that's where you were."

"She's hit," Angie told him. "I shot her. She's dying."

In the middle of the span the Ripper fell to one knee. Then, a mortally wounded animal, she slipped over the side and plunged into the dark river beneath the Bridge.

Lights blazed on the water, picking out her body. She was sinking, unable to stay afloat. Blood gouted from her open mouth. "Damn you!" she screamed. "Damn all of you!"

She was gone.

The waters rippled over her grave.

Angie was convulsively gripping the automatic, the pearl handle cold against her fingers.

Cold.

GHOSTS

(BBC, 1995–)
Directed by Monique Charlesworth
Starring: Douglas Henshall, Dan Mullane &
Jacqueline Leonard
Story: 'Three Miles Up' by Elizabeth Jane Howard

Ghosts, **which the BBC brought to the small screen in February 1995, is the latest genre series, and its adaptation of several highly-regarded short stories of the supernatural has brought the programme popularity with viewers, critical acclaim from the press and the strong likelihood that it will continue in the future. Noteworthy among the tales which** *Ghosts* **presented were 'The Shadowy Third' based on Ellen Glasgow's much anthologized story of a bedridden wife (played by Cheryl Campbell) who believes her husband (Tim Piggot-Smith) is scheming to get control of her money; Stephen Volk's 'The Double' about a murderer (Derrick O'Connor) serving a life sentence in prison who suspects his wife (Anita Dobson) of having an affair and uses the supernatural to find out; and 'Three Miles Up' by Elizabeth Jane Howard. This story of two brothers on holiday sailing a narrow boat along the lonely and ominous-looking Fens of Norfolk who pick up a mysterious young women from the bank and soon find themselves in a nightmare situation was moodily filmed on location in East Anglia and** captured all the eerie and unsettling qualities of the original story. The result was a 'subtle and genuinely spine-tingling hour of television,' according to the reviewer in *The Times*.

Elizabeth Jane Howard (1923-) is one of Britain's finest contemporary novelists and her recently completed tetralogy, *The Cazalet Chronicles*, which ended with *Casting Off* (1995), has been described by the *Daily Telegraph* as 'a dazzling saga of peace and war.' Although Elizabeth has not written a great many short stories during her career, 'Three Miles Up' reveals her interest in the supernatural and for its theme draws on the time she spent in the late forties as the secretary of the Inland Waterways Association in London. After this she was for a time an editor in two London publishing houses before becoming a book reviewer and then full-time writer. A collection of ghost stories, *We Are For The Dark*, published in 1951, first brought her to public notice, but it was novels like *The Sea Change* (1959), *Odd Girl Out* (1972) and the recent series about the lives of the prosperous Cazalet family between 1937 to 1947 – which took her seven years to write – that have established her position of pre-eminence among contemporary English writers. 'Three Miles Up' not only made outstanding viewing on the BBC's *Ghosts*, but is equally gripping on the printed page . . .

There was absolutely nothing like it.

An unoriginal conclusion, and one that he had drawn a hundred times during the last fortnight. Clifford would make some subtle and intelligent comparison, but he, John, could only continue to repeat that it was quite unlike anything else. It had been Clifford's idea, which, considering Clifford, was surprising. When you looked at him, you would not suppose him capable of it. However, John reflected, he had been ill, some sort of breakdown these clever people went in for, and that might account for his uncharacteristic idea of hiring a boat and travelling on canals. On the whole, John had to admit, it was a good idea. He had never been on a canal in his life, although he had been in almost every kind of boat, and thought he knew a good deal about them; so much indeed, that he had embarked on the venture in a light-hearted, almost a patronizing manner. But it was not nearly as simple as he had imagined. Clifford, of course, knew nothing about boats; but he had admitted that almost everything had gone wrong with a kind of devilish versatility which had almost frightened him. However, that was all over, and John, who had learned painfully all about the boat and her engine, felt that the former at least had run her gamut of disaster. They had run out of food, out of petrol, and out of water; had dropped their windlass into the deepest lock, and, more humiliating, their boathook into a side-pond. The head had come off the hammer. They had been disturbed for one whole night by a curious rustling in the cabin, like a rat in a paper bag, when there was no paper, and, so far as they knew, no rat. The battery had failed and had had to be re-charged. Clifford had put his elbow through an already cracked window in the cabin. A large piece of rope had wound itself round the propeller with a malignant intensity which required three men and half a morning to unravel. And so on, until now there was really nothing left to go wrong, unless one of them drowned, and surely it was impossible to drown in a canal.

"I suppose one might easily drown in a lock?" he asked aloud.

"We must be careful not to fall into one," Clifford replied.

"What?" John steered with fierce concentration, and never heard anything people said to him for the first time, almost on principle.

"I said we must be carful not to fall *into* a lock."

"Oh. Well there aren't any more now until after the Junction. Anyway, we haven't yet, so there's really no reason why we should start now. I only wanted to know whether we'd drown if we did."

"Sharon might."

"What?"

"Sharon might."

"Better warn her then. She seems agile enough." His concentrated frown returned, and he settled down again to the wheel. John didn't mind where they went, or what happened, so long as he handled the boat, and all things considered, he handled her remarkably well. Clifford planned and John steered: and until two days ago they had both quarrelled and argued over a smoking and unusually temperamental primus. Which reminded Clifford of Sharon. Her advent and the weather were really their two unadulterated strokes of good fortune. There had been no rain, and Sharon had, as it were, dropped from the blue on to the boat, where she speedily restored domestic order, stimulated evening conversation, and touched the whole venture with her attractive being: the requisite number of miles each day were achieved, the boat behaved herself, and admirable meals were steadily and regularly prepared. She had, in fact, identified herself with the journey, without making the slightest effort to control it: a talent which many women were supposed in theory to possess, when, in fact, Clifford reflected gloomily, most of them were bored with the whole thing, or tried to dominate it.

Her advent was a remarkable, almost a miraculous piece of luck. He had, after a particularly ill-fed day, and their failure to dine at a small hotel, desperately telephoned all the women he knew who seemed in the least suitable (and they were surprisingly few), with no success. They had spent a miserable evening, John determined to argue about everything, and he, Clifford, refusing to speak; until, both in a fine state of emotional tension, they had turned in for the night. While John snored, Clifford had lain distraught, his resentment and despair circling round John and then touching his own smallest and most random thoughts; until his mind found no refuge and he was left, divided from it, hostile and afraid, watching it in terror racing on in the dark like some malignant machine utterly out of his control.

The next day things had proved no better between them, and they had continued throughout the morning in a silence which was only occasionally and elaborately broken. They had tied up for lunch beside a wood, which hung heavy and magnificent over the canal. There was a small clearing beside which John then proposed to moor, but Clifford failed to achieve the considerable leap necessary to stop the boat; and they had drifted helplessly past it. John flung him a line, but it was not until the boat was secured, and they were safely in the cabin, that the storm had broken. John, in attempting to light the primus, spilt a quantity of paraffin on Clifford's bunk. Instantly all his despair of the previous evening had contracted. He hated John so much that he could have murdered him. They both lost their tempers, and for the ensuing hour and a half had conducted a blazing quarrel, which, even at the time, secretly horrified them both in its intensity.

It had finally ended with John striding out of the cabin,

there being no more to say. He had returned almost at once, however.

"I say, Clifford. Come and look at this."

"At what?"

"Outside, on the bank."

For some unknown reason Clifford did get up and did look. Lying face downwards quite still on the ground, with her arms clasping the trunk of a large tree, was a girl.

"How long has she been there?"

"She's asleep."

"She can't have been asleep all the time. She must have heard some of what we said."

"Anyway, who is she? What is she doing here?"

Clifford looked at her again. She was wearing a dark twill shirt and dark trousers, and her hair hung over her face, so that it was almost invisible. "I don't know. I suppose she's alive?"

John jumped cautiously ashore. "Yes, she's alive all right. Funny way to lie."

"Well, it's none of our business anyway. Anyone can lie on a bank if they want to."

"Yes, but she must have come in the middle of our row, and it does seem queer to stay, and then go to sleep."

"Extraordinary," said Clifford wearily. Nothing was really extraordinary, he felt, nothing. "Are we moving on?"

"Let's eat first. I'll do it."

"Oh, I'll do it."

The girl stirred, unclasped her arms, and sat up. They had all stared at each other for a moment, the girl slowly pushing the hair from her forehead. Then she had said: "If you will give me a meal, I'll cook it."

Afterwards they had left her to wash up, and walked about the wood, while Clifford suggested to John that

197

they ask the girl to join them. "I'm sure she'd come," he said. "She didn't seem at all clear about what she was doing."

"We can't just pick somebody up out of a wood," said John, scandalized.

"Where do you suggest we pick them up? If we don't have someone, this holiday will be a failure."

"We don't know anything about her."

"I can't see that that matters very much. She seems to cook well. We can at least ask her."

"All right. Ask her then. She won't come."

When they returned to the boat, she had finished the washing up, and was sitting on the floor of the cockpit, with her arms stretched behind her head. Clifford asked her; and she accepted as though she had known them a long time and they were simply inviting her to tea.

"Well, but look here," said John, thoroughly taken aback. "What about your things?"

"My things?" she looked enquiringly and a little defensively from one to the other.

"Clothes and so on. Or haven't you got any? Are you a gipsy or something? Where do you come from?"

"I am not a gipsy," she began patiently; when Clifford, thoroughly embarrassed and ashamed, interrupted her.

"Really, it's none of our business who you are, and there is absolutely no need for us to ask you anything. I'm very glad you will come with us, although I feel we should warn you that we are new to this life, and anything might happen."

"No need to warn me," she said and smiled gratefully at him.

After that, they both felt bound to ask her nothing; John because he was afraid of being made to look foolish by Clifford, and Clifford because he had stopped John.

"Good Lord, we shall never get rid of her; and she'll fuss about condensation," John had muttered aggressively as he started the engine. But she was very young, and did not fuss about anything. She had told them her name, and settled down, immediately and easily: gentle, assured and unselfconscious to a degree remarkable in one so young. They were never sure how much she had overheard them, for she gave no sign of having heard anything. A friendly but uncommunicative creature.

The map on the engine box started to flap, and immediately John asked, "Where are we?"

"I haven't been watching, I'm afraid. Wait a minute."

"We just passed under a railway bridge," John said helpfully.

"Right. Yes. About four miles from the Junction, I think. What is the time?"

"Five-thirty."

"Which way are we going when we get to the Junction?"

"We haven't time for the big loop. I must be back in London by the 15th."

"The alternative is to go up as far as the basin, and then simply turn round and come back, and who wants to do that?"

"Well, we'll know the route then. It'll be much easier coming back."

Clifford did not reply. He was not attracted by the route being easier, and he wanted to complete his original plan.

"Let us wait till we get there." Sharon appeared with tea and marmalade sandwiches.

"All right, let's wait." Clifford was relieved.

"It will be almost dark by six-thirty. I think we ought to have a plan," John said. "Thank you, Sharon."

"Have tea first." She curled herself on to the floor with her back to the cabin doors and a mug in her hands.

They were passing rows of little houses with gardens that backed on to the canal. They were long narrow strips, streaked with cinder paths, and crowded with vegetables and chicken huts, fruit trees and perambulators; sometimes ending with fat white ducks, and sometimes in a tiny patch of grass with a bench on it.

"Would you rather keep ducks or sit on a bench?" asked Clifford.

"Keep ducks," said John promptly. "More useful. Sharon wouldn't mind which she did. Would you, Sharon?" He liked saying her name, Clifford noticed. "You could be happy anywhere, couldn't you?" He seemed to be presenting her with the widest possible choice.

"I might *be* anywhere," she answered after a moment's thought.

"Well you happen to be on a canal, and very nice for us."

"In a wood, and then on a canal," she replied contentedly, bending her smooth dark head over her mug.

"Going to be fine tomorrow," said John. He was always a little embarrassed at any mention of how they found her and his subsequent rudeness.

"Yes. I like it when the whole sky is so red and burning and it begins to be cold."

"*Are* you cold?" said John, wanting to worry about it: but she tucked her dark shirt into her trousers and answered composedly:

"Oh no. I am never cold."

They drank their tea in a comfortable silence. Clifford started to read his map, and then said they were almost on to another sheet. "New country," he said with satisfaction. "I've never been here before."

"You make it sound like an exploration; doesn't he, Sharon?" said John.

"Is that a bad thing?" She collected the mugs. "I am going to put these away. You will call me if I am wanted for anything." And she went into the cabin again.

There was a second's pause, a minute tribute to her departure; and, lighting cigarettes, they settled down to stare at the long stretch of water ahead.

John thought about Sharon. He thought rather desperately that really they still knew nothing about her, and that when they went back to London, they would in all probability, never see her again. Perhaps Clifford would fall in love with her, and she would naturally reciprocate, because she was so young and Clifford was reputed to be so fascinating and intelligent, and because women were always foolish and loved the wrong man. He thought all these things with equal intensity, glanced cautiously at Clifford, and supposed he was thinking about her; then wondered what she would be like in London, clad in anything else but her dark trousers and shirt. The engine coughed; and he turned to it in relief.

Clifford was making frantic calculations of time and distance; stretching their time, and diminishing the distance, and groaning that with the utmost optimism they could not be made to fit. He was interrupted by John swearing at the engine, and then for no particular reason he remembered Sharon, and reflected with pleasure how easily she left the mind when she was not present, how she neither obsessed nor possessed one in her absence, but was charming to see.

The sun had almost set when they reached the Junction, and John slowed down to neutral while they made up their minds. To the left was the straight cut which involved the longer journey originally planned; and curving away to the right was the short arm which John advocated. The canal was fringed with rushes, and there was one small cottage with no light in it. Clifford went into the cabin to tell Sharon where they were, and then, as they drifted slowly in the middle of the Junction, John suddenly shouted: "Clifford! What's the third turning?"

"There are only two." Clifford reappeared. "Sharon is busy with dinner."

"No, look. Surely that is another cut."

Clifford stared ahead. "Can't see it."

"Just to the right of the cottage. Look. It's not so dark as all that."

Then Clifford saw it very plainly. It seemed to wind away from the cottage on a fairly steep curve, and the rushes shrouding it from anything but the closest view were taller than the rest.

"Have another look at the map. I'll reverse for a bit."

"Found it. It's just another arm. Probably been abandoned," said Clifford eventually.

The boat had swung round; and now they could see the continuance of the curve dully gleaming ahead, and banked by reeds.

"Well, what shall we do?"

"Getting dark. Let's go up a little way, and moor. Nice quiet mooring."

"With some nice quiet mudbanks," said John grimly. "Nobody uses that."

"How do you know?"

"Well, look at it. All those rushes, and it's sure to be thick with weed."

"Don't go up it then. But we shall go around if we drift about like this."

"*I* don't mind going up it," said John doggedly. "What about Sharon?"

"What about her?"

"Tell her about it."

"We've found a third turning," Clifford called above the noise of the primus through the cabin door.

"One you had not expected?"

"Yes. It looks very wild. We were thinking of going up it."

"Didn't you say you wanted to explore?" she smiled at him.

"You are quite ready to try it? I warn you we shall probably run hard aground. Look out for bumps with the primus."

"I am quite ready, and I am quite sure we shan't run aground," she answered with charming confidence in their skill.

They moved slowly forward in the dusk. Why they did not run aground, Clifford could not imagine: John really was damned good at it. The canal wound and wound, and the reeds grew not only thick on each bank, but in clumps across the canal. the light drained out of the sky into the water and slowly drowned there; the trees and the banks became heavy and black.

Clifford began to clear things away from the heavy dew which had begun to rise. After two journeys he remained in the cabin, while John crawled on, alone. Once, on a bend, John thought he saw a range of hills ahead with lights on them, but when he was round the curve, and had time to look again he could see no hills: only a dark indeterminate waste of country stretched ahead.

He was beginning to consider the necessity of mooring, when they came to a bridge; and shortly after, he saw a dark mass which he took to be houses. When the boat had crawled for another fifty yards or so, he stopped the engine, and drifted in absolute silence to the bank. The houses, about half a dozen of them, were much nearer than he had at first imagined, but there were no lights to be seen. Distance is always deceptive in the dark, he thought, and jumped ashore with a bow line. When, a few minutes later, he took a sounding with the boathook, the water proved unexpectedly deep; and he concluded that they had by incredible good fortune moored at the village wharf. He made everything fast, and joined the others in the cabin with mixed feelings of pride and resentment; that he should have achieved so much under such difficult conditions, and that they (by 'they' he meant Clifford), should have contributed so little towards the achievement. He found Clifford reading Bradshaw's *Guide to the Canals and Navigable Rivers* in one corner, and Sharon, with her hair pushed back behind her ears, bending over the primus with a knife. Her ears are pale, exactly the colour of her face, he thought; wanted to touch them; then felt horribly ashamed, and hated Clifford.

"Let's have a look at Bradshaw," he said, as though he had not noticed Clifford reading it.

But Clifford handed him the book in the most friendly manner, remarking that he couldn't see where they were. "In fact you have surpassed yourself with your brilliant navigation. We seem to be miles from anywhere."

"What about your famous ordnance?"

"It's not on any sheet I have. The new one I thought we should use only covers the loop we planned. There is precisely three quarters of a mile of this canal shown on the present sheet and then we run off the map. I suppose there must once have been trade here, but I cannot imagine what, or where."

"I expect things change," said Sharon. "Here is the meal."

"How can you see to cook?" asked John, eyeing his plate ravenously.

"There is a candle."

"Yes, but we've selfishly appropriated that."

"Should I need more light?" she asked, and looked troubled.

"There's no should about it. I just don't know how you do it, that's all. Chips exactly the right colour, and you never drop anything. It's marvellous."

She smiled a little uncertainly at him and lit another candle. "Luck, probably," she said, and set it on the table.

They ate their meal, and John told them about the mooring. "Some sort of village. I think we're moored at the wharf. I couldn't find any rings without the torch, so I've used the anchor." This small shaft was intended for Clifford, who had dropped the spare torch-battery in the washing-up bowl, and forgotten to buy another. But it was only a small shaft, and immediately afterwards John felt much better. His aggression slowly left him, and he felt nothing but a peaceful and well-fed affection for the other two.

"Extraordinary cut off this is," he remarked over coffee.

"It is very pleasant in here. Warm, and extremely full of us."

"Yes. I know. A quiet village, though, you must admit."

"I shall believe in your village when I see it."

"Then you would believe it?"

"No he wouldn't, Sharon. Not if he didn't want to, and couldn't find it on the map. That map!"

The conversation turned again to their remoteness, and to how cut off one liked to be and at what point it ceased to be desirable; to boats, telephones, and, finally, canals: which, Clifford maintained, possessed the perfect proportions of urbanity and solitude.

Hours later, when they had turned in for the night, Clifford reviewed the conversation, together with others they had had, and remembered with surprise how little Sharon had actually said. She listened to everything and occasionally, when they appealed to her, made some small composed remark which was oddly at variance with their passionate interest. She has an elusive quality of freshness about her, he thought, which is neither naïve nor stupid nor dull, and she invokes no responsibility. She does not want us to know what she was, or why we found her as we did, and curiously, I, at least, do not want to know. She is what women ought to be, he concluded with sudden pleasure; and slept.

He woke the next morning to find it very late, and stretched out his hand to wake John.

"We've all overslept. Look at the time."

"Good Lord! Better wake Sharon."

Sharon lay between them on the floor, which they had ceded her because, oddly enough, it was the widest and most comfortable bed. She seemed profoundly asleep, but at the mention of her name sat up immediately, and rose, almost as though she had not been asleep at all.

The morning routine which, involving the clothing of three people and shaving of two of them, was necessarily a long and complicated business, began. Sharon boiled water, and Clifford, grumbling gently, hoisted himself out of his bunk and repaired with a steaming jug to the cockpit. He put the jug on a seat, lifted the canvas awning, and leaned out. It was absolutely grey and still; a little white mist hung over the canal, and the country stretched out desolate and unkempt on every side with no sign of a living creature. The village, he thought suddenly: John's village: and was possessed of a perilous uncertainty and fear. I am getting worse, he thought, this holiday is doing me no good. I am mad. I imagined that he said we moored by a village wharf. For several seconds he stood gripping the gunwale, and searching desperately for anything, huts, a clump of trees, which could in the darkness have been mistaken for a village. But there was nothing near the boat except tall rank rushes which did not move at all. Then, when his suspense was becoming unbearable, John joined him with another steaming jug of water.

"We shan't get anywhere at this rate," he began; and then . . . "Hullo! Where's my village?"

"I was wondering that," said Clifford. He could almost have wept with relief, and quickly began to shave, deeply ashamed of his private panic.

"Can't understand it," John was saying. It was no joke, Clifford decided, as he listened to his hearty puzzled ruminations.

At breakfast John continued to speculate upon what he had or had not seen, and Sharon listened intently while she filled the coffee pot and cut bread. Once or twice she met Clifford's eye with a glance of discreet amusement.

"I must be mad, or else the whole place is haunted," finished John comfortably. These two possibilities seemed to relieve him of any further anxiety in the matter, as he ate a huge breakfast and set about greasing the engine.

"Well," said Clifford, when he was alone with Sharon. "What do you make of that?"

"It is easy to be deceived in such matters," she answered perfunctorily.

"Evidently. Still, John is an unlikely candidate you must admit. Here, I'll help you dry."

"Oh no. It is what I am here for."

"Not entirely, I hope."

"Not entirely." She smiled and relinquished the cloth.

John eventually announced that they were ready to start. Clifford, who had assumed that they were to recover their journey, was surprised, and a little alarmed, to find John intent upon continuing it. He seemed undeterred by the state of the canal, which, as Clifford immediately pointed out, rendered navigation both arduous and unrewarding. He announced that the harder it was, the more he liked it, adding very firmly that "anyway we must see what happens."

"We shan't have time to do anything else."

"Thought you wanted to explore."

"I do, but . . . what do you think, Sharon?"

"I think John will have to be a very good navigator to manage that." She indicated the rush and weed-ridden reach before them. "Do you think it's possible?"

"Of course it's possible. I'll probably need some help though."

"I'll help you," she said.

So on they went.

They made incredibly slow progress. John enjoys showing off his powers to her, thought Clifford, half amused, half exasperated, as he struggled for the fourth time in an hour to scrape weeds off the propeller.

Sharon eventually retired to cook lunch.

"Surprising amount of water here," John said suddenly.

"Oh?"

"Well, I mean, with all this weed and stuff, you'd expect the canal to have silted up. I'm sure nobody uses it."

"The whole thing is extraordinary."

"Is it too late in the year for birds?" asked Clifford later.

"No, I don't think so. Why?"

"I haven't heard one, have you?"

"Haven't noticed, I'm afraid. There's someone anyway. First sign of life."

An old man stood near the bank watching them. He was dressed in corduroy and wore a straw hat.

"Good morning," shouted John, as they drew nearer.

He made no reply, but inclined his head slightly. He seemed very old. He was leaning on a scythe, and as they drew almost level with him, he turned away and began slowly cutting rushes. A pile of them lay neatly stacked beside him.

"Where does this canal go? Is there a village further on?" Clifford and John asked simultaneously. He seemed not to hear, and as they chugged steadily past, Clifford was about to suggest that they stop and ask again, when he called after them: "Three miles up you'll find the village. Three miles up that is," and turned away to his rushes again.

"Well, now we know something, anyway," said John.

"We don't even know what the village is called."

"Soon find out. Only three miles."

"Three miles!" said Clifford darkly. "That might mean anything."

"Do you want to turn back?"

"Oh no, not now. I want to see this village now. My curiosity is thoroughly aroused."

"Shouldn't think there'll be anything to see. Never been in such a wild spot. Look at it."

Clifford looked at it. Half wilderness, half marsh, dank and grey and still, with single trees bare of their leaves;

clumps of hawthorn that might once have been hedge, sparse and sharp with berries; and, in the distance, hills and an occasional wood: these were all one could see, beyond the lines of rushes which edged the canal winding ahead.

They stopped for a lengthy meal, which Sharon described as lunch and tea together, it being so late; and then, appalled at how little daylight was left, continued.

"We've hardly been any distance at all," said John forlornly. "Good thing there were no locks. I shouldn't think they'd have worked if there were."

"*Much* more than three miles," he said, about two hours later. Darkness was descending and it was becoming very cold.

"Better stop," said Clifford.

"Not yet. I'm determined to reach that village."

"Dinner is ready," said Sharon sadly. "It will be cold."

"Let's stop."

"You have your meal. I'll call if I want you."

Sharon looked at them, and Clifford shrugged his shoulders. "Come on. I will. I'm tired of this."

They shut the cabin doors. John could hear the pleasant clatter of their meal, and just as he was coming to the end of the decent interval which he felt must elapse before he gave in, they passed under a bridge, the first of the day, and, clutching at any straw, he immediately assumed that it prefaced the village. "I think we're nearly there," he called.

Clifford opened the door. "The village?"

"No, a bridge. Can't be far now."

"You're mad, John. It's pitch dark."

"You can see the bridge though."

"Yes. Why not moor under it?"

"Too late. Can't turn round in this light, and she's not good at reversing. Must be nearly there. You go back, I don't need you."

Clifford shut the door again. He was beginning to feel irritated with John behaving in this childish manner and showing off to impress Sharon. It was amusing in the morning, but really he was carrying it a bit far. Let him manage the thing himself then. When, a few minutes later, John shouted that they had reached the sought after village, Clifford merely pulled back the little curtain over a cabin window, rubbed the condensation, and remarked that he could see nothing. "No light at least."

"He is happy anyhow," said Sharon peaceably.

"Going to have a look round," said John, slamming the cabin doors and blowing his nose.

"Surely you'll eat first?"

"If you've left anything. My God it's cold! It's *unnaturally* cold."

"We won't be held responsible if he dies of exposure will we?" said Clifford.

She looked at him, hesitated a moment, but did not reply, and placed a steaming plate in front of John. She doesn't want us to quarrel, Clifford thought, and with an effort of friendliness he asked: "What does tonight's village look like?"

"Much the same. Only one or two houses you know. But the old man called it a village." He seemed uncommunicative; Clifford thought he was sulking. But after eating the meal, he suddenly announced, almost apologetically, "I don't think I shall walk round. I'm absolutely worn out. You go if you like. I shall start turning in."

"All right. I'll have a look. You've had a hard day."

Clifford pulled on a coat and went outside. It was, as John said, incredibly cold and almost overwhelmingly silent. The clouds hung very low over the boat, and mist was rising everywhere from the ground, but he could dimly discern the black huddle of cottages lying on a little slope above the bank against which the boat was moored. He did actually set foot on shore, but his shoe sank immediately into a marshy hole. He withdrew it, and changed his mind. The prospect of groping round those dark and silent houses became suddenly distasteful, and he joined the others with the excuse that it was too cold and that he also was tired.

A little later, he lay half conscious in a kind of restless trance, with John sleeping heavily opposite him. His mind seemed full of foreboding, fear of something unknown and intangible: he thought of them lying in warmth on the cold secret canal with desolate miles of water behind and probably beyond; the old man and the silent houses; John, cut off and asleep, and Sharon, who lay on the floor beside him. Immediately he was filled with a sudden and most violent desire for her, even to touch her, for her to know that he was awake.

"Sharon," he whispered; "Sharon, Sharon," and stretched down his fingers to her in the dark.

Instantly her hand was in his, each smooth and separate finger warmly clasped. She did not move or speak, but his relief was indescribable and for a long while he lay in an ecstasy of delight and peace, until his mind slipped imperceptibly with her fingers into oblivion.

When he woke he found John absent and Sharon standing over the primus. "He's outside," she said.

"Have I overslept again?"

"It is late. I am boiling water for you now."

"We'd better try and get some supplies this morning."

"There is no village," she said, in a matter of fact tone.

"What?"

"John says not. But we have enough food, if you don't mind this queer milk from a tin."

"No, I don't mind," he replied, watching her affectionately. "It doesn't really surprise me," he added after a moment.

"The village?"

"No village. Yesterday I should have minded awfully. Is that you, do you think?"

"Perhaps."

"It doesn't surprise you about the village at all, does it? Do you love me?"

She glanced a him quickly, a little shocked, and said quietly: "Don't you know?" then added: "It doesn't surprise me."

John seemed very disturbed. "I don't like it," he kept saying as they shaved. "Can't understand it at all. I could have sworn there were houses last night. You saw them didn't you?"

"Yes."

"Well, don't you think it's very odd?"

"I do."

"Everything looks the same as yesterday morning. I don't like it."

"It's an adventure you must admit."

"Yes, but I've had enough of it. I suggest we turn back."

Sharon suddenly appeared, and, seeing her, Clifford knew that he did not want to go back. He remembered her saying: "Didn't you say you wanted to explore?" She would think him weak-hearted if they turned back all those dreary miles with nothing to show for it. At breakfast, he exerted himself in persuading John to the same opinion. John finally agreed to one more day, but, in turn, extracted a promise that they would then go back whatever happened. Clifford agreed to this, and Sharon for some inexplicable reason laughed at them both. So that eventually they prepared to set off in an atmosphere of general good humour.

Sharon began to fill the water tank with their four-gallon can. It seemed too heavy for her, and John dropped the starter and leapt to her assistance.

She let him take the can and held the funnel for him. Together they watched the rich even stream of water disappear.

"You shouldn't try to do that," he said. "You'll hurt yourself."

"Gipsies do it," she said.

"I'm awfully sorry about that. You know I am."

"I should not have minded if you had thought I was a gipsy."

"I do like you," he said, not looking at her. "I do like you. You won't disappear altogether when this is over, will you?"

"You probably won't find I'll disappear for good," she replied comfortingly.

"Come on," shouted Clifford.

It's all right for *him* to talk to her, John thought, as he struggled to swing the starter. He just doesn't like me doing it; and he wished, as he had begun often to do, that Clifford was not there.

They had spasmodic engine trouble in the morning, which slowed them down; and the consequent halts, with the difficulty they experienced of mooring anywhere (the banks seemed nothing but marsh), were depressing and cold. Their good spirits evaporated: by lunch-time John was plainly irritable and frightened, and Clifford had begun to hate the grey silent land on either side, with the woods and hills which remained so consistently distant. They both wanted to give it up by then, but John felt bound to stick to his promise, and Clifford was secretly sure that Sharon wished to continue.

While she was preparing another late lunch, they saw a small boy who stood on what once had been the towpath, watching them. He was bare-headed, wore corduroy, and had no shoes. He held a long reed, the end of which he chewed as he stared at them.

"Ask him where we are," said John; and Clifford asked.

He took the reed out of his mouth, but did not reply.

"Where do you live then?" asked Clifford as they drew almost level with him.

"I told you. Three miles up," he said; and then he gave a sudden little shriek of fear, dropped the reed, and turned to run down the bank the way they had come. Once he looked back, stumbled and fell, picked himself up sobbing, and ran faster. Sharon had appeared with lunch a moment before, and together they listened to his gasping cries growing fainter and fainter, until he had run himself out of their sight.

"What on earth frightened him?" said Clifford.

"I don't know. Unless it was Sharon popping out of the cabin like that."

"Nonsense. But he was a very frightened little boy. And, I say, do you realize . . ."

"He was a very foolish little boy," Sharon interrupted. She was angry, Clifford noticed with surprise, really angry, white and trembling, and with a curious expression which he did not like.

"We might have got something out of him," said John sadly.

"Too late now," Sharon said. She had quite recovered herself.

They saw no one else. They journeyed on throughout the afternoon; it grew colder, and at the same time more and more airless and still. When the light began to fail, Sharon disappeared as usual to the cabin. The canal became more tortuous, and John asked Clifford to help him with the turns. Clifford complied unwillingly: he did not want to leave Sharon, but as it had been he who had insisted on their continuing, he could hardly refuse. The turns were nerve wracking, as the canal was very narrow and the light grew worse and worse.

"All right if we stop soon?" asked John eventually.

"Stop now if you like."

"Well, we'll try and find a tree to tie up to. This swamp is awful. Can't think how that child ran."

"That child . . ." began Clifford anxiously; but John, who had been equally unnerved by the incident, and did not want to think about it, interrupted. "Is there a tree ahead anywhere?"

"Can't see one. There's a hell of a bend coming though. Almost back on itself. Better slow a bit more."

"Can't. We're right down as it is."

They crawled round, clinging to the outside bank, which seemed always to approach them, its rushes to rub against their bows, although the wheel was hard over. John grunted with relief, and they both stared ahead for the next turn.

They were presented with the most terrible spectacle. The canal immediately broadened, until no longer a canal but a sheet, an infinity, of water stretched ahead; oily, silent, and still, as far as the eye could see, with no country edging it, nothing but water to the low grey sky above it. John had almost immediately cut out the engine, and now he tried desperately to start it again, in order to turn round. Clifford instinctively glanced behind them. He saw no canal at all, no inlet, but grasping and close to the stern of the boat, the reeds and rushes of a marshy waste closing in behind them. He stumbled to the cabin doors and pulled them open. It was very neat and tidy in there, but empty. Only one stern door of the cabin was free of its catch, and it flapped irregularly backwards and forwards with their movements in the boat.

There was no sign of Sharon at all.

PHANTOMS

(Miramax Productions, 1996)
Produced by Dean Koontz
Story 'The Black Pumpkin' by Dean Koontz

Every Halloween, television networks on both sides of the Atlantic make a point of taking advantage of the night's reputation for being the one time of the year when ghosts are free to haunt the earth as the *raison d'etre* to broadcast late night horror programmes – sometimes consisting of old horror movies or else productions made especially for TV. *Phantoms*, a book which Dean Koontz wrote in 1983, has been described as one of the key works in his *oeuvre* and its terrifying account of a group of people desperately fighting an awesome supernatural foe has been bought by Miramax for turning into a television movie for showing at Halloween. Although Dean today enjoys the reputation of being one of the most popular writers of macabre fiction in the world – he dislikes being categorized as a 'horror' writer and has in fact written on a much wider scale – his books adapted for the cinema including *Demon Seed* (1977 starring Julie Christie and Fritz Weaver), *Watchers* (1988 produced by Roger Corman with Corey Haim and Barbara Williams) and *Whispers* (1990 with Victoria Tennant and Jean LeClerc) have not been as successful or well received as might be expected. On TV, however, his 1977 novel, *The Face of Fear*, which was produced for CBS' *Television Movie of the Week* in September 1990, directed by Farhad Mann with Pam Dawber and Lee Horseley, fared much better and has been called 'the most faithful film of any Koontz work.' There are now high hopes for *Phantoms . . .*

Dean Ray Koontz (1945–) is a publishing phenomenon whose books have sold over 125 million copies world-wide. Born into an impoverished family, he escaped into books of fantasy and remembers ghost stories being an important formative influence. "As a kid I read spooky stories in my room, huddled under the covers, using a flashlight to illuminate the pages," he recalls. Charles Dickens' classic, *A Christmas Carol*, is, he believes, the greatest ghost story of all time, and its mixture of the frightening along with a message of hope, charity and love is something that finds its way into even the blackest of his own novels and short stories. Of his books, the supernatural features most prominently in *The Funhouse* (1980), *The Mask* (1981), *Darkfall* (1984), *The Servants of Twilight* (1984), *Hideaway* (1992), and *Strange Highways* (1995). 'The Black Pumpkin' is one of my favourite Dean Koontz short stories and is, I think, overdue for adaptation on television – to be shown on Halloween, of course! It appeared originally in December 1986 in the pages of *Twilight Zone* – the fondly remembered magazine associated with the famous TV series – complete with this editorial introduction, 'Tommy Sutzmann's jack-o'-lantern brimmed with a strange magic – a dark and evil magic that paid everyone exactly what they'd earned.' It makes for a perfect conclusion to this anthology and after you have read it . . . do sleep well!

The pumpkins were creepy, but the man who carved them was far stranger than his creations. He appeared to have baked for ages in the California sun, until all the juice had been cooked out of his flesh. He was stringy, bony, and leather skinned. His head resembled a squash, not pleasingly round like a pumpkin, yet not shaped like an ordinary head, either: slightly narrower at the top and wider at the chin than was right. His amber eyes glowed with a sullen, smoky, weak – but dangerous – light.

Tommy Sutzmann was uneasy the moment he saw the pumpkin carver. He told himself that he was unnecessarily apprehensive, maybe even paranoid. He had a tendency to overreact to the mildest signs of anger in others, to panic at the first vague perception of a threat. Some families taught their twelve-year-old boys honesty, integrity, decency, and faith in God. But by their actions, Tommy's parents and his brother Frank had taught him caution and paranoia. In the best of times his mother and father treated him as an outsider; in the worst of times, they enjoyed punishing him as a means of releasing their anger and frustration at the rest of the world. To Frank, Tommy was simply – and always – a target. Consequently, uneasiness was Tommy Sutzmann's natural condition.

Every December this vacant lot was full of Christmas trees, and during the summer, itinerant merchants used the space to exhibit Day-Glo stuffed animals or paintings on velvet. As Halloween approached, the half-acre property, tucked between a supermarket and a bank on the outskirts of Santa Ana, was an orange montage of pumpkins, all sizes and shapes, lined in rows and stacked in neat low pyramids and tumbled in piles, maybe two thousand of them, the raw material of pies and jack-o'-lanterns.

The Black Pumpkin

The carver was in a back corner of the lot, sitting on a tube-metal chair. The vinyl-upholstered pads on the back and seat of the chair were dark and mottled and webbed with cracks – not unlike the carver's face. He sat with a pumpkin on his lap, whittling with a sharp knife and other tools that lay on the dusty ground beside him.

Tommy Sutzmann did not remember crossing the field of pumpkins. He recalled getting out of the car as soon as his father parked at the curb – and the next thing he knew, he was in the back of the lot, a few feet from the strange sculptor.

A score of finished jack-o'-lanterns were propped atop mounds of other pumpkins. This man did not merely hack crude eye holes and mouth holes, but carefully cut the skin and the rind of the melon in layers, producing features with considerable definition and surprising subtlety. He also used paint to give each creation its own demonic personality: four cans, each containing a brush, stood on the ground beside his chair – red, white, green, and black.

The jack-o'-lanterns grinned and frowned and scowled and leered. They seemed to be staring at Tommy. Every one of them.

Mouths agape. Pointy teeth bared. None had the blunt, goofy teeth of ordinary jack-o'-lanterns. Some even had long fangs.

Staring, staring. And Tommy had the peculiar feeling that they could *see* him.

When he looked up from the pumpkins, he discovered that the old man was also watching him intently. Those amber eyes, full of smoky light, seemed to brighten as they held Tommy's own gaze.

"Would you like one of my pumpkins?" the carver asked. He had a cold, dry voice that gave each word the sound of brittle October leaves blown along a stone walkway.

Tommy could not speak. He tried to say, *No, sir, thank you, no*, but the words stuck in his throat as if he were trying to swallow the cloying pulp of a pumpkin.

"Pick a favorite," the carver said, gesturing with one withered hand toward his gallery of grotesques – but never taking his eyes off Tommy.

"No, uh . . . no, thank you," the boy finally said, his voice thin and with a slightly shrill edge.

What's wrong with me? he wondered. Why am I hyping myself into a fit like this? He's just an old guy who carves pumpkins.

"Is it the price you're worried about?" the carver asked.

"No."

"Because you pay the man out front for the pumpkin, same price as any other on the lot, and you just give me whatever you feel my work is worth."

He smiled, and every aspect of his squash-shaped head was changed by that expression. Not for the better.

The day was mild. Sunshine found its way through holes in the overcast, brightly illuminating some orange mounds of pumpkins while leaving others deep in cloud shadows. In spite of the warm weather, a chill gripped Tommy and would not release him.

Leaning forward with the half-sculpted pumpkin in his lap, the carver said, "You just give me what you want . . . though I'm duty-bound to say that you get what you give."

Another smile. Worse than the first one.

Tommy said, "Uh . . ."

"You get what you give," the carver repeated.

"No shit?" Frank said, stepping up to the row of leering

jack-o'-lanterns. Evidently he had overheard everything that had been said. He was two years older than Tommy, muscular where Tommy was slight, with a self-confidence that Tommy had never known. Frank hefted the strangest of all the old guy's creations. "So how much is this one?"

The carver was reluctant to shift his gaze from Tommy to Frank, and Tommy was unable to break the contact first. In the man's eyes Tommy saw something he could not define or understand, something that filled his mind with images of disfigured children, deformed creatures he could not name, and dead things.

"How much is this one, gramps?" Frank repeated.

At last, the carver looked at Frank – and smiled. He lifted the half-carved pumpkin off his lap, put it on the ground, but did not get up. "As I said, you pay me what you wish, and you get what you give."

Frank had chosen the most disturbing jack-o'-lantern in the eerie collection. It was big, not pleasingly round but lumpy and misshapen, narrower at the top than at the bottom, with ugly crusted nodules like ligneous fungus on a diseased oak tree. The old man had compounded the unsettling effect of the pumpkin's natural deformities by giving it an immense mouth with three upper and three lower fangs. Its nose was an irregular hole that made Tommy think of camp-fire tales about lepers. The slanted Asian eyes were as large as lemons but were not cut all the way through the rind except for a pupil – an evil elliptical slit – in the center of each. The stem in the head was dark and knotted like a thrusting cancerous growth. The maker of jack-o'-lanterns had painted this one black, letting the natural orange color blaze through in only a few places to create character lines around the eyes and mouth, and to add emphasis to the tumorous growths.

Frank was bound to like *that* pumpkin. His favorite

223

movies were *The Texas Chainsaw Massacre* and all the *Friday the 13th* sagas of the mad, murderous Jason. When Tommy and Frank watched a movie of that kind on the VCR, Tommy was always on the side of the victims, while Frank cheered the killer. Watching *Poltergeist*, Frank was disappointed that the whole family survived; he kept hoping that the little boy would be eaten by something in the closet and that his stripped bones would be spit out like watermelon seeds. "Hell," Frank had said, "they could have at least ripped the guts out of that stupid dog."

Now, Frank held the black pumpkin, grinning as he studied its malevolent features. He squinted into the thing's slitted pupils as if the jack-o'-lantern's eyes were real, as if there were thoughts to be read in those eyes – and for a moment he seemed to be mesmerized by the pumpkin's gaze.

Put it down, Tommy thought urgently. For God's sake, Frank, put it down and let's get out of here.

The carver watched Frank intently. The old man was still, like a predator preparing to pounce.

Clouds moved, blocking the sun.

Tommy shivered.

Finally breaking the staring contest with the jack-o'-lantern, Frank looked at the carver and said, "I give you whatever I like?"

"You get what you give."

"But no matter what I give, I get the jack-o'-lantern?"

"Yes, but you get what you give," the old man said cryptically.

Frank put the black pumpkin aside and pulled some change from his pocket. Grinning, he approached the old man, holding out a nickel.

The carver reached for the coin.

"No!" Tommy said.

Both Frank and the carver looked at him.

Tommy said, "No, Frank, it's a bad thing. Don't buy it. Don't bring it home, Frank."

For a moment, Frank stared at him in astonishment, then laughed. "You've always been a wimp, but now are you telling me you're scared of a *pumpkin?*"

"It's a bad thing," Tommy insisted.

"Scared of the dark, scared of high places, scared of what's in your bedroom closet at night, scared of half the other kids you meet – and now scared of a damn pumpkin," Frank said. He laughed again, and his laugh was full of scorn and disgust as well as amusement.

The carver took his cue from Frank, but the old man's dry laugh contained no amusement at all.

Tommy was pierced by a cold fear that he could not explain, and he wondered if he was just a wimp after all, afraid of his shadow, maybe even unbalanced. The counselor at school said he was "too sensitive." His mother said he was, "too imaginative," and his father said he was "impractical, a dreamer, too self-involved." Maybe he was all those things, and perhaps he would wind up in a sanitarium some day, in a room with rubber walls, talking to imaginary people, eating flies. But, damn it, he *knew* the black pumpkin was a bad thing.

"Here, gramps," Frank said, "here's a nickel. Will you really sell it for that?"

"I'll take a nickel for my carving, but you still have to pay the usual price of the pumpkin to the fella who runs the lot."

"Deal," Frank said.

The carver plucked the nickel out of Frank's hand.

Tommy shuddered.

Frank turned from the old man and picked up the pumpkin again.

Just then, the sun broke through the clouds, and a shaft of light fell on their corner of the lot. But only Tommy saw what happened in that radiant moment. The sun brightened the orange of the pumpkins, imparted a gold sheen to the dusty ground, gleamed on the metal frame of the chair – but did not touch the carver himself. The light parted around him as if it were a curtain, leaving him in shade. It was an incredible sight, as though the sunshine shunned the carver, as though he were composed of an unearthly substance that *repelled* light. Tommy gasped, and the old man fixed him with a wild look, his amber eyes aglow with promises of pain and terror, and abruptly the clouds covered the sun again.

The old man winked.

We're dead, Tommy thought miserably.

Having lifted the pumpkin again, Frank looked craftily at the old man as if expecting to be told that the nickel sale was a joke. "I can really just take it away?"

"I keep telling you," the carver said.

"How long did you work on this?" Frank asked.

"About an hour."

"And you're willing to settle for a nickel an hour?"

"I work for the love of it." The carver winked at Tommy again.

"What are you, senile?" Frank asked in his usual charming manner.

"Maybe. Maybe."

Frank stared at the old man for a moment, perhaps sensing some of what Tommy felt, but he finally shrugged and turned away, carrying the jack-o'-lantern toward the front of the lot, where their father was buying a score of uncarved pumpkins for tomorrow night's big party.

Tommy wanted to run after his brother, beg Frank to return the black pumpkin and get his nickel back.

"Listen," the carver said fiercely, leaning forward once more.

The old man was so thin and angular that Tommy was half-convinced he had heard the other's ancient bones scraping together within the inadequate padding of his desiccated body.

"Listen to me, boy . . ."

No, Tommy thought. No, I won't listen, I'll run, I'll run.

However, the old man's power was like solder, welding Tommy to that piece of ground, rendering him incapable of movement.

"In the night," the carver said, his amber eyes darkening, "your brother's jack-o'-lantern will grow into something other than what it is now. Its jaws will work. Its teeth will sharpen. When everyone is asleep, it'll creep through your house . . . and give what's deserved. It'll come for you last of all. What do you think you deserve, Tommy? You see, I know your name, though your brother never used it. What do you think the black pumpkin will do to you, Tommy? Hmmm? What do you deserve?"

"What *are* you?" Tommy asked.

The carver smiled. "Dangerous."

Suddenly Tommy's feet tore loose of the earth to which they had been stuck, and he ran.

When he caught up with Frank, he tried to convince his brother to return the black pumpkin, but his explanation of the danger came out as mere hysterical babbling, and Frank laughed at him. Tommy tried to knock the hateful thing out of Frank's hands. Frank held on to the jack-o'-lantern and gave Tommy a hard shove that sent him sprawling backwards over a pile of pumpkins. Frank laughed again, purposefully tramped hard on Tommy's right foot as the younger boy struggled to get up, and moved away.

Through the involuntary tears that were wrung from him by the pain in his foot, Tommy looked toward the back of the lot and saw that the carver was watching.

The old man waved.

Heart beating double time, Tommy limped out to the front of the lot, searching for a way to convince Frank of the danger. But Frank was already putting his purchase on the back seat of the Cadillac. Their father was paying for the jack-o'-lantern and for a score of uncarved pumpkins. Tommy was too late.

Frank took the black pumpkin into his bedroom and stood it on the desk in the corner, under the poster of Michael Berryman as the demented killer in *The Hills Have Eyes*.

From the open doorway, Tommy watched.

Frank had found a fat, scented decorative candle in the kitchen pantry, and now he put it inside the pumpkin. It was big enough to burn for a couple of days. Dreading the appearance of light in the jack-o'-lantern's eyes, Tommy watched as Frank lit the candle and put the pumpkin's stem-centered lid in place.

The slitted pupils glowed-flickered-shimmered with a convincing imitation of demonic life and malevolent intellect. The serrated grin blazed bright, and the fluttering light was like a tongue ceaselessly licking the cold rind lips. The most disgusting part of the illusion of life was the leprous pit of a nose, which appeared to fill with moist, yellowish mucous.

"Incredible!" Frank said.

The scented candle emitted the fragrance of roses.

Though he could not remember where he had read of

such a thing, Tommy recalled that the sudden, unexplained scent of roses supposedly indicated the presence of spirits of the dead. But of course, the source of this odor was no mystery.

"What the hell?" Frank said, wrinkling his nose. He lifted the lid of the jack-o'-lantern and peered inside. The inconstant orange light played across his face, queerly distorting his features. "This is supposed to be a *lemon*-scented candle."

In the big airy kitchen, Lois and Kyle Sutzmann, Tommy's mother and father, were standing at the table with the caterer, Mr Howser. They were looking over the menu for tomorrow night's flashy Halloween party, reminding Mr Howser that all the food was to be prepared with the very best ingredients.

Tommy circled behind them, hoping to remain invisible. He took a can of Coke from the refrigerator.

Now, his mother and father were hammering at the caterer about the need for everything to be "impressive." Hors d'oeuvres, flowers, the bar, the waiters' uniforms, and the buffet dinner must be so elegant and exquisite that every guest would feel himself to be in the home of true California aristocracy.

This was not a party for kids. In fact, Tommy and Frank would be required to remain in their rooms tomorrow evening, permitted to engage only in the quietest activities: no television, no stereo, no slightest peep to draw attention to themselves.

This party was strictly for the movers and shakers on whom Kyle Sutzmann's political career depended. He was now a California State Senator, but in next week's election he was running for the United States Congress. This party was a thank you to his biggest financial backers and to the power brokers who had pulled strings to insure his nomination last spring. Kids verbotten.

Tommy's parents seemed to want him around only at major campaign rallys, media photography sessions, and for a few minutes at the start of election-night victory parties. That was okay with Tommy. He preferred to remain invisible because, on those rare occasions when they took notice of him, his folks invariably disapproved of everything he said and did, every movement he made, every innocent expression that crossed his face.

Lois said, "Mr Howser, I hope we understand that large shrimp do *not* qualify as finger lobster."

As the caterer reassured her of the quality of his operation, Tommy sidled silently away from the refrigerator and quietly extracted two Milanos from the cookie jar.

"These are important people," Kyle informed the caterer for the tenth time, "and they are accustomed to the very best."

In school, Tommy had been taught that politics was the means by which many enlightened people chose to serve their fellow men. He knew that was baloney. His parents spent long evenings plotting his father's political career, and Tommy had never once overheard either of them talk about serving the people or improving society. Oh sure in public, on campaign platforms, that was what they talked about— "the rights of the masses, the hungry, the homeless" – but never in private. Beyond the public eye, they endlessly discussed "forming power bases" and "crushing the opposition" and "shoving this new law down their throats." To them and to all the people with whom they associated, politics was a way to gain respect, make some money, and – most important – acquire power.

Tommy understood why people liked to be respected

because he got no respect at all. He could see why money was desirable. But he did not understand this power thing. He could not figure why anyone would waste a lot of time and energy trying to acquire power over other people. What fun could you get out of ordering people around, telling them what to do? What if you told them to do the wrong thing, and then what if, because of your orders, people were hurt or wound up broke or with other bad problems? And how could you expect people to like you if you had power over them? Frank had power over Tommy – complete power, total control – and Tommy *loathed* him.

Sometimes, he thought he was the only sane person in his family. At other times, he wondered if they were all sane and if he was mad. Whatever the case, crazy or sane, Tommy always felt that he did not belong in the same house with his own family.

As he slipped stealthily out of the kitchen with his can of Coke and two Milanos wrapped in a paper napkin, his parents were querying Mr Howser about the quality of the champagne.

In the back hallway, Frank's door was open, and Tommy paused for a glimpse of the pumpkin. It was still there, fire in every aperture.

"What you got there?" Frank asked, stepping into the doorway. He grabbed Tommy by the shirt and yanked him into the room, slammed the door, took away the cookies and Coke. "Thanks, snotface. I was just thinking I could use a snack." He went to the desk and put the booty beside the glowing jack-o'-lantern.

Taking a deep breath, steeling himself for what resistance would mean, Tommy said, "Those are mine."

Frank pretended shock. "Is my little brother a greedy glutton who doesn't know how to share?"

"Give me back my Coke and cookies."

Frank's grin was sharklike. "Good heavens, dear brother, I think you need to be taught a lesson. Greedy little gluttons have to be shown the path of enlightenment."

Tommy would have preferred to walk away, to let Frank win, to go back to the kitchen and get another Coke and more cookies. However, he knew that his life, already intolerable, would get worse if he did not make an effort, no matter how futile, to stand up to this stranger who was supposedly his brother. Total, willing capitulation would enflame Frank and encourage him to be even more of a bully than he already was.

"I want my cookies and my Coke," Tommy insisted.

Frank rushed him. They fell to the floor, pummeling each other, rolling, kicking, but producing little noise. They neither shouted nor squealed because they didn't want to draw their folks' attention. Tommy was reluctant to let his parents know what was happening because they would invariably blame the ruckus on him. Athletic, well-tanned Frank was their dream child, their favorite son, and he could do no wrong. Frank probably wanted to keep the battle secret because their father would put a stop to it, thereby spoiling the fun.

Throughout the tussle, Tommy had brief glimpses of the glowing jack-o'-lantern, which looked down on them, and he was sure that its grin grew steadily wider, wider.

At last beaten, exhausted, Tommy was driven into a corner. Straddling him, Frank slapped him once, hard, rattling his senses, then tore at Tommy's clothes, pulling them off.

"No!" Tommy whispered when he realized that, in addition to being beaten, he was to be humiliated. "No, no."

He struggled with what little strength he still possessed,

but his shirt was stripped off, his jeans and underwear yanked down. With his pants tangled around his sneakers, he was pulled to his feet and half-carried across the room. Frank threw open the door, pitched Tommy into the hallway, and called, "Oh, Maria! Maria, can you come here a momemt, please?"

Maria was the twice-a-week maid who came in to clean and do the ironing, and this was one of her days.

"Maria!"

Naked, terrified of being humiliated in front of the maid, Tommy scrambled to his feet, grabbed at his pants, tried to run and pull up his jeans at the same time, stumbled, fell, and got up again.

"Maria, can you come here, please?" Frank asked, barely able to get the words out between gales of laughter.

Gasping, whimpering, Tommy somehow reached his room and got out of sight before Maria appeared. For a while he just leaned against the closed door, holding up his jeans with both hands, shivering.

With their parents off at a campaign appearance, Tommy and Frank had dinner together, heating up a casserole that Maria had left in the refrigerator. Ordinarily, dinner with Frank was an ordeal, but this time it was uneventful. As he ate, Frank was engrossed in a magazine that reported on the latest horror movies, with an emphasis on slice-and-dice films and with lots of full-color photographs of mutilated and blood-soaked bodies; he seemed oblivious of Tommy.

Later, when Frank was in the bathroom preparing for bed, Tommy sneaked into his older brother's room and stood at the desk, studying the jack-o'-lantern. The wicked mouth glowed. The narrow pupils were alive with fire.

The scent of roses filled the room, but underlying that

233

odor was another more subtle and less appealing fragrance that he could not quite identify.

Tommy was aware of a malevolent presence – something even worse than the malevolence that he could *always* sense in Frank's room. A cold current raced through his blood.

Suddenly he was certain that the potential murderous power of the black pumpkin was enhanced by the candle within it. Somehow, the presence of light within its shell was dangerous, a triggering factor. Tommy did not know how he knew this, but he was convinced that, if he were to have the slightest chance of surviving the coming night, he must extinguish the flame.

He grasped the gnarly stem and removed the lid from the top of the jack-o'-lantern's skull.

Light did not merely rise from inside the pumpkin but seemed to be *flung* up at him, hot on his face, stinging his eyes.

He blew out the flame.

The jack-o'-lantern went dark.

Immediately, Tommy felt better.

He put the lid in place. As he let go of the stem, the candle re-lit spontaneously.

Stunned, he jumped back. Light shone forth from the carved eyes, nose, and mouth.

"No," he said softly.

He edged forward, removed the lid, and blew the candle out again.

A moment of darkness within the pumpkin. Then, before his eyes, the flame reappeared.

Reluctantly, issuing a thin involuntary sound of distress, Tommy reached into the jack-o'-lantern to snuff the stubborn candle with his thumb and forefinger. He was convinced that the pumpkin shell would suddenly snap shut around his wrist, instantly severing his hand, leaving him with a bloody stump. Or perhaps it would hold him fast while dissolving the flesh from his fingers, then would release him with an arm that terminated in a skeletal hand. Driven toward the brink of hysteria by those fears, he pinched the wick, extinguished the flame, and snatched his hand back with a sob of relief at having escaped mutilation.

He jammed the lid in place and, hearing the toilet flush in the bathroom, hurried out of the room. He dared not let Frank catch him there. As he stepped into the hallway, he glanced back at the jack-o'-lantern, and of course it was full of candlelight again.

He went straight to the kitchen and got a butcher's knife, which he took back to his own room and hid beneath his pillow. He was sure that he would need it sometime in the dead hours before dawn.

His parents came home shortly before midnight.

Tommy was sitting in bed, his room illuminated only by the pale bulb of the low-wattage night light. The butcher's knife was at his side, under the covers, and in fact his hand was resting on the haft.

For twenty minutes, Tommy could hear them talking, running water, flushing toilets, opening and closing doors. Their bedroom and bath were at the opposite end of the house from his and Frank's rooms, so the noises they made were muffled but nonetheless reassuring. These were the ordinary noises of daily life, and as long as the house was filled with them, surely no unnatural lantern-eyed predator could be stalking anyone. Soon, however, quiet returned. In the post-midnight stillness, Tommy waited for the first scream.

He was determined not to fall asleep. But he was only

twelve years old, and he was exhausted after a long day and drained by the sustained terror that had gripped him ever since he had seen the mummy-faced pumpkin carver. Propped against a pile of pillows, he dozed off long before one o'clock . . .

. . . and something thumped, waking him.

He was instantly alert. He sat straight up in bed, clutching the butcher's knife.

For a moment he was certain the sound had originated within his own room. Then he heard it again, a solid thump, and he knew that it had come from Frank's room.

He threw aside the covers and sat on the edge of the bed, tense. Waiting. Listening.

Once, he thought he heard Frank calling his name – "Tooommmmyyy" – a desperate and frightened and barely audible cry that seemed to come from the far rim of a vast canyon. Perhaps he imagined it.

Silence.

His hands were slick with sweat. He put the knife aside and blotted his palms on his pajamas.

Silence.

He picked up the knife again. He reached under his bed and found the flashlight he kept there, but he did not switch it on. He went cautiously to the door and listened for movements in the hallway beyond. Nothing.

An inner voice urged him to return to bed, pull the covers over his head, and forget what he had heard. Better yet, he could crawl under the bed and hope that he would not be found. But he knew this was the voice of the wimp within, and he dared to hope for salvation in cowardice. If the black pumpkin *had* grown into something else, and if it was now loose in the house, it would respond to timidity with no less savage glee than Frank would have shown.

God, he thought fervently, there's a boy down here who believes in You, and he'd be very disappointed if You happened to be looking the other way right now when he really, really, really needs You.

Tommy quietly turned the knob and opened the door. The hallway, illuminated only by the moonlight that streamed through the window at end, was deserted.

Directly across the hall, the door to Frank's room stood open.

Still not switching on the flashlight, desperately hoping that his presence would go undetected if he was mantled in darkness, he stepped to Frank's doorway and listened. Frank usually snored, but no snoring could be heard tonight. If the jack-o'-lantern was in there, the candle had been extinguished at last, for no flickering paraffin light was visible.

Tommy crossed the threshold.

Moonlight silvered the window, on which danced the palm-frond shadows of a wind-stirred tree. In the room, no object was clearly outlined. Mysterious shapes loomed in shades of dark gray and black.

He took one step. Two. Three.

His heart pounded so hard that it shattered his resolve to cloak himself in darkness. He snapped on the Eveready and was startled by the way the butcher's knife, in his right hand, reflected the light.

He swept the beam around the room and, to his relief, saw no crouching monstrosity. The sheets and blankets were tumbled in a pile on the mattress, and he had to take another step toward the bed before he was able to ascertain that Frank was not there.

The severed hand was on the floor by the night stand. Tommy saw it in the penumbra of the flashlight, and he brought the beam to bear directly on it. He stared in shock.

Frank's hand. No doubt about its identity, for Frank's silver skull-and-crossbones ring gleamed brightly on one slug-white finger. It was curled into a tight fist.

Perhaps powered by a post-mortem nerve spasm, perhaps powered by darker forces, the fisted hand suddenly opened, the fingers unfolding like the spreading petals of a flower. In the palm was a single, shiny nickel.

Tommy stifled a wild shriek but could not repress a series of violent shudders.

Frantically trying to decide which escape route might be safest, he heard his mother scream from the far end of the house. Her shrill cry was abruptly cut off. Something crashed.

Tommy turned toward the doorway of Frank's room. He knew he should run before it was too late, but he was as welded to this spot as he had been to that bit of dusty ground when the pumpkin carver had insisted on telling him what the jack-o'-lantern would become during the lonely hours of the night.

He heard his father shout.

A gunshot.

His father screamed.

This scream was also cut short.

Silence again.

Tommy tried to lift one foot, just one, just an inch off the floor, but it would not be lifted. He sensed that more than fear was holding him down, that some malevolent spell prevented him from escaping the black pumpkin.

A door slammed at the other end of the house.

Footsteps sounded in the hall. Heavy, scraping footsteps.

Tears slipped out of Tommy's eyes and down his cheeks.

In the hall, the floorboards creaked and groaned as if under a great weight.

Staring at the open door with no less trepidation than if he had been gazing into the entrance of Hell, Tommy saw flickering orange light in the corridor. The glow grew brighter as the source – no doubt a candle – drew nearer from the left, from the direction of his parents' bedroom.

Amorphous shadows and eerie snakes of light crawled on the hall carpet.

The heavy footsteps slowed. Stopped.

Judging by the light, the thing was only a foot or two from the doorway.

Tommy swallowed hard and worked up enough spit to say, *Who's there?* but he was surprised to hear himself say instead, "Okay, damn you, let's get it over with." Perhaps his years in the Sutzmann house had toughened him more thoroughly and had made him more fatalistic than he had previously realized.

The creature lurched into view, filling the doorway.

Its head was formed by the jack-o'-lantern, which had undergone strange and hideous changes. The head had retained its black and orange coloring and its peculiar gourdlike shape, narrower at the top than at the bottom, and all the tumorous nodules were as crusted and disgusting as ever. Once huge, however, once as large as any pumpkin Tommy had ever seen, it was now the size of a basketball, shriveled. The eyes had sagged, though the slitted pupils were still narrow and mean. The nose was bubbling with some vile mucus. The immense mouth stretched from ear to ear, for it had remained large while the rest of the face had shrunk around it. In the orange light that streamed out between them, the hooked fangs appeared to have been transformed from points of pumpkin rind into hard, sharp protuberances of bone.

The body under the head was vaguely humanoid, though it seemed to be composed of thick gnarled roots and tangled vines. The thing looked immensely strong, a colossus, a juggernaut if it wished to be. Even in his terror, Tommy was filled with awe, and he wondered if the creature's body had been grown from the substance that had been leached from its previously enormous head and, more pointedly, from the flesh of Frank, Lois, and Kyle Sutzmann.

The worst was the orange light within the skull. The candle still burned in there, and its leaping flame emphasized the impossible emptiness of its head – how could it move and think without a brain? – and invested a savage and demonic awareness in its eyes.

It raised one thick, twisted, powerful, vinelike arm and thrust a rootlike finger at him. "You," it said, in a deep whispery voice that made him think of wet slush pouring down drain.

Tommy was now less surprised by his inability to move than by his ability to stand erect. His legs felt like rags. He was sure he was going to collapse and lay helpless while the thing descended upon him, but somehow he stayed on his feet, the flashlight in one hand and the butcher's knife in the other.

The knife. Useless. It would do no harm to this adversary, so he let it slip out of his sweaty fingers. It clattered to the floor.

"You," the black pumpkin repeated, its deep voice reverberating moistly through the room. "Your vicious brother got what he gave. Your mother got what she gave. Your father got what he gave. I fed on them, sucked the brains out of their heads, chewed up their flesh, dissolved their bones. Now what do you deserve?"

Tommy could not speak. He was shaking and weeping

silently and dragging each breath into his lungs only with tremendous effort.

The black pumpkin lurched out of the doorway, into the room, looming over him, eyes blazing.

It stood six and a half feet tall, and had to tilt its lantern head to look down at him. Curls of black smoke from the candle's sooty wick escaped between its fangs and out of its leprous nose.

Speaking in a whisper, yet with such force that its words vibrated the windowpanes, the thing said, "Unfortunately, you are a good boy, and I've no right to feed on you. What *you* deserve is what you've got from now on – freedom."

Tommy stared up into the grotesque face, not yet understanding what he had been told.

"Freedom," the demonic beast repeated. "Freedom from Frank and Lois and Kyle. Freedom to grow up without their heels pressing down on you. Freedom to be the best you can be, which means I'll probably *never* get a chance to feed on you."

For a long time they stood there, face to face, boy and beast, and gradually Tommy achieved complete understanding. In the morning, his parents and Frank would be missing. Never to be found. A great and enduring mystery. Tommy would have to live with his grandparents. You get what you give.

"But maybe," the black pumpkin said, putting the cold monstrous hand upon Tommy's shoulder, "maybe there's some rottenness in you, too, and maybe someday you'll surrender to it, and maybe I'll have my chance with you, too, in time. Dessert." Its wide grin widened even farther. "Now get back to your bed and sleep. Sleep."

Simultaneously horrified and joyous, Tommy crossed the room to the doorway, moving as if in a dream.

He looked back and saw the black pumpkin watching him.

He said, "You missed a bit," and pointed to the floor beside the nightstand.

The beast looked at Frank's severed hand. "Ahhhh," the black pumpkin said, snatching up the hand and stuffing that grisly morsel into its mouth. The flame within its skull suddenly burned very bright, a hundred times brighter than before, then was extinguished.